VANNI: A Prequel

Book 4 of the Groupie Saga

By
Ginger Voight

© 2015 by Ginger Voight

ALL RIGHTS RESERVED. This book contains material protected under International and Federal Copyright Laws and Treaties. **Any unauthorized reprint or use of this material is prohibited.** No part of this book may be reproduced or transmitted in any form or by any means, electronic or mechanical, including photocopying, recording, or by any information storage and retrieval system without express written permission from the author/publisher.

Hey girl,

I know it's been a long time since we've been together. Honestly, it feels like it's been too long. Truth be told, I've missed you. A lot, in fact. We've been through a lot, you and me. And deep down I knew that our time together wasn't over. I've just been waiting for the right moment to tell you some things that I've never had the courage to say before.

The scary question, for me at least, is... are you ready to hear them?

You should know that I've been thinking about you and all the time we shared together, when you took time out of your life to follow along with me as I rose to superstardom as the lead singer of the world-renowned rock band, Dreaming in Blue. I couldn't have made it through all that stuff without you. I truly enjoyed that time we spent together, though I know that I drove you crazy more than once. I could be a bastard sometimes, and you were right to hate me. (Confession, I kind of hated me too.)

But what would you say if I told you that was only half of my story? That there was a lot that happened in my life that you never knew?

Truth is the story of how I became "Giovanni Carnevale, The Rock Star" started years before I first sang for you in that bar in Philadelphia. And I know you have plenty of questions of how I got to be the guy I was. After all this time, and after all the love that you've shown me over the years, I think I'm finally ready to share this side of myself with you. I feel like I can trust you. And I sure hope that you can trust me, too.

It's not a pretty story, but you know me. I can't make any promises that it will be a pretty tale, or a happy one. That's not how it usually works with me.

What I can promise is that I will tell it honestly and unflinchingly. In the end, I hope that we will be closer than ever before.

So get comfortable, baby, right here in the crook of my arm. Let me share with things I've never had the courage to share. Because of how much you've believed in me and you've cared about me, I finally feel like I can.

See you at the end... which will take us right back to the beginning where we first met all those years ago. Maybe then you'll understand why I did the things I did... and why I needed you as much as I do.

*Yours forever,
Vanni*

*Bad boys aren't born.
They're created.*

CHAPTER ONE:

Brooklyn, New York
December 21, 2004

"Order up!"

The loudly barked words attempt to rise above the din in the small but crowded Italian restaurant. Cynzia's is a local landmark around Bensonhurst, a diverse neighborhood in Brooklyn. The voices within those narrow brick walls often rise in a chorus of boisterous laughter and conversation, but Santino Amichi had never been shy about letting his voice be heard, particularly when he calls out for his indolent employees. "Joe!" he hollers again.

I chuckle to myself as I shake my head. That crusty old coot would never get it right. "How many times do I have to tell you, Santino? I won't answer you if you don't call me by my real name."

The robust Italian leans over the window to glare my direction. "I did call you by your name, *Joe-vanni*," he says, yet another installment of our long-standing argument how to properly pronounce my name.

I simply flash a brilliant white smile. "Call me that all you want. I'll never answer to it. My name is Gee-oh-vah-nee. You might want to get it right, considering it's going to be famous one day."

Santino grunts as he pushes a couple of plates towards me. They're overflowing with tantalizing pasta, with meatballs as big as a fist, steaming hot and covered in ooey, gooey cheese. "Famous. Right. Let me know when you can get an order right and we'll talk. And put on your hairnet. I'm not telling you again."

"I'm almost off," I say, blowing off the criticism like I always do, with a disarming smile and good humor. These two things have been my saving grace through the years, particularly when I was a hell-raising teenager. I got into more trouble than I knew how to handle, and charm was often my greatest currency to get back out again. A guy's got to have a good time, right? My philosophy has always been if I couldn't find one, I'd make one.

Not a lot of fun can be had in the presence of a hairnet, I'm just saying. If my charm gets me out of trouble, my long locks often get me into it. The girls always love playing with each silky strand within their fingers, and I have never been one to deny the request. I started growing my hair in the fourth grade, to mimic all the popular rock bands I grew up listening to. Girls have always been a fan. Since I have always been a fan of girls, I decided to keep it long after the hair phase had passed.

Santino doesn't understand this, which is why he constantly threatens me with his clippers. "I'm gonna give you a proper haircut one day, Joe-vanni," he'd say.

These are empty threats mostly. I've worked at Cynzia's for almost five years, with my hair intact, thank you very much. It's a small victory and I'll take it.

I mean, sure. I could be depressed about working at a minimum wage job, serving at a restaurant in the neighborhood, living from paycheck to paycheck, and sometimes not even then. But I have plenty of dreams to keep me warm at night. The way I see it, a boy named Gee-oh-vah-nee was born to entertain big plans and even bigger dreams.

So what if I haven't gotten as far as I wanted by the time I turned twenty-six? It's a late start for someone trying to break into the music industry and I know it. A star needs a hook, a gimmick, something that makes him stand out from the crowd. I just haven't found mine yet.

Truthfully, I haven't had much of a chance to look for one. Life doesn't always leave a whole lot of room for dreams, especially the older we get. I'm just like any other guy, just trying to pay my rent and survive from one day to the next. I've done the garage band thing. I've done the bar singer thing. It didn't pay for shit, and I couldn't find anyone to share my groove.

Sadly this means more time spent on Plan B. People always tell us to have a Plan B, since only a small fraction of folks can make Plan A happen for real. People who tell me to have a Plan B rarely understand how painful Plan B really is. The harder I work to make ends miraculously meet, the more out of reach these big dreams seem, and nothing depresses me more than that.

But I'm undeterred. Something way deep inside me drives me to keep chasing that dream, even when all odds are stacked against me that I'll never make anything of it.

Frankly that's part of the appeal.

Let's face it. Statistics are not my friends. I'm not the first boy who fancies himself a rock star. Bars across the country are filled with frustrated singers and musicians who will probably never see the light of day. Only a scant percent ever make it. I know that. All evidence suggests that I'll still be schlepping hot plates for bupkis well into the future.

But the dream won't be denied. It pesters me like a splinter under the skin, especially on my birthday of all days. This isn't just a reminder of where I've been. It offers a glimpse of where I'm was going. I'm still young and still primed to grab life by the balls. And no grumpy boss, no restaurant full of demanding patrons, and certainly no hair net, is going to dampen my enthusiasm.

I'm still in good spirits when I clock out that evening. Santino still yells at me as I unwind the dirty white apron from my hips and head towards the back to change. My coworker, Alicia, catches up with me near my locker.

"Happy birthday, Vanni," she said with that sweet, hopeful smile she always wore when I'm around.

I can't help but indulge her with a smile of my own. It gives her a thrill and I know it, and it's a pretty harmless way to make her day. "Thanks."

"Big plans tonight?"

I'm still grinning as I sit down on the bench to change out of my ugly, slip-resistant work shoes. "Yeah, sort of. My aunt always throws me a big surprise party, though it stopped being a surprise by the time I was seventeen." My voice catches somewhat. "It's the first one without Mama, so I'm sure she'll overcompensate."

Alicia sits next to me on the bench, closer than proper manners might dictate. Immediately I'm on guard. I know that Alicia Amichi has had her eyes on me from the minute we met five years before. She was only twelve then, so her instant crush was a lot harder to hide. In the years since, her hero-worship of me has been the well-known secret of Cynzia's, which often includes an endless line of teasing at my expense.

Personally I think that's why old Santino never misses an opportunity to bust my balls. His passionate daughter grows lovelier and bolder by the day. I figure I've got a year left before I'm either betrothed or Santino will find a brand new use for that nasty old hairnet, namely tying up my junk and whacking it right off with his trusty meat cleaver.

I certainly couldn't blame him. I can tell by the look on her face that her nerves are on fire just sitting next to me. If I were a different man, one who might take advantage of a seventeen-year-old girl, then Santino would be well within his rights to deal with it. If a guy like me got next to my daughter, I'd break out the meat cleaver too.

"Maybe I could stop by or something," she suggests with that same hopeful, doe-eyed stare.

I cock my head to the side. "Your dad would have my balls."

She shrugs off my concerns. "You know Papa. His bark is way worse than his bite." I laugh at the visual. "Besides. I'm almost eighteen."

I lean close to run a fingertip along the curve of her slender nose. "Almost," I agree. It's a very important word. I haven't dated anyone under eighteen since I've been able to drive, and I have no plans to start now.

"Besides," I add with a smirk I can't control, "Lori is going to be there."

Alicia immediately makes a face, which makes me chuckle. I kiss her forehead. "See you tomorrow, kiddo," I promise before hopping up from the bench and heading out the back door.

Cynzia's is roughly six blocks from the brownstone I share with my great aunt, Susan Faustino. The house itself was built in the 1930s, in a neighborhood that became home to many Italian-Americans throughout the early 20th century. Susan has lived in that cozy, three-bedroom, two-story home from the second she was born, and every inch of it is a proud testament to her long life there. From the tchotchkes on the mantle to the lovingly embroidered doilies on the furniture, every square inch of the place is an extension of my dynamic great-aunt Susan. Since she has never married, there has never been any need to move. Instead she took care of her parents there until they both passed away by the 1990s. When my mother, Rose, and I hit hard times in Philadelphia eleven years back, she was the first to offer us a place to stay.

We had been bouncing around in rat-trap apartments and tenement housing back in the day. Strangely, the minute I walked into Susan's cozy brownstone, I knew for the first time in my whole life, I had a home.

Some things you just know in an instant.

Aunt Susan has always been just as welcoming as her old house. We're talking about woman who has watched the neighborhood change and grow around her for seven decades, which makes her a cornerstone for our community. Even at seventy-one, she is still active in the church she's attended since birth. I always thought she was a frustrated nun at heart, though she had dropped that particular pursuit at seventeen. No one knows why. It's a secret she'll take to her grave. But it is safe to say that no one I know is as devout as Susan Faustino. Her passion has never been for a man, or even another woman. No, her only true passion was and is music. She has taught generations of kids how to play the piano and sing in the choir, right in her homey front room.

I'm blessed to say that this includes me. When I showed up at her door in 1994, six feet of gangly attitude at the ripe ol' age of fifteen, she used music to turn me around before I could happily traipse down the one-way road to ruin. Thanks to the crowd I was running around with at the time, that was a legitimate concern.

I knew within an afternoon that she'd never put up with my shit, which was a revelation. My mother, Rose, was a saintly woman who had given her all to be both mother and father to me after my father skipped out on us. I was just a toddler then, so there's no question that her burden had been heavy for a long, long time. I knew that she carried a lot of guilt, both for picking the wrong kind of man to father her child, as well as the inability to make him change or stay once I was in the picture. She hadn't been much of a disciplinarian as a result.

Susan changed all that. There are rules to live in Susan's house. I went from running around the Philadelphia streets at all hours to having a curfew. I couldn't cuss, which I learned the hard way after boldly using the worst curse word I could think of to back her down. She promptly washed my mouth out with the worst tasting homemade soap she could concoct.

I also learned to contribute to the household almost immediately. She had me mowing lawns and walking dogs from the moment we moved in. These are usually favors for the members of her church who are old or infirm, unable to do these things for themselves, things she still does to this day.

By the time I was old enough to get a "real" job that paid, I was already in the habit of spending huge chunks of my time in the service of other people. As a result I think I'm a better worker than most, no matter what old Santino might say. Sure I am prone to daydream, but I think that's true of most people who long for a day we don't have to work menial jobs just to keep a roof over our heads.

Fortunately Susan's brownstone was paid off even before she took possession of it, so our needs have always been relatively few. Then Mama got sick and everything changed. After she was diagnosed with breast cancer, much like my grandmother before her, we scrimped and saved every penny to get her the best treatment we could afford.

That was the day I went to Cynzia's for a job. I'm proud to say I haven't missed one day since.

I credit Susan entirely for that work ethic. Hell, I credit Susan for just about everything. My mother, God rest her soul, was the heart of me, who taught me compassion and selflessness and unconditional love.

Susan is my spiritual mirror through and through.

I wear a smile as I take the concrete steps two at a time to reach the front door. The narrow entryway is quiet and dark. I have to laugh to myself. We go through this ruse every single year. The non-surprise of it is more of a tradition than the party itself. I had legitimately feigned surprise the first few years to humor her, but eventually it became the running joke. I have to get creative with my surprise faces now, because every single time they jump out at me, someone snaps a photo. Susan has kept every single one of those shots in a photo album that she always threatens to show my kids someday. I tell her I may not have any kids. She in turn threatens to once again wash my mouth out with soap.

I head to the homey kitchen in the back, where Susan and members from her church, neighbors and my new girlfriend, Lori, lay in wait. The minute I hit the light, everyone pops out from their hiding places, cheering, "Surprise!" as loud as they can.

By no surprise at all, the room instantly fills with love. Who am I to complain?

I offer my shocked face for the obligatory photo, before holding up my arms like a champ. Thereupon I get passed from one pair of arms to another. There are more people at this party than there had been a year ago, and I have a pretty good idea why. This is my first birthday without my mother, and my beloved aunt has clearly enlisted the help of her entire community to fill the gaping hole left behind.

Of course nothing can, but the thought sure counts. When I finally get to Susan, who is wider than she was tall, I hug her extra tight. "You spoil me, *Cara Mia*." Normally I never use Italian, certainly not like my fluent aunt. But I speak it for her since I know nothing pleases her more.

She hugs me back just as strong. Those very same hugs held me together when my mom was so sick and eventually passed. They still hold me together now. "Impossible," she tells me. "You are my superstar, are you not?"

I lift her easily, though she instantly struggles. As a bigger woman, she worries about things like that–though I have always told her that it never mattered to me. Sometimes I wondered if that was the reason that she never married. Was she so worried about being too heavy for a man that she never tried? That's the only explanation I can think of. I can't imagine anyone ever meeting my great-aunt and not falling head over heels in love with her. Still, she is conscious of every single pound and I know that. Instantly I return her to her feet before kissing her on the tip of her nose.

"I hope you can share your superstar," a feminine voice drifts over my shoulder. I turn to face Lori Flannigan, a sunny blonde who has an immediate smile for me as I pull her into my arms.

"Hey, baby," I say, in that sleepy bedroom voice that always makes her tremble in my arms. I swear it makes me feel like a superhero. I'm butter in her hands as she kisses me, even if it has to be a modest kiss because we're standing in front of my conservative great-aunt and all her friends.

Susan grabs me by the arm and pulls me further into the kitchen, where a veritable feast awaits. There's pasta and meatballs, eggplant parmesan, baked ziti and Susan's renowned ravioli. And for dessert she has prepared a decadent favorite of mine, scrumptious homemade tiramisu.

My mouth waters as Susan pours the Prosecco for everyone. Lori cuddles closely, fitting nicely in the crook of my arm. It's a good hiding place for her since she's never been one for crowds of people she didn't know. She'd much prefer our private celebration later, when I can sneak her away to my room. (I kind of prefer that, too.)

Thanks to all the people present I don't really know, who mill around me, talking in their own little groups, I am able to do that sooner rather than later. I close the door behind us before I take the tiny blonde back into my arms. Lori is short, like Susan, but she is also fairly petite. Lifting her into my arms is like picking up a bird. From the moment she entered our home for piano instruction five months ago, I have been completely fascinated by her. She's tiny and fragile, like one of Susan's old porcelain dolls she kept packed away so that they didn't crack.

The similarity between the two makes me want to wrap myself around Lori like living body armor to keep her safe.

Whether it was her fair, freckled skin, that slight body, or her full, heart-shaped face, one that hovered somewhere between adolescence and adulthood even years after she came of age, there is just something about her that would jump-start the white knight complex in any guy prone to such tendencies. Fun fact about me: I'm one of those guys. She held me off for a good four months before we finally consummated our relationship. Since that amazing night three weeks ago, she had proven to be an enthusiastic partner.

"I'm just making up for lost time," she'd say before she'd wind her arms around my neck. I'd then trail my fingers across her satiny flesh, which would spring up to meet my touch as she gasped against my ear.

In fact she is so passionate and responsive to my touch, it remains a mystery how she stayed a virgin until she met me.

"I just know what I want," she'd tell me if I dare asked. And who the hell needed to talk after that?

I lift her against my 6'3-foot frame and press her against the door. I toy with her lips momentarily before I murmur, "So where's my birthday gift?"

She giggles against me, which shoots electricity through my core. "You're holding it."

I can't help but growl against her mouth as I lift her up and carry her towards my single bed. We barely fit, which makes it even sexier. "Just what I wanted."

We topple together on the bed. She allows it for a brief, passionate moment before she withdraws. "Vanni. Everyone is here."

"So?" I say as I kiss my way along the fragrant line of her neck. She smells like citrus and spice, fresh and bright, like a summer morning.

"So, it's disrespectful. They came here to share your birthday with you."

"Fuck 'em," I say as I continue to explore the nape of her neck.

She glares at me out of the corner of her eye. "Vanni."

"Fine. You're right," I admit with a sigh, before I caress the curve of her lovely face. "You're too good for me, you know that right?"

"I know," she chirps happily. She springs to her feet, pulling me up with her.

When we return to the shindig, my best buddy Tony Biello has arrived. It is now officially a party.

"Hey, buddy," he greets as he hands off a bottle of whiskey with a blue bow on it. He can't possibly remember that is my favorite color, since guys don't really think about those things. I know it's a happy accident. It makes me appreciate it even more. "Birthday greetings," he says as he takes me in a side hug, effectively putting himself in the middle of Lori and me as we head back towards the kitchen.

"I thought you forgot," I accuse.

"Me? Forget?" he says as he withdraws a long envelope with yet another blue bow. Maybe it isn't an accident after all.

"What's this?"

"Open it," he tells me.

I withdraw three tickets. "Holy shit," I breathe. They are tickets to Madison Square Garden, to catch a concert I had been jonesing to attend for months, but the tickets are outrageously expensive. "How'd you get these?"

He shrugs. "Client at the firm had some and didn't want them. Score one for corporate America."

I am contrite as I face him. Tony and I had been thick as thieves since I moved to Bensonhurst. We met on the street corner down the block, right in between our two houses, and we had been inseparable ever since. We attended the same high school, shared many of the same classes. He was always the better student, even though he was just as likely as I was to be caught ditching afternoon classes and smoking a J in the parking lot with the rest of us slackers. We loved the same music, which connected us on a deep level almost immediately. I always picked my friends by how versed they were on the rock music I've loved by my whole life. If I can sing a tune and someone can sing the next lyric, we're automatically bonded for life.

Somewhere around junior year, Tony got serious about his future. His parents were ragging on him to give up his delinquent behavior, so that he could get into college. His dad had worked two jobs just to pay for his first year. Tony ended up paying for the rest.

He got a job in Manhattan after he graduated, and had been moving up the corporate ladder in the last few years since. I tease him mercilessly because of it. A million years ago, we had talked about forming our own garage band and touring all over the country, singlehandedly bringing rock back to the forefront of popular music. Now he is a suited lackey with an expensive shoebox of an apartment in the city he now called home.

But he is a suited lackey who could acquire coveted concert tickets. I am sincere when I tell him, "Thanks, man. This means a lot."

"Of course it does," he shoots back with an affable grin. "Who knows you better than your best friend? You're taking me with you, you know. Unless I'm some kind of third wheel."

"Never," Lori assures him immediately as she places her hand on his arm. "We'd love for you to go."

"Excellent," he says with a smile. "Now where's that ziti? My mouth has been watering for it all day."

We don't break away from the crowd until the last of the guests leave. In the case of Susan's peers, that means about ten o'clock, after all the food is put away and the dishes are washed. Also a tradition: Susan shoos away every good Samaritan that wants to help her. Eventually we all land on the front stoop.

Though it's frigid and the light clouds above are threatening snow, we do not dare to go back in until she's done. Instead I sit on the concrete step, cuddling a shivering Lori in my lap.

Tony turns to me. "So what time do you want me to pick you up for the concert?"

"Oh right," I say. With the chaos of the party, I've forgotten all about one of my favorite gifts. "What day is it, again?"

"Thursday. Christmas Eve-eve," he clarifies with a lopsided grin.

"Good, because if I miss Christmas Eve at the church with Aunt Susan, she'll fill my stocking full of coal."

"You got that right," Susan says as she walks out onto the porch where we sit. "My Vanni always sings for the church."

"*O Holy Night,*" I tell them. It's her favorite. It always makes her cry when I sing it.

"You should come," she tells them, and Tony instantly shakes his head.

"My family is getting together Christmas Eve. The house should be full of about thirty people."

"Then they will hardly miss one, will they?" Susan teases. I know she doesn't mean it. Family is the most important thing to my beloved *prozia*, so she'd never stand in anyone's way to enjoy it.

Tony grins as he stands. He leans over to kiss her cheek. She's as much his family as I am by now. "It was a great party, Susan. Thanks for inviting me."

She pats his shoulder. "You're a good boy, Tony. I had my doubts but you've really come a long way."

He laughs. "Guess it's time to get Vanni in shape."

Her dark eyes meet mine. The love there takes my breath away. "Vanni's all right," she assures him.

Tony claps his hand on my shoulder as he trots down the steps. "See you Thursday," he tells Lori and me.

"What's Thursday?" Susan wants to know.

"Concert," I tell her. "He got some tickets through his firm."

"That's generous of him to give them to you," she says as she collapses on the bench on the porch with a happy sigh. "I'd say everything shaped up to be even better than last year."

For a moment I can say nothing. Yes, it had turned out to be a pretty great birthday. I got some killer concert tickets, I ate like a king and I have a beautiful woman sitting on my lap. There is only one thing missing. "Almost," I finally say.

Susan realizes her error with widened eyes. "I'm sorry, Vanni."

"It's okay," I assure her with a smile. She had tried so hard to make the evening special. It wasn't her fault the universe or God or whatever anyone wanted to call it had decided to call Mama home the year before. And I know Susan feels the loss every bit as much as I do. "It was truly a beautiful night. Really."

She smiles. "Anything for you, dear boy."

I notice that she's shivering. "On that note, I think you should probably get inside and defrost."

She nods. It is cold, and cold isn't as easy for her to shake off these days. She rises with a little difficulty. I immediately put

Lori on her feet next to me and hover over my aunt, who won't take my outstretched hand, but won't begrudge how I shadow her to make sure she doesn't fall.

Lori follows us into the house.

I hate that Susan doesn't seem to be getting around like she used to. When Mama and I first came to live with her, she had the energy of women half her age. Now she moves a little slower, she holds onto furniture to stabilize herself and often overexerts herself with simple tasks like cooking dinner or doing the laundry. "You need some help to your room?" I ask, knowing she wouldn't ask for it even if she needed it.

She brushes me off with an impatient wave of her hand. "I can still see myself to bed, thank you very much." She stops only to kiss me, and I can feel her tremble from the effort it took to walk a few measly feet. I know that she had pushed herself too hard today. Instantly I feel guilty.

"Giovanni. *Mi amore*," she says as she caresses my face with both hands. "Happy birthday, beautiful boy."

We watch her leave the room, heading for her downstairs bedroom. The door closes behind her before either Lori or I say anything. Lori breaks the silence as she wedges herself back into my arms. "She loves you," she says as she runs her fingers through my long hair.

"More than anyone has or will," I reply softly.

She tightens her hold around my neck. "Oh, I wouldn't say that."

My eyes meet hers. I love how they shine like sapphires in the dim amber light of the hallway. "Baby," I say as I reach for another kiss. Her mouth opens under mine eagerly, which only makes me hungrier for more. I lift her easily into his arms and carry her up the narrow stairs to my bedroom.

She has pushed my shirt from my shoulders before I have a chance to close the door behind us. We land together on the bed, tearing away each piece of fabric in the way of our curious fingers. God, how I love it when she touches me. Her soft skin feels like a feather brushing across my nerve endings. Lori wasn't the first girl I had been with, not by a long shot. But she *is* the first one I'd ever worked up to. Not to toot my own horn, but finding a romantic partner had always been a bit like shooting fish in a barrel. I'd always had confidence to go after what I wanted, and girls seem to respond to that. Not Lori. I had to try harder with her. Lines didn't work. The flirting, the smirking, the innuendo didn't work. Instead I had to learn how to be a patient, respectful gentleman. A good Catholic boy. I had to open doors, say please and thank you, talk about the future, talk about my feelings... and listen to hers.

That somehow made the grand prize more appealing.

Needless to say I had fucked plenty by the time I was twenty-six years old. But I had only really made love to one woman, and she is the one beneath me on my tiny single bed.

She wears a blue dress, and I know that is no accident. I easily turn her over onto her tummy to pull down the zipper with my teeth. She giggles as my hair brushes against her back. I watch goose bumps rise along her spine. I kiss my way down the sexy line of her back to the gentle swell of her ass. She trembles beneath me. I'm instantly hard as I hear her breath catch as I hover over her, my breath hot against her satin panties. "Time for dessert," I say as I loop my thumbs on either side of her underwear and peel them from her body.

I turn her onto her back and spread her legs. Her thighs quiver as I snake my tongue up the delicate expanse of flesh. She arches her back and moans as I dive in between her legs. I love to make a woman come. It's brilliant, like a ray of sunlight shining through every single facet of a diamond all at once. They are never more beautiful, and never more themselves, until they finally let go of each and every inhibition holding them back.

I learned this lesson when I was sixteen. Like I told you before, my aunt insisted that I provide services in the community. One summer I mowed the lawn for a thirty-something single mom just down the way. This was just after my last growth spurt, when I stood about a foot taller than the rest of the kids in my class. I wore my stubble proudly, and strutted with all the confidence of a man.

It only took three weeks for her to turn me into one. Over that summer, she taught me everything I needed to know about pleasing a woman. Through her I learned all about multiple orgasms and cunnilingus and g-spots. She had all sorts of toys and was never shy about teaching me how to use them.

I went to the tenth grade a changed man. Not only could I get a sexy, grown woman, I could make her scream. Regularly.

Now, with Lori writhing under me, arching her hips towards my face as she unsuccessfully tries to muffle her cries of pleasure, all I can say is: *Thank you, Myra.*

I love everything about sex. I love the sounds, the smells, the tastes, the exploration. The minute our clothes come off, I'm excited to see what new things we could discover about each other. Lori tastes like honey on my tongue, I spiral in lazy circles until she's begging me to stop teasing her. "I want you inside me, Vanni," she pants.

I wear a smile as I climb up her body, kissing her sweet-smelling skin as I go. I latch onto one tightly puckered nipple as I slam myself inside her. She gasps hard against me before she grabs a handful of my hair. It shoots volts down my spine. I love it when they lose control. I love it when they take control.

Most of all, I love how tightly she wraps herself around me, pulling me in tightly where I love to go.

I bite my lip before I say something dirty. Myra loved it, but girls like Lori were sweet, nice girls. They didn't want to hear me tell them that I love shoving my big hard cock inside them.

These are the girls you make love to.

These are the girls you marry.

That's my thought as I come hard, as if my body understands what kind of decision it's making for me. Of all the variables in front of me as I face a new birthday, this life decision I can wrap up tight with a huge, happy bow. I gather her close in my arms to catch my breath, feeling her body continue to quiver all around me as she gently drifts back down to earth.

If I ever wanted to order a wife, Lori has a lot of green checkmarks already in her favor. She is a devout Catholic, which means Aunt Susan loves her. She comes from a large, Irish-American family that instilled in her a strong work ethic and ambition to see things through. Hardworking, moral, faithful and ambitious? Check, check, check, check.

She is everything a guy could want, all in one sexy package. I kinda like the fact that most guys pass her over when she walks into the room. It's like I alone have solved the riddle. I alone discovered the treasure. One day people would look at her and think, "How did she land a rock star?"

And I alone would know the secret.

I honestly can't wait to see her backstage at one of my concerts. She'll wait patiently for me to dominate the crowd and win over legions of fans. Rag mags would write about my longtime sweetheart, while groupies gnashed their teeth, waiting for the chance to get me into bed.

Only it would never come. Lori is the kind of woman that demands better of me, and I have been waiting for a girl like that for a long, long time. I'd keep myself true. She is much too perfect to lose.

I break our kiss to stare down into her face. "I'm the luckiest guy on earth."

She smiles happily. "Remember that."

"I'll never forget," I promise, bending for another kiss, repeating the word 'never' over and over again.

This time she pulls away. "You really mean that, Vanni?"

"Of course. How can you question it?"

She clearly mulls something over as she toys with one lock of my hair, which had escaped over my strong, bare shoulder and clung to my damp skin. "I don't question you," she clarifies at once. "But I do question our future."

My eyes roll. I can't even help it. A perfectly nice moment and she has to ruin it. Ever since she decided to sleep with me, her thoughts had turned to the future, and exactly what I might be doing (or not doing) to secure it. I lift away from her. "Not this again."

She doesn't even bother to cover herself as she sits up. "Vanni, you're twenty-six. Don't you think it's time to have a serious discussion about what you want to do with your life?"

"I already told you what I wanted to do with my future. I want to sing." It is her turn to roll her eyes. which only angers me further. "Thanks a lot," I grit out between clenched teeth as I hop off the bed to dress.

"Vanni," she says as she jumps up after me. "You know that's not what I meant."

I whip around to glare at her. "Then what did you mean?"

She tries to wrap herself into my arms, but I keep them rigidly locked at my side. This routine is getting old. And I can't believe she'd bring it up on my birthday. It's like she didn't have faith in me at all. She reads me like a book. "You can have a career in music," she assures at once. "But you have to be smart about it. Becoming some rock star is a pipe dream. Look at that brochure I brought you, for that music school in the city. You could learn to run a sound board, you could produce. Hell, you could even learn to play an instrument. Those are the dreams to reach for, baby. Everything else is just wishful thinking."

"What if it's not?" I challenge, since that is the question that keeps me ramming my head against every closed door. Sure it doesn't happen for everyone. But it happens for some. What if I'm that guy and I never know it? What if my story is different? Isn't that a question that deserves to be answered? "I know my chances are one in a million, babe. But it's still a chance, isn't it? I'd rather try to make it and fail than have one more regret to ponder on my death bed."

"And I get that," she tells me as she finally releases my arms to wrap around her. "No one wants to see you make it more than I do. I just… I just don't want to see you get hurt, that's all. I love you, Vanni," she says at last. My eyes widen as he stared down at her. Aside from Mama and Aunt Susan, no one had ever said those words to me before. Not even my oversexed Myra, who had taught me all the finer points of lovemaking. "This isn't just your future anymore, Vanni. It's ours. At least, I want it to be. If you do," she adds in a scared, small voice.

Suddenly I understand why she feels she needs to drive me. It's not just me she's pushing towards something better… it's *us*.

What a great word to hear on my birthday.

I lift her into my arms. "It wouldn't be my dream if you weren't in it," he say at last, before walking her back to the bed, where we fall together.

That night I dream of performing in front of a large crowd, with my biggest, most faithful fan, Lori, standing backstage. I wake knowing there is only one way to assuage her fears about a future together. I have to show her how great it could be. And I won't stop until I do.

CHAPTER TWO:

The antsy crowd waiting to enter Madison Square Garden has more to do with the music than the blustery Christmas Eve-Eve. Flakes drift from the sky, with one landing right on Lori's upturned nose. I grin as I kiss it away. It dissolves under my touch, as does Lori.

I love how wholesome she looks on my arm, such blonde, blue-eyed innocence. She wears a long white sweater over a leather miniskirt, with tights to keep her legs warm. I know she's indulging me. The music I love, the raunchy rock and roll I grew up with, doesn't do much for her. She prefers the classics, and by classics I mean classical.

In the relatively short time she's been studying under Aunt Susan, she has already perfected some of the most complicated sheet music Susan could throw at her. It impresses my formidable aunt more than she'll let on.

I wonder momentarily if our children will be musically inclined.

My mother never was. There are times I wonder if my father had been, but there is no one to ask anymore.

I'm not entirely sure I want to know. Anything I may have in common with this man would soften me towards him, and he doesn't deserve that, not after what he did.

Sometimes I fantasize that one day I'll be so rich and so famous that he won't be able to run from me anymore. What would I say if he showed up right in front of my face?

I have so many questions, which all circle back to the big one: "Why did you leave us?"

I grew up in the streets of Philadelphia. Most kids I knew had a father missing in action. Whether the guy split or ended up in jail, it was all the same.

We grew up without a man to guide us.

What would my father say to me now, I wonder? Would he encourage me to chase my dreams, like Aunt Susan? Or would he caution that I needed to keep my head out of the clouds, like Tony or Lori?

Looking around at the ecstatic bunch of revelers waiting to file into the entrance of the Garden, I know it doesn't really matter what he would say. He got his chance to live his life his way when he walked out, which–by no strange coincidence–is exactly when I got my chance to the do the same. I wrap my arm around Lori's waist and start inside.

Tony pulls me back, allowing others who had fallen in line behind us to go ahead. I am flabbergasted as I stare at him. "What are you doing?"

Tony just grins as he reaches inside his jacket. "Just the second part of your gift, man."

He pulls out a lanyard and loops it around my neck. I hold the tag up in my hand. "It's a backstage pass," I murmur incredulously.

"Fuck yeah, it is," Tony smiles as he pulls me into a side hug. "Nothing's too good for one of my boys."

I want to hug him, but we do have an image to maintain, especially Tony, who is still single. I see how he eyes the single girls around us, who are dressed to the nines for their favorite rock idols. I've seen my man Tony in action before. He could hone in on a girl who caught his eye like a bird of prey. I have seen many a girl crumble under his charm. And now he had the job and the apartment in the city to lure new flies onto his web. He wears a leather jacket that still smells brand new, one I have coveted ever since he bought it with his first big paycheck. It intoxicates a redhead nearby, who flashes him a wide smile when he puts his own backstage pass around his neck.

My buddy doesn't miss a beat. He winks back at her, causing her to giggle.

When I was single, Tony and I were pretty scandalous as we prowled for a little female companionship. We knew all the dude tricks to leave them wanting more. It got complicated every now and then, with pissed off boyfriends that would try to run us down, or jealous girls who wanted to stake a claim. I cuddle my girl closer under my arm, glad to be done with all that drama for once. I only want three things out of life. I want to take care of my aunt

Susan. I want to make love to my girl, Lori. And I want to make music.

The lights finally go down for the first act. I don't really know their music but I don't care. I'm on my feet, my fist pumping in the air, trying to sing along with every song. It's all so fucking intoxicating, man. It's like ingesting pure ecstasy. When the band I've come to see hits the stage, I lose my mind like every star-dazed groupie in the crowd. I know all the songs, which I sing loudly and on key, not that anyone can hear me. The massive amplifiers are almost as loud as the roar coming from the crowd.

Lori can't see much, so I lift her up in my arms. I hear her try to sing along as best she can. I know she's trying. I reward her with a kiss for the whole damn world to see. When our kiss breaks, I sing to my audience of one. I don't care about the crowd around us. I don't care about the band in front of us. All I care about is the possibility of the future. I lean forward to shout into her ear, "One day I'll perform here. And you'll be front row!"

She laughs as she wraps her body around mine. I know she thinks I'm daydreaming again, but I'm dead serious.

When we finally head backstage to meet a few of my idols, I am full of questions. "Such a fan, man. That show was killer."

"Thanks, man. Glad you enjoyed it."

"Hey, do you think you have a few words of wisdom for an aspiring singer?"

"You sing?"

"I want to."

The older man just chuckles. "It's a yes or no answer, dude. You want to sing, you gotta sing. Period. Only a handful of people get anywhere in this business. What sets us apart is we're willing to go for broke and make it happen. You can be a dreamer. Or you can be a doer. Your choice, man."

I nod my head. I know he's right. And I know this next year is my opportunity to do something about it. I'm sure as hell not getting any younger. The clock ticks louder every year.

I convince myself that my birthday officially starts my new year, ten days ahead of schedule. By the time I turn twenty-seven, I want to make music my focus. No more schlepping pizza or wearing hairnets.

I'm ready to become a star, to live the life I see all around me, with fans and excitement and music and sheer creative orgasmic bliss.

I'm still flying high as we head to SoHo, to the club where Lori works. We squeeze in past the pretty people who are there to see a local band. More music? I'm game. I follow as Lori leads us to one of the VIP tables on the top floor. We start with beer, but I couldn't care less about the alcohol. I'm already drunk on my dreams. It's exhilarating. I pull Lori close and plant hot kisses along her neck. The fact that we're in public only makes it more exciting. Let them see. I want every guy in the joint to gnash his teeth that the prettiest girl will be leaving with me.

"Vanni," she says as she pushes me slightly away. "Come on. This is where I work."

"You're not on duty tonight," I tell her as I nibble her sensitive earlobe. She sighs against me and tries a little harder.

"Come on, Vanni. I'm serious."

I slip my hand up her shirt, around her soft tummy and along her smooth side. She wears no bra, which makes me instantly hard. I drag her hand to my lap so she can know how crazy she makes me. "So am I."

She pulls a little stronger. "Vanni."

"Fine," I relent. "But there will come a day you'll want me to prove to a room full of sexy strangers that you belong to me. About a year from now almost exactly, I'd say."

She offers a benign smile. It's nothing she hasn't heard before. I dreamed of being a rock star long before Lori walked into my aunt's living room for the first time.

Tony, however, leans across the table. "It's a tough road," he cautions at once. "If you ever want to explore Plan B, I can probably get you something where I work. I mean, it'd be something in the mail room to start you out, but it pays more than Cynzia's."

I roll my eyes. *Mail room*, good God. "There is no Plan B," I tell my friend. There are a variety of reasons I don't accept Tony's generous offer. First and foremost, I don't want to leave Brooklyn. What would happen if Susan needed me and I was working all the way in the city? I need to be close for her, especially the older she gets. She'd smack me for saying it, but she's gotten noticeably feeble in the last year, after Mama died. I know Mama's cancer took every bit as much out of her as it did out of me, arguably even more so. Mama was like a daughter to her.

Two, I can't leave old Santino, even if he was a grumpy slave master. He gave me a job when no one else would. He deserves my loyalty. Starting off in some mail room where nobody knows my name, where I become a faceless cog in the machine, has never interested me. I love to interact with people, and Cynzia's was one of the places I could sing while I worked, often charming the girls and the ladies who would tip me very well for the privilege of hearing me croon to them as I presented the daily specials. Those tips make working at Cynzia's more profitable than some entry level position in the city.

And fuck the hair net… some hoity toity big corporation would probably force me to cut my hair entirely. If I'm going to be on stage within a year, singing and fronting a band of my own, I want to be a wild carefree rocker, not some button-downed, clean cut milquetoast corporate drone.

I glance over Tony, who had cut his own ponytail off by the time he trotted off to college. We used to look like brothers. Now we're like some before and after photos, with me stuck in perpetual, rebellious youth. I guess that's who I am, who I've always been. As a rock star, I can stay that way. I can be me and be totally and completely accepted and loved for it.

Sounds like heaven to me.

Lori, who sits practically in my lap, runs her hand over my arm. "You might to reconsider, babe," she tells me. "It's always good to have a five-year plan."

"I do have a five-year plan," I say. Down below where we sit, the band everyone is waiting to see takes the stage and the place erupts in wild, wonderful chaos as the crowd goes crazy. I point at the lead singer, who looks like some random punk on the subway. He's got spiked black hair, smudged black liner around his dark eyes, a chain slung across his shoulder, holding his guitar in place while his fingers, tipped with black nail polish, grip the neck. He wears jeans, T-shirt and biker boots, but the minute he opens his mouth, he has the crowd captivated. I have to shout for Lori to hear me. "That's me in five years, but in bigger, better venues. That's the life I want, babe. And I'm ready to go for broke."

She scowls immediately as she scoots of my lap. "Emphasis: broke."

My mouth drops open as I stare at her. I can't believe she is making a deal about this. She knew what I wanted to do with my life the minute we started going out. Here I am ready to make a commitment and she's trying to bring me down to earth?

I want to soar, with her, through the stars.

And I know I can do it. The only thing left to do is prove it to her.

"I'm going to go get a drink," I tell her as I scoot out from the booth. She doesn't fight me. Inside I'm glad.

I make my way downstairs, past the bar and towards the stage. I need to get up close to watch this guy work the crowd. He's good, I have to admit. He knows how to get the crowd involved. He sings a couple of cover tunes that everyone knows the words to, so the crowd is delirious to be a part of the show. When they get to their original material, the crowd is already on their side. The material is good, too. Solid rock music, with a heavy beat I can feel in the center of my chest.

It's like sex, with its raw, primal rhythm. God, it gets me so pumped. I figure that Tony or Lori must not feel it the same way I do, way down deep in their bones. If they did, they'd understand why my passion to make music happen drives me, even when it makes no logical or rational sense. I want to be a part of something beautiful and magical and epic. Staying in the crowd, lost in the numbers, physically pains me.

Giving up is not an option. Plan B is a prison sentence.

I thrust my fist into the air along with the rest of the crowd. This is the essence of rock and roll. It's the Don't Give a Fuck aspect that pumps the blood through my veins. It's heaven and hell, pleasure and pain, sex and heartache, all rolled into one. It's fucking fantastic and I'm a part of it whenever the music starts to play. I can't even stop it anymore. I sing the songs I know the words to, and race to learn those songs I'm unfamiliar with in order to keep up with the high octane band onstage.

By the end of their set, I've forgotten about Lori and Tony. I linger by the stage as the musicians load out their equipment. The guitarist carefully puts away the three guitars he's brought along to perform. He's got long hair as black as night, which contrasts with his pale skin. "Hey, man, great show," I tell him.

His dark eyes meet mine. "Thanks."

He tries to go back to his task, but I need to know more. "You can really shred. Have you had formal study?"

The slight man offers a shrug. "You could say that." I don't say anything as I wait for him to fill in the blanks. Finally he says, "Julliard."

"No shit?" I say, immediately impressed.

He finally smiles. I get the feeling he doesn't do that often. "No shit," he answers.

I reach out my hand. "Giovanni Carnevale."

He looks down at my hand, as if he debates whether or not he should engage me. "Yael Satterlee," he responds as he shakes my outstretched hand.

I love it. Sounds exotic and interesting. "Nice to meet you. I'm an aspiring performer myself. I have to say that set was quite inspiring. Maybe I could buy you guys a round and pick your brains about the business."

The man named Yael chuckles humorlessly. "If you can tie Marty down, more power to you." He nods off towards the bar, where nearly a dozen girls surround the lead singer. He has his arm around one, while he chats up two or three more. He's literally got his hands full.

"Girl in every port?" I ask.

"Something like that. It would sell tickets if he didn't give them all away. He likes to fluff up the crowd with sexy girls at every show. I tell him they'll buy them, but I think he prefers other types of payment."

Watching the man named Marty work his groupies, I figure Yael is probably right.

"Just you then," I say. "You have to tell me about Julliard. That's like a dream come true for someone like me."

Yael raises an eyebrow. "You play?"

I shrug. Aunt Susan has tried her best to get me to play an instrument, but I really have no patience for it. "Chopsticks, mostly," I answer. We laugh.

He looks down at his packed guitars for a moment before he finally says, "Sure, why not? I could use a beer."

I notice that there are no groupies surrounding the stage for Yael. He seems perfectly happy with that. His fulfillment comes from elsewhere, and that's a beautiful, fascinating thing. "Let me help you," I say as I reach for one of the cases. He doesn't argue, so I carry the case and follow him outside through the exit behind the stage.

The December air turns our breath to frost the moment the heavy steel door closes behind us. Neither of us wears a jacket, so we trot over to his tiny, second-hand car parked close to the building in the private lot. As much as their act had filled the small club, his car is beat to shit. I can see why he'd be miffed that the lead singer gave away so many tickets for free.

As beloved as they seemed to be, they are still living hand to mouth just like I am, busting my ass at Cynzia's. This realization doesn't deter me in the slightest. I know that it's not the fault of the music, but a boneheaded decision on behalf of one of the important members of the band. With the right lead singer, Yael could be selling out venues all over the world. No, shit. He is that good.

We make it back into the bar, where I buy him that promised beer. His hands still shake from the cold outside as he brings the frosty glass to his lips. "Tell me about your band," I say.

He shrugs as he places the mug back onto the polished bar. "I guess you could say we're getting there. We've done a few demos that have been passed around town. No offers yet."

"Is that what you want?"

"Isn't that what we all want?" he shoots back. "I just want to play. I'm never more alive than when it's just me and that guitar. I can't stay away from it." I nod. I completely understand. "So I'd rather work for peanuts doing what I love than make someone else rich. It's a hard life, but it's worth it when you hit the right note, or compose the right song."

"I work at a pizza joint right now," I tell him, reaching for my own beer. "Singing is the only thing that keeps me sane. If I could do it full time, that'd be a dream come true."

He glances over me with wise, knowing eyes. "So what's stopping you?"

I sigh. I ask myself that same question dozens of times a day. "You name it, I've got an excuse for it, I guess. I live with my great aunt. She's in her seventies. She helped take care of me and my mom until my mom passed away. I guess I feel like I owe her something. How can I take away what little income we have left? Just doesn't seem practical."

Yael chuckles. "There's no room in rock music for practicality, my friend. If we were all rational, sane people, we'd get a nice, safe nine-to-five just like everyone else. We live off of the danger. We get an adrenaline rush from the uncertainty. Not a whole lot of people are built to sustain this life, and even fewer people actually make it. Knowing you can do nothing else has to be enough sometimes."

I nod. I get it.

"One person," he goes on to say. "That's all you need. Convince one person you're a rock star and that person will convince another and another. It's like a ripple in a pond." He gestures to Marty, who now sits in one of the booths near the bar, flanked on every side by an adoring fan. "Marty may not be the best singer in the world, but he's convinced enough people that he's a star. He believes it, right down to his bones. It fills in all the gaps of mediocrity."

The comment takes me by surprise. I thought Marty was a decent singer. Or maybe he had convinced me he was with his swagger and stage presence, just like Yael says. It had amped me up and sold me on his rock-n-roll image from the moment he stepped out into the spotlight.

"What about you?" I ask. I can tell by his face that he's not use that question. It's almost as if he's familiar in the anonymous, darkened shadows behind the more dynamic frontman.

He chuckles again. It's a wry little laugh that immediately makes me smile. "He's got swagger, I've got skill. Whether I play backup for him or backup for some other singer, it doesn't matter. As long as I get to play."

"You deserve to play in front of sell-out crowds," I tell him sincerely. I recognized his skill when he improvised a guitar solo on one of the cover tunes. "He's not the only one convincing people he's a rock star."

Yael shakes his head. "Yeah, I don't know about all that."

I hold up my beer mug. "I'm only one person, but you convinced me."

He mulls over what I said before he clinks his glass to mine. "Guess it's your turn to go convince someone."

I glance up towards the VIP section above the stage. "You are absolutely right." I toss some bills on the bar to pay for our drinks before I head up the spiral stairs to find Lori.

I don't have to go too far. Tony and Lori begin their descent right as I reach the middle of the staircase. I wait until they reach me. "Early night?"

Both nod. "I get enough of this place when I work," she says, stifling a yawn. She's indulged me yet again like the good girlfriend she is. I take her into my arms. "Let's head back to the house, then."

She pulls away ever so slightly. "Actually, I'm going to stay in town tonight." I immediately pout, so she touches my arm to reassure me. "I have an early train to Boston tomorrow. It just makes sense."

I nod. Her family is from Boston, and I forget that people with large families tend to have other obligations on the holidays. It's just me and Aunt Susan now. "Sure, okay," I say, but I still pout.

She giggles and stands on her tiptoes to kiss me on the lips. Even with the extra steps, she has to strain to reach me. I bend happily to meet her halfway. "Maybe I could stay with you tonight," I murmur against her lips.

She giggles again. "I told you I have to get up early tomorrow. This weekend is going to be chaos. I need some sleep."

I wrap my arms around her tiny waist. "You can sleep on the train."

She indulges my passionate kiss for a moment before she finally pulls away. "I'll see you on Monday," she promises.

"You need some cab fare?" I offer, but Tony shakes his head.

"Her apartment is on the way to my place. I'll just give her a ride. If that's okay."

I nod. Of course it's okay. It reassures me to know she's with someone I trust, someone who can protect her against the mean streets of New York City. Of course, as an Irish-American from Boston, with four older brothers the size of linebackers, I know that despite her diminutive size, Lori is quite capable of taking care of herself. But still, it's Christmas Eve-Eve and the streets were especially crowded, even with the frigid weather.

"Thanks for everything, man," I tell him as I envelop him into a bro-hug.

"My pleasure," Tony says.

"Next time you'll come to see me play," I promise with a wide smile.

"I wouldn't be anywhere else," he assures me before he takes Lori by the arm and escorts her down the stairs. I glance back to the bar, to see if Yael is still there. Perhaps I'll join him again. I have no place to be for the next few hours.

But the reclusive guitarist has disappeared, as has the horny front man, Marty. I stay only for one more drink, where I stare at the empty stage the way a homeless guy might stare at a hot meal on somebody else's table. I want this. I *need* this. I have to make this happen.

When I make it home a little over an hour later, I find Aunt Susan asleep in her chair, a book opened across her lap. My heart fills with love for this woman. She's the one who gave me the gift of music. There's only one way to repay her. I have to make myself a huge success so that I can give her the life she deserves. No more waiting on all of us, no more struggling to make ends meet, no more worries that the roof might leak or the plumbing might fail.

I would treat her like a queen. And I knew I would always be her prince.

I kneel down beside her, propped up on my knees as I circle her generous waist with both arms. I'm holding her tight, my head on top of the book on her lap, when she stirs. "Giovanni," she murmurs as she strokes my hair. "Did you just get home?" I nod but say nothing. "Did you have a good time?"

I lift my head to look at her. "The best."

A tender smile appears on her face. "Good. You deserve it."

"You deserve more," I tell her. "And one day, I'm going to give it to you."

"Oh, Vanni," she says as she cups my face with that gnarled but gentle hand. "You already did."

"I mean it," I assert. "I wouldn't even know to sing if it hadn't been for you."

She chuckles as she pulls me back into her lap to stroke my hair. I cuddle her closer. "You were born a singer, Giovanni. I just lit the way. If it hadn't been me, the music would have found you eventually. That's how destiny works."

I squeeze her tightly. God, how I needed to believe that. "Do you really mean that? You're not just saying it, right?"

She whacks me softly on the back of my head with an open palm. "You would really accuse me of lying?"

I shake my head, instantly chagrined.

"Many singers have darkened these doors. They learn all the notes. They can sing perfectly on pitch. But you, my sweet, sweet boy. You have a gift. When you open your mouth to sing, people stop to listen. They know you have something to say, something to share. That's reason enough to share it whenever you get the chance."

"Tony and Lori say that I should have a Plan B."

She plays with my hair for a long moment before she says, "Tony and Lori need a Plan B. Some people just do. There's nothing you can do about that." She tips my chin to look me in the eye. "But this isn't their path to walk, Vanni. You have to do what's right for you. You follow your heart, *tesorino*. It will never lead you astray."

I smile at her. "And you'll still love me if all I'll ever be is some low-paid singer in a bar?"

She gathers my face in her hands. "I'll love you till my dying day and beyond, Vanni. Never question that." There are tears in her eyes, so I wouldn't dare. "I just want you to be happy. If chasing rainbows makes you happy, chase away. You never know when you might actually catch one."

I chuckle as I lift up to take her into a warm bear hug. "I've already got my pot of gold right here."

She laughs. "You keep sweet-talking like that and you might just become a star yet." I know she's teasing from the glint in her eye. "Someone has got to make it," she says, bringing the conversation back on point. "Might as well be you."

I nod. "It might make things hard around here for a while. There's no steady paycheck in chasing rainbows."

She shrugs. "We made it before. We'll make it again. I never want to be the reason you don't try."

How could she think such a thing? "You're the reason I wake up in the morning," I tell her. Aside from my mother, Aunt Susan is the truest love of my life. "And if I make it, you'll be the reason why."

She grabs my chin in her hand. "*When*," she corrects. "If this is what you want, then it's up to you to make it happen. I believe in you," she adds, which fills my heart with joy. Those are about the four best words anyone can say to another. It proves she loves me best of all.

With her on my side, I can't lose.

I rise to my feet and pull her up to hers. "We have a big day tomorrow," I tell her. I wrap my arm around her, pulling her close to me as I assist her to her bedroom, accepting no argument this time. "You're my first groupie," I tell her with a grin. "I have to take care of you."

I make sure she is safely tucked into bed before I leave her room. I take the stairs two at a time to my room, where I can shamelessly dream of conquering the world.

CHAPTER THREE:

    The sun burns bright into my bedroom by the time my eyes finally peel apart. After spending much of my night burning the midnight oil, I didn't fall into bed until sometime before dawn. But it's totally worth it. I have a list of at least five places to audition. Sure, I don't expect much to happen until the holidays are over, but I like to have a plan.

    There is also a slip of paper on my nightstand, where I have written, half-asleep, lyrics for my very first song. Aunt Susan's voice lingers in my ear to "*Make it Happen*," so of course I have to pay homage to my favorite muse with my tentative verse. I find that my words don't come as easily as hers.

    But there's time to fix all that. After the bustle of our annual Christmas events die down, I can corner Aunt Susan at her old piano to help me pound out a melody for the song. Hopefully I can pick her brain for more nuggets of wisdom.

    I smile as I think of how much it will please her to do so. She is my biggest cheerleader–my good luck charm.

    I sit up and the cotton sheets slide down my half-naked body. I hadn't even bothered with pajamas, despite the cold night. I know I have to dress quickly. Susan's probably ready to dig out her old yard stick to beat some Christmas spirit back into me if I don't appear downstairs for our traditional Christmas Eve breakfast. My mouth waters just thinking of the hearty holiday meal, which consists of eggs over easy, crispy bacon, sausage and a warm slice of her cranberry coffee cake.

    Usually there's enough for us to nibble on all day so that we can run around like crazy people trying to prepare everything for the big Christmas celebration. This often includes last minute preparations with the choir for the church performance every Christmas Eve, including my customary solo singing "*O Holy Night*" a capella.

    When I grab a robe and head into the hall towards the upstairs bathroom, I expect to hear the chaos down below. Even with my mother's noticeable absence, our neighborhood–and my aunt's parish–are full of boisterous Italian women ready to pitch in to make enough food to feed an army. And they all prepare like they're going straight into battle, fending off hunger one ravioli at a time.

It's a tradition, you see. No matter how cold, snowy or inclement the weather, my Aunt always hosts a holiday meal for everyone in the neighborhood. It starts in the evening, generally around sundown, and goes all the way until we all walk down to the massive church five blocks from the house for midnight mass. Honestly, though, the party starts somewhere around noon.

With a smile, I glance down at my watch. To my surprise, it's nearly noon. She really must have let me sleep in. I rush to the bathroom to shower and change.

It only takes me ten minutes to rush through my morning routine. Steam fills the hall as I open the bathroom door. I dry my hair with a towel as I skip down the steps. My brow creases as I land on the bottom step. The drapes are still pulled and none of the lights are on, nor is there a fire burning in the small fireplace, all the things I have seen every single Christmas Eve for over ten years.

Even odder, there is no smell of food coming from the kitchen, like there usually is every waking moment of my aunt's life. I glance towards her door, which is still shut. Before I can turn that direction, someone pounds on the front door.

Maybe she had to go to the market. I was gone all day the day before, so I hadn't been able to do any last-minute errands for her. Every single Christmas for more than ten years, there have always been errands. And now that Mama was gone, only Susan or I could ensure it was all done.

I smile as I walk to the entryway to pull open the heavy wooden door with the cheerful stained glass panel across the top. I expect to see my elderly aunt with an armful of bags from the market down the street, all those leftover incidentals we always seem to forget until the last minute.

However my face instantly falls when I open the door. It's not Aunt Susan on the stoop. It's Mrs. D'onofrio from next door. "Merry Christmas, Giovanni!" she greets with a smile. She juggles four big pans, which I know are full of every comfort food known to Italy. She promptly plops them in my arms. "I would have been here earlier but I swear, the older I get the more scatterbrained I get. Usually Susan calls me to pick something up at the store, which reminds me to get my fanny in gear." She laughs. "Guess she forgot too."

I look again towards her closed bedroom door. My gut instantly sinks, but Mrs. D'onofrio practically drags me to the kitchen.

"I've prepared all the dishes. They just need to be heated. Since it's so late now, I guess we should get started."

She flips on the light in the kitchen, which is as spic and span as the night before. There are no breakfast goodies, leftover from my sleeping in. There is no warm, spicy fragrance of coffee cake rising in the air, long after she had pulled the decadent treat from the oven. And it's all wrong. Very, very wrong.

Mrs. D'onofrio and I share a startled glance before I dump the pans on the kitchen table with a bang. She grabs my arm as I race from the room and down the hall.

"Vanni!" she calls, but I can't stop. My heart settles somewhere near my stomach as I reach Aunt Susan's door. *"She's asleep,"* I tell myself over and over again. Of course she's never slept in before, but she was up late last night… waiting for me.

Oh God…

I don't even bother knocking on the door. My hand shakes as I grab the knob and turns it, opening to a darkened room, with all the drapes shut tight.

Aunt Susan is still in bed. She faces the window, just like I left her the night before.

"Vanni," Mrs. D'onofrio says softly from the doorway, but I don't stop. My feet shuffle towards the bed as I focus on the silhouette of her body under the covers, searching in vain to see the reassuring rise and fall of her chest.

She remains completely still.

Tears pour from my face but I barely notice. "Aunt Susan?" I call, and my strained voice croaks in the quiet stillness of the room.

I round the bed where I can see her face. Her mouth has fallen open, but her lovely, dark eyes are shut. The closer I get, the more I see the purple tint crawling up her neck and towards her face. My knees buckle and I land on the floor next to the bed. A cry of anguish immediately erupts from my soul. From another room I hear Mrs. D'onofrio call 9-1-1.

I can't even form a coherent thought as my shaking hand hovers over her beautiful, wizened, weathered face.

I was there in the room when my Mama passed at last. She had been in hospice for a week before she died, and every waking moment was spent staring at her, waiting for the moment she'd heave that last breath and depart her earthly dwelling for the great unknown. I didn't want to miss one minute. I never wanted to have one regret.

Now that sonofabitch Grim Reaper had stolen my last known family away from me in the still of the night… Christmas Eve no less. I didn't get to say goodbye. I didn't get to tell her… *thank you*… for all the things she had done for me.

Tears course down my face as I touch her cold skin. It feels like paper underneath my hands. "*Prozia*," I repeat, hoping that she'd hear me, hoping she's still near enough to find her way back. She has to come back if I'm being a good boy, right? Isn't that how this works? The universe can't be this cruel… it just can't. "*Ti amo. Per favore*," I say. I want to beg her to stay, and I think I remember what to say but I'm probably mangling every single syllable. My Italian has always been rudimentary at best, something that would make her whack me upside the head sometimes to correct. But I can't stop. If she can hear me, if she can hear me…

"Vanni," Mrs. D'onofrio says as she places her hands on my shoulders. "Come on."

"I'm not leaving!" I scream. I never should have left her the night before. If she had called out in her sleep, I could have helped her.

"Come on. Let me get you some tea."

"I don't want any fucking tea!" I bellow at the generous woman who is just trying to be kind. And of course I know that. But I'm so angry. I'm so hollow. Instantly and completely. I just want to rage. My mouth opens and I release one long, angry wail as I clutch the blanket on her bed.

Mrs. D'onofrio sinks to her knees beside me and cradles me as I sob into the blanket. Her hand gently caresses my hair, which is still damp from my shower.

It had been only minutes, but my whole world had changed.

I do not leave the room until the paramedics come, and even then I can only make it to the doorway. Mrs. D'onofrio tries to turn me away, so I can't watch. The minute they roll her over onto her back, I see that her entire left side is dark purple. I collapse against the door.

"Come on, hon," Mrs. D'onofrio says. "There's nothing more you can do here."

Finally I relent and allow her to guide me out into the living room, which has begun to fill with people. Any other Christmas Eve, those people would have been boisterous and jovial. But it has ceased to be a holiday celebration.

Our time of mourning Susan Luisa Faustino has officially begun.

I sit in her chair in the living room, positioned right next to the humble Christmas tree. The smell of pine races up my nose as mourner after mourner passes by, offering me words of comfort I can't even hear. It all devolves into some indiscernible hum.

I barely understand when the paramedics tell me that it was a massive coronary, and that she likely went quickly. I think that's supposed to make me feel better, but it doesn't. This isn't the way it's supposed to go. This isn't the plan. This can't be real. Maybe I'm having a weird nightmare. I pray each and every second that Aunt Susan will be nudging me awake, for the holiday we were supposed to have. The kind of holiday we always had.

Instead the nightmare drags painfully on. She stays in that room until the coroner comes, which is mercifully within an hour. I stand on the stoop with other people I haven't the presence of mind to identify. We all huddle together, fending off the cold and the sorrow as the EMT's roll the gurney from the house. I hear weeping behind me as someone realizes she's covered head to toe, as if it is some revelation that she is really gone.

Father Genovese arrives to console me. We sit together in the living room. Someone has prepared hot buttered rum, which I cradle within my hands. I don't speak much. I may shake my head or nod, but I hear nothing. Words jumble together like perfect nonsense.

Nothing makes sense to me now. Just yesterday... *just hours ago*... I had a plan. I had a dream. I had a *family*. Now I am alone. More alone than I have ever been.

As alone as I feel, it doesn't take long for people to fill the tiny brownstone to overflowing. Everyone from the neighborhood stops to pay their respects. There's more food than anyone wants to eat. There are stories, many stories, of Susan and her giant heart. I hear laughter mingle with the sobs as everyone reminisces on the amazing woman who had somehow just left the planet.

Already the world seems smaller without her.

I let the world spin on without me. I watch everyone bustle around the small house as if they are all in fast forward. The hands on the grandfather clock keep spinning, even though my heart stopped beating hours ago. I sit in that chair, staring into the Christmas tree that someone had finally turned on. "She loved Christmas," I hear someone say.

Their use of past tense punctures my heart.

They are right. She loved Christmas. She loved the hope of it. "Every day of your life should feel like Christmas morning," she would say.

Tears keep pooling in my eyes. I have no shame as I let them fall. Nothing matters anymore.

It is after six o'clock in the evening before I find the presence of mind to call Lori. But I figure she deserves to have a nice holiday with her family. I can't just call her and drop this kind of bombshell. Susan would never forgive me.

In the blink of an eye it is nine o'clock, when everyone begins their migration to the church. They need the comfort of those four walls now more than ever. Mrs. D'onofrio sits on the sofa next to me. "You should go. It will make you feel better. Perhaps you could sing in her honor," she offers but I shake my head.

I'm not sure I can ever sing again. And I know I'll never sing *that* song again. I can't, not without her to hear me.

"Then I can stay," she says. Again I shake my head.

As nice as everyone has been, I need to be alone. I'm exhausted from their constant attention, as well-meaning as it is. I need to rip off every scab by myself, in private.

Mrs. D'onofrio is not convinced. She purses her lips as she stares at me. I notice how her eyes are bloodshot and her nose is red. This has been a hard day for her too. I struggle to smile as I touch her hand. "Thank you for everything," I tell her. I will never forget that she was there for me on my most difficult day.

She leans forward and cups my face with her hand. It reminds me so much of Aunt Susan that it rips fresh tears from my eyes. "I'm always here. Right next door if you need me. For anything."

I nod and she bends forward to kiss my forehead. She stands and gathers her things, bringing up the rear of all the departing mourners. I can't even rise to lock the door behind them. What difference does it make anyway? What is there left to steal? Every good thing is gone, including my heart.

A deafening silence falls over the house the instant the door closes behind them. It's quieter than it has ever been, so quiet that I can distinctly hear the quiet tick-tock of the grandfather clock, the steady heartbeat of my lonely home. How time keeps marching forward, I have no idea. Doesn't it know? Doesn't it care? One of the most amazing women on the planet is gone, and yet she left with no fanfare, no applause or standing ovation for her final curtain call. Just one final breath in the darkness of night and it was over.

I stare at the tree. There are several boxes under it; all cheerfully wrapped, waiting for the intended recipient to rip them open on Christmas morning. It breaks my heart all over again that her boxes will never be opened. She'll never gasp with glee when she opens up the box with the colorful scarf I had purchased way back in August, when life was still normal. There is a small box with a gold pendent, an eighth note, which I bought with my Christmas bonus. She had never been one for jewelry, but the simple design and the emotional significance inspired me to buy it.

My eyes travel to the upright piano in the corner of the room. I stare at it for a long time as I remember every muggy summer afternoon that I spent there, learning how to play piano because it gave my hands "something productive to do," after I'd been picked up for tagging an ugly, old abandoned building in the neighborhood.

I could almost picture myself sitting there years ago, all legs and swagger, and not one iota of common sense. I could see her standing over me, patient and unmoving as she guided me through those reluctant lessons. I would get so frustrated that I was ready to tip over the bench and say to hell with all of it. She'd wind up her metronome and let it sway back and forth, telling me to concentrate. To breathe. To count out the beats and everything would be okay.

I took a deep breath as I counted each second on the clock, subconsciously willing it to go backwards. Take me back to those humid afternoons, take me back to the first day I stepped foot in this house, when I first understood the concept of "family." Up until then it had been just me and Mama against the world.

What a revelation it had been that we weren't alone anymore.

Now I am alone. Irrefutably and heartbreakingly alone.

The clock strikes midnight before I move from that chair. I haven't eaten. I haven't spoken. And, for about three hours at least, I haven't cried. The fire someone started in the fireplace has burned out its last ember, allowing a chill from the cold night air outside to filter into the room.

I don't bother with anything. I leave all the lights on, including those twinkling on the Christmas tree. I don't worry about putting away the grief buffet in the kitchen. I can't do anything more than lumber up the steps towards my room, simply because I need to sleep. I need to close my eyes and forget.

I stumble to my bed, where I fall on the mattress without shedding one article of clothing. I realize then that I had left my cell phone on my nightstand all day long. More out of habit than anything, I grab it to check if I had any missed calls. I have more than a dozen, with five of those belonging to Lori.

I sigh as I put my phone back on the nightstand. I'll call her tomorrow, at a decent hour. There's no reason that the both of us should fight through that first shitty night on Planet Earth without Susan, trying to cope with the knowledge my beloved *prozia* would never smile, or laugh, or joke, or console, or correct, or hug… or love… ever again.

Fresh tears spring into my eyes as I reach for the lamp by my bed. I need that light. I need to see what's coming from now on. That bastard death stole my aunt in the middle of a dark night like the cowardly shit that it is. When it comes for me, I want to see its hateful face.

As my hand pulls away from the chain, I see the scrap of paper with my meager songwriting scrawled across it like chicken scratch. Grief closes my heart in a vice as I realize that Aunt Susan would never be able to help me finish the song like I had hoped. She'll never even hear it.

For that reason alone, it was no longer worth singing.

I pull the covers up to my ears, close my eyes, and pray for morning.

CHAPTER FOUR:

I let Christmas 2004 come and go without me. I don't answer the phone. I don't rise from the bed unless I have to go to the bathroom, the one pressing physical need that cannot be denied. Each minimal task is done with effort, including a return call to Lori at last, sometime around two-thirty in the afternoon, Christmas Day. I might not have called her at all, but I figure she needs to know what is going on, and it's better to hear it from me.

Her sobs reduce me once again to tears, as I relive the moment where I found my aunt, cold and dead in her bed.

"I can be there in a few hours," she promises. I shake my head, though she cannot see. There's no one to see. No one. My throat closes over the painful lump I just can't swallow.

"Stay with your family, Lori. It's Christmas."

"You shouldn't be alone," she says. Little does she know that's all I want.

"I'll be okay," I promise, though it's complete and utter bullshit.

Bullshit. That's a word I can use now. Gone is the threat of foul-tasting homemade soap. It seems a hollow victory, but he minute I get off the phone with Lori, I try the words out, speaking them to the cold empty room. It is as each word can summon Susan to return, if only to beat me with her yardstick for being such a naughty boy.

"Fuck this shit," I say, slowly, annunciating every word. "You cock-sucking, motherfucking, ass-munching son of a bitch." My voice rises with my anger. I don't know who I'm attacking. Death, maybe. God, probably. The capricious hand of fate. Either way, "You fucking suck!"

Finally I bring out the big guns. "Goddamn you, motherfucker. Is this some kind of fucking game? Are we just your goddamn pawns to push around? You can suck my big, fat cock!"

Just saying the words fuels me, like pumping gas into a car running on fumes. I hop out of the bed, buzzing with newfound adrenaline. I grab a baseball bat from my closet. I string together any curse words I can think of as I swing at my computer, my desk, my dresser drawers, my bed. Every crack and boom is strangely rewarding.

Debris flies everywhere as I dismantle my room. It was the first real room I had ever had, but it's meaningless now. Now that Aunt Susan is dead, I probably won't get to stay here in her house anyway. I'm used to things being taken right out from under me, something that started when I was two years old. Why should my home, the last thing I have in this world, be any different?

Let them sell it now, I think to myself as I start bashing big holes in the walls. At some point I start crying again, though I'm not sure when.

Finally I end up on my knees amidst the carnage. Feathers float around the room like snow, released from my down pillow and comforter with repeated blows from my baseball bat.

I look around the room. It's wrecked every bit as wrecked as I am.

Yet the door doesn't open. Aunt Susan doesn't charge in, her trusty yard stick in one hand and a big chuck of soap in the other.

I realize with a start that there's no one there to stop me from self-destructing anymore. There's no one to put me in check. There's no one left who gives that much of a damn.

I toss my bat aside and leave the room I can no longer face. There's no one there to pick up the pieces anymore, either.

I grab my jacket and my keys, but leave my phone. It, like the house phone, has been ringing non-stop, but I can't face any of it. I'll have to think about things like funerals and work and life soon, but I'm not ready. Instead I head down to the liquor store down the street and around the block. Three hundred and fifty-two steps. I know, because I count each one. Since I can't even stomach the thought of food, I decide to pour vast amounts of whiskey on the hurt. I buy at least two bottles.

Both Mama and Aunt Susan had an aversion to hard liquor. We usually always had wine in the house, or maybe some rum or liqueurs for baking. (Aunt Susan's rum balls were the envy of the entire neighborhood this time of year.) But they drew the line when it came to anything else, and I knew this had everything to do with my dad. My old man would win very few prizes, but drunk of the year was right at the top of that list.

The lucky sonofabitch. He got to miss all the heartache and the struggle just by crawling into a bottle. Suddenly that's all I want to do, too.

When I get back home, Mrs. D'onofrio waits for me on the stoop. She has yet another casserole dish, but just seeing that white dish with blue flowers makes me want to puke. Nothing will ever be as good again as Aunt Susan's cooking. This realization chases away any appetite.

I want my Christmas breakfast. I want my cranberry streusel cake.

I want my aunt back.

Mrs. D'onofrio offers to come inside to help me take care of things. It's all I can do to refuse. She tells me that I shouldn't eat alone, that food is meant to be shared. I stop short of asking her if she plans to come over every meal for the rest of her life, because eating alone is no longer an option for me. Finally she gets the hint and leaves, but only after I take her casserole.

Italian women, I think to myself with a half-smile. They'll never let you go hungry, no matter what's going on. Sick? Here's a bowl of minestrone. Funeral? Here's some ziti. Zombie apocalypse? Here. Have a cannoli.

I take the dish into the kitchen, which I realize has been cleaned by all the mourners who had stopped by the day before. I am a part of their community, so I know they won't leave me hanging, any more than Aunt Susan would have left any other neighbor hanging in their time of need.

Her good deeds are finally being rewarded, but to the wrong person. I figure I'll have to craft a "Do Not Disturb" sign for the window if I want any real privacy.

I shove the dish into the overfilled refrigerator before grabbing a tumbler from the cupboard, along with a pad of paper and a pencil from the drawer next to the fridge.

It still has her half-crafted grocery list on top. My gut lurches to see her recognizable handwriting. It had never changed, in all the years I had known her. Where mine was barely readable, her beautiful cursive had graceful lines and loops, picture perfect like it was lifted from all those grade school wall decorations to teach proper handwriting.

If my aunt did it, she made sure it was done right. Likewise I take care as I write my door sign in big bold letters. "IN MOURNING. PLEASE DO NOT DISTURB."

I place it in the window just to the side of the door, next to the doorbell. I know if I hear this sound, I will shatter into a gazillion pieces.

Only the silence, and my lonely little cocoon, holds me together.

The lights from the Christmas tree still twinkle as I sink to the floor next to it. I could turn on the television for some noise, but I don't think I could make it through some schmaltzy holiday cheer-fest surely playing nonstop all Christmas Day.

Instead I fill the glass. It burns going down but somehow that feels right. It gives me something else to think about than the dead weight in my chest. I fill the glass again. It burns going down again. But my brain mercifully starts to cloud as I force myself to chug each glassful at a time.

After I kill the first bottle, I feel removed enough from my grief to introduce noise into my surroundings. I begin at the piano, because where else would I begin? I drag myself from the floor, staggering just a tad as I amble over to the piano.

I settle onto the hard wooden bench and lift the fall board. I have always loved the promise of the keys, sitting uniformly side by side, just waiting for the touch of a human hand to make some of the most beautiful music on earth. Every Christmas for the last eleven years, I listened to my Aunt Susan play every single Christmas carol I could think of to request.

I only know one song, because it was all I had the patience to learn. I set my half-empty glass of booze to the side as I stumble clumsily through Chopsticks. Every missed note resounds in the tiny living room. I growl under my breath in muted frustration before I try it again.

I play the stupid song for two hours straight, until I can get through it without missing any notes. When I glance up at the music rack, I notice that the book of Christmas songs sits right on top. Likely she had been using that to teach her students. I open the book and skim through. "*Silent Night*"? No way. "*O Holy Night*"? Never, never again. Finally I settle on "*Away in a Manger.*" I study the notes on the page, trying my damnest to remember Aunt Susan's lessons. "Open space–FACE," I could hear her say. "Every line: Every Good Boy Does Fine."

I search every working brain cell to figure out which key goes to which note, and stumble through the first few bars of the song. If I get frustrated, I stop, wind the metronome, and let it calm me down, just like Aunt Susan told me to.

By the end of the night, I finally teach myself one song.

Then, and only then, do I stumble in a drunken stupor back to the sofa, where I am forced to sleep after destroying my bedroom.

The snow finally arrives the day after Christmas, bringing with it my girlfriend and my best buddy, who don't care a whit about my *Do Not Disturb* sign in the window. Lori and Tony bang on the door until I pull it open, nursing a serious hangover for the first time in my life.

Lori steps right into my arms, holding me tight as she sobs against my chest.

There are tears in Tony's eyes as he reaches for a random but powerful hug as well. Fortunately I've exhausted most of my tears by this point. I'm numb. It is a welcome relief.

Their condolences go in one ear and out the other as we all walk into the living room, where unopened presents still sit under the twinkling, festive tree.

It's the only thing that brings light into my darkened home.

They say nothing as they watch me fill yet another glass. I haven't eaten in days. My stomach growls loud enough for all to hear, but I know anything solid I shove down my gullet will come right back up again.

Unlike everyone else, Lori and Tony don't say much. Lori sits next to me on the couch, her soft hand against my back and her head on my shoulder. Tony sits in Susan's chair, absently tracing the dainty doilies on either arm. We all miss her. We all share her loss. We don't talk about Christmas, or family, or music. We all sit and silently reflect.

Finally Tony heads into the kitchen to retrieve two more glasses. He pours a drink for both Lori and himself, before holding up the glass. "To Susan," he says, with a catch in his throat. Lori softly sobs as she drinks. Tears I didn't know I had left to shed spring instantly to my eyes, but I don't let them fall.

I can't.

If I start crying, I don't think I'll ever stop. And that's not the image of a man I ever want to display for Lori. She deserves a true man, one who can cowboy the fuck up whenever shit goes down. My aunt didn't raise me to be weak.

To honor her, I'd never be weak again.

Night falls without us saying much of anything. They break into the grief buffet, with Lori preparing some of the dishes so we could have some semblance of dinner. She brings me a plate but I don't touch it. Her hand lingers on my shoulder. "You need to eat, baby," she says.

All I hear is Susan's voice. I shake my head. "I'm not hungry," I croak at last.

It's near ten by the time she says, "Have you made any arrangements?"

I shake my head. "I can't think about that right now."

"Now is the time to think about that," she corrects gently. "I think it will help."

I glare at her. "How can anything help?"

She appears contrite and confused. She's handling wet dynamite and she knows it. "Do you know where… where they took her?"

I swallow the lump in my throat. I had been so self-absorbed I have no idea. It makes me feel even more like a shit. Aunt Susan has one last errand for me on this earth, and that is to put her away with all the love and respect she deserves.

"I don't know where to start," I confess at last.

Lori nods. "I'm here," she promises. "I'll help you."

Finally I let her take me into her arms.

Tony leaves around midnight. By then, Lori has discovered what I did to my room. She brings blankets down to the living room so we can sleep together on the couch. As I cuddle her warm body next to mine, I stare at the blinking lights on the Christmas tree. Christmas used to be my favorite holiday, though I can't even tell you why. When I was a kid, I had only one wish each and every year. I wrote Santa every August like clockwork, figuring he'd need a little time to pull off the Christmas miracle I was seeking. I wanted my Dad to come home. "Bring him home by the 21st," I'd request in every letter my mother would help me write. "That way I can see him for my birthday too!"

It dawns on me how difficult that must have been for her. She was the parent who stayed behind, and yet all I could think about was the selfish asshole that left us.

I guess the rotted apple doesn't fall too far from the tree.

Each and every Christmas was a disappointment, despite how hard she tried to make it nice for me. Our resources were so limited, my name usually ended up on a tree in a mall somewhere, so good Samaritans could patch up all the holes with presents that would miraculously appear under my tree.

For a kid, a present with your name on it means you're in the club. Somebody loves you.

How hard it must have been for Mama. She probably had just as many dreams and plans as I did. But life made a habit of kicking her in the teeth.

That all changed when we moved in with Aunt Susan, who gave us the home we'd always wanted.

Now I am an orphan in every sense of the word. Just days ago I was planning for this grand future, and now I didn't even know where I'll be living when 2004 gives way to 2005.

Fortunately Lori, though undeniably saddened by my aunt's death, isn't burdened by the same crushing sorrow that I am. The next day, she calls Father Genovese first thing. As it turns out, Aunt Susan had all her arrangements in place. Even in death, she is looking out for all of us, trying to ease our burdens and make our lives a little better.

Lori then calls the mortuary where my aunt's body has been delivered. She schedules an appointment to finalize the funeral arrangements, and to bring in the clothes in which we wanted Susan buried. She asks me if I have a preference. I shake my head. "Blue," is all I can offer.

We both love the color blue.

Lori puts together an outfit, one of Susan's nicest blue dresses, with a lace overlay. She wore it for my high school graduation, which at the time warranted a special celebration. I was a problem kid, so that diploma was a victory not only for me, but for those who whipped me into shape. Tops on that list? My Aunt Susan. It was her accomplishment every bit as it was mine.

After I dress to go with Lori to the mortuary, I pause only briefly to pull a couple of gifts out from under the tree. I bought them for Susan. I want her to have them, and this is my last chance to give them to her.

The mortuary isn't that far from the house, so we brave the snow and the cold to walk the mile or so it takes to get there. I clasp Lori's hand in mine, but we say very little on our journey. I say even less as we approach the modest brick building housing the funeral home.

Funeral home. What a depressing fucking name for a building. The décor inside isn't much better. It looks like an actual home, which is supposed to be comforting, but it's not. I know behind several closed doors are caskets filled with corpses. The sickly sterile stench, mixed with an obnoxious combination of fresh flowers, nearly chokes me. I can't fathom what my aunt is even doing in a place like this.

The director, Bob or Frank or Johnny or fuck-all, greets us, shakes our hands, and speaks in hushed, sympathetic tones. It's almost as if everyone is afraid to speak too loudly for fear of actually waking the dead. It lends itself to this whole charade, that the bodies in this wretched place were actually sleeping guests, rather than human remains.

Remains, I think with a sinking gut. That's all that's left of any of us, eventually.

He leads us to his office, where his assistant takes the clothes from Lori. He tells us what arrangements my aunt had prepared in advance. While they talk about the wake and the funeral service, I stare at the crucifix hanging behind the funeral director's desk.

It's all meaningless to me now.

Lori steps up to the plate like a champ. She loves Susan almost as much as I do, and her faith is equally important. Thanks to Lori, I know my aunt will have the respectful sendoff she wanted. As we walk back to the house, I hold Lori close to me. I've never needed her more, and that scares me.

It reassures me how strongly she hugs back.

When the guests come, she's the one who manages everything. I sit in Susan's chair and itch for another drink, but I won't tarnish Aunt Susan's memory amongst her closest friends by turning into a profanity-spewing drunk for everyone to see.

Instead I sit quietly, and nod through all the stories from all the people who, in their fruitless attempt to make me feel better, pull my nerves to the breaking point. How little it comforts me to hear that Aunt Susan is likely teaching Jesus to play piano in heaven now, when her piano sits silent across the room. When her bedroom is locked tight like a tomb, or her kitchen isn't full of the delicious aroma of her cooking, and each and every thing I see or hear is a reminder of her loss.

God could have anyone in all of time and space that he wanted, from Beethoven to Liberace. Susan was all I had, and it fucking hurts that she's gone.

Lori shoos all our guests away by eight o'clock that night. I start drinking and do not stop until I pass out in Susan's recliner.

We hold the vigil on the 28th of December, and her funeral on the 29th. Both our brownstone and the parish itself are filled to overflowing.

Fortunately, for the wake, I'm allowed to drink all I want. It makes it easier to stomach all the eulogies given as each sad guest extols Susan Faustino's many virtues to the grieving crowd. My nerves are dead by the time we make it to the funeral. I barely even crumble as I spot the golden eighth note around her neck as I pass by the casket to offer my final respects.

Her color has been artificially restored, so she looks like an old woman sleeping within the satin interior of a cozy box. She doesn't look like Susan, though. Her dress barely fits over her shrunken body, and her eyes look as if they have been sewn shut, and they probably have been.

There is no twinkle to be found, no smile to remember. She is, simply, *gone*.

It makes my job as pallbearer much easier.

I don't have to volunteer for this job. Plenty of good strong men are willing to do it for me, including Tony, who shows up with his entire family for the ceremony.

But honestly it is the last thing I could do for my aunt, and I want to do it.

I carry her to her final resting place, where I stand, stoic as a statue, as she's lowered into the ground.

With every fiber of my being I want to throw myself on the casket, to pull her out of that cramped little box and keep her with me always. But these are her wishes, and I will abide, even if it kills me.

As each hour passes, I pray that it does.

"*My beautiful boy*," I can almost hear her whisper. My chin trembles but I do not cry. I've thrown my fits in private, but I won't do it here. Aunt Susan had spent more than a decade making me a man. By God I was going to act like one.

That night, all the mourners are finally gone as the macabre ritual completes. I still get screaming drunk, and this time I pull Lori to me, the first time in days. Her body is soft and warm and alive underneath me. I sink into her and it's like piercing the fog that has surrounded me for days. I say nothing. I'm afraid to say anything. Fucking her on my aunt's sofa in the middle of her living room, despite the watchful eyes from family portraits or even Jesus himself, from where he is impaled silently and forever on the cross, separates me further from that good Catholic boy Susan had raised me to be.

    It's a damn shame I have given up on being a rock star.

    That's where bad boys like me belong.

CHAPTER FIVE:

The days leading up to Susan's funeral had flown by in such a haze I could barely distinguish them. The days afterwards, while we are all trying to put the pieces back together again, drag minute by excruciating minute. That New Year's Eve is smack dab in the middle only serves to make it weirder. For such a festive holiday, I know I'll never look at it the same way again. I spend the end of 2004 on my aunt's couch alone, simply because Lori had to work.

Of course I'm not entirely alone. I have several bottles of booze to keep me company.

I pass out before the ball drops.

Santino had paid his respects at the funeral, where he offered me a week off, which I gladly take. I still don't want to face life yet, not with everything up in the air. It's kind of like picking up the pieces after a bomb detonates. I don't know where to start.

"*How do you eat an elephant?*" I hear the echo of Susan's voice asking me, something she had said in all those times I got so frustrated with music and homework and chores. "*One piece at a time.*"

The first order of business is actual business. At nine o'clock the first Monday of 2005, I sit across from my aunt's attorney, Donald Meir, in his Brooklyn office. Like everyone else in my aunt's life, her lawyer is from the neighborhood, someone she had known for years and obviously trusted implicitly.

I am not quite as convinced. I'm sure that he is about to toss me out of the only home I've ever known, and where I'll go from there is anyone's guess. What he says instead blows my mind. My mouth falls open, as does Lori's, who has come along with me. "What do you mean, it's mine?"

Donald links his fingers on top of the open folder in front of him. "She willed the house to you, Giovanni. You are her last living relative. Most of her estate is split between you and her parish, with you retaining most items of any value. That includes the house, some stock, along with her modest life insurance policy."

He goes on, but I stop listening after '*the house*'. "I don't understand. You're not asking me to leave?" The news is so unexpected I think I'm in shock.

Donald chuckles. "No, of course not. Your aunt owned the property free and clear. Aside from property taxes, you don't have a monthly mortgage or rent. In fact," he adds as he pulls a piece of paper from the stack. "You have an income from her other investments."

He slides the graph my way. A single number is circled. My eyes widen. "Are you serious?"

Donald shrugs. "Granted it's not enough to live on. What is, these days? But it'll help keep you afloat."

I stare at him. I barely blink. What he called 'not enough to live on,' was more than my salary at Cynzia's easy. I could take time off if I wanted. I could pursue music–

No, I think suddenly. No, I can't.

"And of course if you ever need additional income, you can always sell the brownstone. In today's market, it could pull in a tidy little profit, especially now that the entire area is being renovated. You could sell it like that," he says as he snaps his fingers.

"No," I say at once. "I'm not selling the brownstone."

That house has been in my family since the day it was built. I'll never sell it. No matter what.

"Fine," Donald says with a raised hand. "Just know there are options. Should I call the church and schedule a pickup for all the belongings bequeathed to them in her will?"

"As soon as possible," I find myself saying. I feel guilty how relieved I am that most of her things will be given away. Sure, it's charitable for the church, but deep down I hope that, with her things gone, I won't feel as haunted every single night by every single shadow looming near her now dark, quiet room. "Tomorrow works for me. Noon, maybe?"

He nods as he makes a note of it on the folder. "I'll let them know. I guess that's it, then. Unless you have any questions."

Since he has already blown my mind, I honestly can't think of a single one. I shake my head as I rise from the chair.

Donald rises also, taking a long, slender envelope from the file folder. I know it holds a check. My knees nearly buckle under me when I see the number $38,492 under the *Pay the Amount Of* section.

"That's her $50,000 life insurance policy less the cost of her final expenses. Again, I know it's a modest amount. For the record I always advised her to get more."

More? I'm stunned there is even this.

I remain stunned all the way back out to the street, where we head back on foot towards the house.

My house.

Lori threads her arm through mine. There's a skip in her step that wasn't there before. "Can you believe it?" she finally says. "We should go somewhere to celebrate."

"We're not going out to eat," I decide at once, annoyed she'd even suggest such a thing. "We wouldn't even have this money if she were alive." My voice softens. I'm still so, so angry, but it's useless to yell at anybody. "I'd rather have her here."

"Vanni," Lori admonishes. "Your great-aunt was a seventy-one-year-old woman. What did you think? That she'd live forever?"

I narrow my eyes as I glare at her. "Yes," I say. She can judge me all she wants but my aunt was not old. She was not feeble. She had complete control of her senses and relative mobility. She also had more life in the tip of her pinky than most have in their entire bodies. The world has lost its color with her passing. Why can't Lori see that?

She broaches the next topic very carefully. "I suppose now you have the freedom to pursue your music."

My throat tightens. Yes, I suppose I *could*, but there is no way. Not now. I shrug. "Like Donald said, it isn't a whole lot of money. I'd rather have it in the bank than gamble it on some kind of what if."

She nods as her features relax on her face. I can tell she's relieved that I won't be pursuing a career in music, but I really can't understand why. Like being a waitress in a New York City bar was any more secure.

It's a moot point, so I decide to let the subject drop.

We compromise on dinner out by stopping in Cynzia's, where I pick up my check and schedule. "You can take more time if you need it, Giovanni."

I know Santino must be concerned. He actually got my name right.

"I'm fine," I assure him. "Everything is done anyway, and sitting around that quiet house is driving me crazy. I could use the money, man," I finally admit, which softens old Santino even more.

"Fine. I could use some help tomorrow. Dinah's due any day, so she finally took her maternity leave."

"I'll be here with bells on," I promise.

"Just the hairnet!" he calls after me.

It's after nine o'clock in the evening when we return home. I carry our leftovers in a greasy flat box, which won't fit inside our loaded refrigerator.

"Can't we give this back to the church or something?" I ask Lori, but she shakes her head.

"It's perishable. Speaking of church, who is supposed to be here tomorrow when they come for Susan's things?"

"Shit," I breathe as I bring my hand to my forehead. I had completely forgotten.

"I've got a late shift tomorrow," she says as she finally finds a spot for the storage container full of our leftover pizza. "I can do it."

I smile at her. She really has been my rock through this whole troubling period. I know there are no words to tell her how much that means to me. "Thanks, Lori."

She stands to her feet and slides her arms around my waist, linking her hands behind my back. I bend for a kiss. "You taste like wine," I mutter against her lips.

"So do you," she whispers back.

I lift her easily into my arms, cupping her ass with both hands as I bring her mouth to mine for a more thorough exploration. She shudders against me. "Let's go to bed," she begs.

"Let's stay here," I offer instead, depositing her on the kitchen table. Her eyes widen as she stares up at me.

"Vanni," she says with a slight shake of her head.

"Why not?" I ask as I pin her to the table with my weight on top of her. "Who's going to stop us? It's my house," I finally say out loud.

She tries again. "Vanni. That's just the vino talking."

"Then let's listen what it has to say." I bury my face in her neck, dragging my mouth along her sensitive skin.

I don't care if it's the wine, frankly. I just need to feel *something*. I'm tired of feeling so fucking empty. Everything flows through me like wind through a dead, hollow tree. My hands are urgent as they slide up her body. It is such a warm body, so smooth under my palm. I rise to a standing position above her, keeping my eyes on her face as I peel away my shirt, which makes her lick her lips in anticipation.

She's mine now and I know it. I can't help but smirk in self-satisfaction as I crawl in between her legs for one of the best meals available to me on that table now that lovingly prepared Italian feasts were no longer an option. I spread her legs even wider before one of my large hands holds Lori open, to study her under the bright light. My tongue finds her clit easily and she writhes around me as I work my magic. Each cry gets louder than the last. It gets me so pumped. I feel so powerful, like a genie, there to grant her every wish.

I roll her onto her stomach and I take her from behind. I don't ask for permission. She's begging me to fill her, and I'm more than happy to oblige. It's all I want to do. Blood pumps through my body as I start to feel something again, finally. Sure it's something titillating, something naughty, but it almost has to be. Like jumping out of a plane or riding a bull, it's an adrenaline rush to push back at some of the boundaries I had always accepted.

By the time I come I utter a warrior cry.

We spend another night on that tiny, cramped sofa in the living room. I know I'll have to buy bedroom furniture again, considering I had decimated every single piece it in my bedroom upstairs. I'd destroyed the bedroom itself, which poses the question of what other rooms I can use going forward. The master bedroom on the ground floor is the largest of the three, but I wonder if I'm even capable of moving anything into Susan's room after all her things are gone.

I'm glad I picked up a shift at Cynzia's. The busy shift keeps me hopping all afternoon. I figure old Santino told everyone about my Aunt Susan, because the customers tip me handsomely all day long. My wallet nearly bursts a hole through my pocket by the time I head home.

When I open the door, I smell a glorious aroma from the kitchen. I smile as I head straight for the back of the house, where Lori prepares our meal. I slip my arms around her waist and bend to kiss her neck. "This is an unexpected surprise."

She smiles wide as she turns for a kiss. "I was here all day, waiting for the church to pick up your aunt's stuff. Remember?"

"Oh yeah," I nod as I peer over her shoulder to see what she's cooking. "What smells so good?"

"Roast chicken, garlic potatoes and steamed broccoli."

I laugh. "I think that's the healthiest meal ever prepared on this stove. It may go into shock."

"I can cook all that other stuff," she says. "I can make anything." She spins around into my arms. "But I thought it may bring up too many bad memories. I know I'm just a pale substitute for the real thing."

I hold her tight. "You are no substitute."

She gives me a happy smile as she pulls me closer. "We can have a new start, Vanni. Your house. Your future. Our future," she corrects awkwardly, hopefully. I'd never thought about a future I'd share with somebody else before. Right now it sounds damned good. I reward her with a deep kiss. She melts against me for a long, sweet moment before I push her away with a smile.

"Feed me first, woman," I tease, which makes her giggle.

I head over to the table in the corner. I avoid looking at the kitschy salt-and-pepper shakers on the table. Aunt Susan collected them. She had a whole shelf devoted to them in the china cabinet in the formal dining room. She would rotate them out on a weekly basis, almost like a ritual. "It's the only way I'll get to enjoy them all," she'd say when I poked fun at her for it.

Now looking at them reminds me of all I don't have, which is something I've been trying to avoid like a bad habit after the last eleven days. I take them from the table and head straight for the china cabinet.

Only I discover as I pass through the swinging door to the formal dining room that I no longer have one. "Lori!" I holler.

She runs in behind me. "What?"

Her sweet voice does nothing to calm me. "Where's my aunt's furniture?"

"They picked it up."

"What does a church need with a china cabinet?" Then it dawns on me what is also missing. "Where are the salt-n-pepper shakers?"

She seems reluctant to answer, sensing my darkening mood. "The people from the church. Susan wanted to give them something to remember her by. She assigned them all." Her eyes fall to the ones in my grasp. "She wanted you to have those."

I look down at the Laurel & Hardy figurines. We had spent many Saturday afternoons watching these shows after I came to live with her. I remember how her laugh was always so clear and true, full of life. It was contagious. Eventually I laughed more because her joy was infectious, rather than the slapstick comedy on the screen.

My throat tightens as I glance around the bare room, left only with portraits on the wall. "Where am I supposed to put them? Christ," I say, empowered by the forbidden word. "What else did they take?"

For some reason I had believed they would only take the things from her bedroom. The clothes she would never wear. The bed where she drew her last breath. I know now this is just wishful thinking, as if it will make her absence sting a little less if I have fewer reminders.

"They took what was on her list," Lori offers feebly. "Didn't you read it?"

I glare at her before I turn down the hall and open the door to Susan's bedroom. It's completely empty. From the wide-open closet door, I know that everything is gone from there too. Pictures on the wall, even the drapes. It's all gone. "Well, they certainly didn't miss a spot, did they?"

She touches my arm. "It was what she wanted for you. A clean slate."

I wrench from her and stalk to the living room. I flip on the light to see in clear detail what all had changed. Her recliner is gone, that I see right away. The sofa is present and accounted for, though, as is the grandfather clock. "I told them we needed the sofa still, until we get some furniture of our own. The grandfather clock she wanted you to have. Said that her father bought it, and she wanted to keep it in the family."

I nod as I turn to the wall opposite the window, where I had spent summer after summer learning the piano.

Only nothing is there, except for the outline of the upright piano the sun had burned into the ages-old wallpaper. No piano, no metronome... it's all gone. "Where?" I grit between my teeth.

"She wanted the church to have it."

I spin on her. "Susan? Or you?"

She drops her hands to her side. "You don't even know how to play, Vanni."

"That's not the point!"

"Then what is the point?"

"I don't know who I am without her, okay?" I hurl one of the shakers against the wall, where it demolishes into dust on impact. It only takes me a second to realize that I can't replace it. I can't replace it and I can't replace her. I drop the other one to the hardwood floor, where it cracks in half. I grab my coat from the peg on the wall and slam out the door.

CHAPTER SIX:

I sit next to Tony at the bar where we nurse our beers. I'm on my third, but I'm not numb enough yet. I know I have to keep going. I signal the bartender, a cute black girl with mocha skin and hair that bounces in spiral, ebony curls around her face. She wears color in her hair, a vibrant purple. It catches my eye whenever the light hits it. "That money's not going to last forever, Tony," I tell my friend.

"No, it won't. You gotta be smart about it, Vanni."

I snort as I tilt my bottle for another chug of beer. "Are you saying I should invest?"

"In a manner of speaking, yes. Invest in you." Off my look, he expounds, "School, dude."

I shake my head. I had never been a great student before. I can't imagine all this time away helped matters at all. "I wouldn't even know where to start."

"That's easy. What do you want to do with your life? And don't say rock star. I'm serious."

I offer a helpless shrug. "There is nothing else to say, Tony. There never has been. I honestly can't see myself as anything else."

He heaves a beleaguered sigh. When you're kids, best friends will support you if you want to fly a unicorn to the moon. As adults, most friends prefer to keep their friends grounded in reality. I know I've tested this to the breaking point with Tony. "And you're willing to gamble every dime you have on seeing if you can be one of the small percent of singers who actually make it, is that it?"

"No," I say softly. I had buried that dream when I had buried my aunt. "But if you ask me what I can plug into its place after years of targeting just one bulls eye, I'm afraid you've got me stumped."

"No Plan B, right," Tony says. "I can still get you into the mail room. It's not much, but it's a start. It's a future," he adds, though the concept of future has definitely lost its sheen over the past dozen days.

I kill my beer and reach for the other. I'm finally numb enough. "Might as well," I slur at last.

Lori takes the news of my new career well. In fact, she is relieved. "That's where Tony started, and look where he is now. It could mean big things."

I caress her hair with my hand. "He has an education under him."

"You can, too. I was looking around at some of the city colleges. Your money could go a long way there."

"That's great. But I have no idea what I'd be studying for."

She shrugs as she runs her fingers along my chest. "You can figure that out as you go along."

I scoff. "Yeah, and what if I spend tens of thousands of dollars only to figure out I still can't figure it out?"

"A degree still means something. The time won't be wasted. Future employers will take it as a sign of dedication and commitment. It will open doors no matter what you want to do."

I swear to God, all I can think about is how I can't see how some business degree would help me be a singer. My mind has decided not to pursue my dream, but the message hasn't made it all the way to my heart now. *It's just too soon*, I assure myself.

I guess I need mourning for that, too.

I pull Lori to me and get lost within her kiss so I don't have to think about anything else.

It takes a few weeks for me to start my job at McKinley, Donnelly and Roth, the financial consulting firm in a gleaming Manhattan skyscraper in the financial district. It's in the mail room, like Tony had said. I wear a white button-up dress shirt and slacks, while I run around to all different floors of the company daily. My long hair doesn't pose a problem for this job, which, as an entry-level position, usually held by students and fresh-faced graduates anyway. Tony did warn me that I would have to cut it eventually if I want to be taken seriously, especially by my boss, Stu Plimpton.

Stu isn't any older than me, but he has the Ivy League education behind him. He's a proper button-down corporate climber, who clearly wants to run the business one day. He's a by-the-book kind of guy, who takes particular glee in showing me who's boss on a regular basis.

I suspect he's not a very happy person. He's rail thin, with thick glasses and comb-over before he's thirty. But there's a smirk on his face whenever he corrects me, as if that position of power is the only thing he has in the world to elevate him. I take it in stride most days, but it's clear he thinks I'm stupid. If I dare say anything to Lori, she brings up the whole college conversation again.

"People will take you as seriously as you take yourself, babe," she says, before she launches into another conversation about my hair.

She buys me clothes now. I've almost completely disappeared from the guy I knew mere months before.

Still not sold on college, I keep my job at Cynzia's nights and weekends. I owe him my loyalty, sure. But part of it is that I know who I am there. The guy who stares back at me through the perfect mirrors in the men's bathroom of McKinley, Donnelly and Roth is a stranger to me. I don't know him, and I don't understand him. I'm not sure I even like him. He swallows a lot of shit for a little bit of money and a whole lot of hope that one day it will all be worth it.

After a month of working in the city, even that old hair net starts to look like a long lost friend.

Things are changing fast. Thanks to the windfall from Susan's life insurance policy, I'm able to fill the house with furniture of my own. Lori helps me, since I really don't know what the hell I'm doing. She's thinking long-term, what kind of furniture would be practical for our future, something with quality and nothing too trendy.

I fight her only once. I want a platform bed. I know that the king-sized model won't fit in the upstairs bedrooms. There's only one room to fit it, and I haven't been able to walk into it for weeks.

Lori suggests that we tear down the wallpaper and paint it. She hopes that by making it into a new room entirely, we'll exorcise any lingering ghosts.

Truth is I no longer feel Susan there anywhere, and haven't ever since all her furniture and belongings were taken away. That's part of the overall problem. The me I used to be is fading just like her presence, like wisps of smoke in the wind. I don't know who I'm becoming, but I it's clearer by the day I don't like this guy. I have less and less in common with him as I watch him scurry from Brooklyn to Manhattan, running around like all of the other rats in the maze. When Stu gives him a dressing down every other day, for not following some procedure in which he's never been versed or trained, he stands there and takes it–a pawn in someone else's chess game.

I drink more heavily these days. I'm so exhausted when I walk home from Cynzia's nightly that all I want to do when I get home is eat, drink till my eyes cross and fuck Lori like we've never fucked before.

In many ways, she's the only way I know I'm still alive. When I'm inside her, I'm not Old Vanni or this new mutated Vanni. I'm a god, the star of the show, the one who controls her like a puppet on my strings, making her scream because she can't help herself.

That comes to mean more to me than the booze.

Despite our active sex life, our relationship strains simply because we never see each other, and the rare times we do, she's nagging in my ear about college. She wants me to quit Cynzia's and pursue a degree that could get me promoted in the company.

The only problem is that I don't want to be promoted. I don't like the assholes at work, who drink a gallon of coffee to get through hectic days and frenzied nights, working late to make other people rich. They in turn treat everyone around them as rungs on their own private ladders. Even Tony looks about ten years older than he really is. Talking to him about anything is useless. He's done his time with the likes of Stu and advises me to just cowboy the fuck up and soldier on. Then he parrots what Lori tells me, all about planning for the future. It's like they share the same brain some days.

But I don't want some crappy fifty-hour workweek doing the same crap, and swallowing the same shit, day after monotonous day until I can retire with a gold watch and neat little pension in exchange for all my years of service. In exchange for my *life*. Supposedly I'm laying bricks with each frustrating, unsatisfying day, where every sacrifice I make in the moment will serve me in some far-off future I can't even picture. It's like I'm waiting to live, and I have a long way to go until I see these seeds I'm planting grow into something even remotely gratifying.

Call me impatient, but I need more. Something is missing and I don't know what it is.

I figure it out late January, when I can't stop staring at the faded outline against the far wall in the living room. What's missing is music, which has become a painful reminder for all I've lost. I avoid it purposefully, which is completely unlike me. I've never gone this long without it before. But these past few weeks have been torture. Thinking about music reminds me that I have nothing left to dream about, which depresses me way down deep in my core.

I had never wanted a regular life. I wanted my name up on a marquee, with thousands of screaming fans in the front row. I wanted the thunder of a band behind me and the impossible dream set forth before me, right within my reach.

"*Then make it happen*," Aunt Susan's ghost whispers in my ear. I have to smile because that's just what she would have said, despite it all. It gets me thinking. Why *can't* I have the life of my dreams? I think I've forgotten the answer.

Since I have a rare night off, I stay in Manhattan. There's no need to rush home; Lori is working the late shift, and suddenly I want to be a part of the big world outside my tiny brownstone in Bensonhurst.

It's hard to deny music in New York City. Many popular genres have taken root there, so it is a veritable stroll through time from jazz and doo-wop to disco and hip-hop. And there's no shortage of live music venues to explore. I don't need one drop of alcohol as I hit some of my old haunts, clubs that cater to my passion for rock. Just being a part of the crowd is a high in and of itself. Is it a surprise, really, that I want to do this and this only for the rest of my life? It's like one of those machines where you can self-dose heavy pain medication whenever you feel down or hopeless. That's what art does. It takes what life is and makes it better. It takes hope and makes it a tangible thing that you can see, hear or touch.

With music, it takes pain and makes it something beautiful. A guy can sing about heartbreak or a girl can sing about an unrequited love, and the swell of empathy from the audience helps lift the shadows so you can once again see the sun.

I can't see the sun in any florescent-lit mail room.

Returning to the club scene invigorates me. That night, when I surprise Lori at work and we take the train home, I practically finger-fuck her as we make out on the deserted subway car. I thrill her with my newly charged passion, though she has no idea why I'm so fucking happy for once. But if we're both happy, does it really matter why?

The next day I cut my hours back at Cynzia's. I don't tell Lori because I don't want the lecture. And what she doesn't know won't hurt her. It's not like I'm auditioning to be in a band. I just need to be a part of the music in some way, otherwise I'll disappear entirely. It's my only anchor now.

I hide my alternative life until the end of February. It starts with a horrible day at the office, where I'm late to work. This means my day starts with being reamed by Stu. He's in a mood most days, and I'm his favorite whipping boy. Days that start with an ass-chewing usually means shit will roll downhill all day long.

And of course, it does. He spots streaks on our incoming correspondence, which is printed by our massive printers that cost thousands of dollars. I don't know much about them, other than how to change the ink or refill the paper. That doesn't seem to matter to Stu. "Clean it up, Carnevale. Show some professionalism."

"How am I supposed to clean them?" I ask, because I've never had to clean a big printing machine before.

"It's not my job to figure that out," he tells me with that know-it-all smirk that makes my fists clench. "It's yours. So get it done."

I spend most of the morning going through endless files to find the operator's manual for the printer, in order to figure out how to clean the glass panel. Finally I find it. It says to wipe the pane down with isopropyl alcohol.

I head down to the lobby of our high-rise, to the quickie store. The only alcohol on the shelf is rubbing alcohol. I just know if I buy this alcohol and try it on the expensive printer, I'll ruin it. Not only will I get yet another lecture, but I'll likely have to pay for it too. I take a deep breath before I call Stu on my cell. "Yeah, Stu. It's Vanni. I found a manual that said to use isopropyl alcohol on the printer to clean it. I'm downstairs at the quickie mart, but all they have is rubbing alcohol."

He heaves a dramatic sigh, one he often utilizes when he has to explain anything to a mere high school graduate like me. He loves to throw my lack of education in my face, something Lori uses to motivate me to go to school.

All it really motivates me to do is shove a stapler up his ass.

"Rubbing alcohol *is* isopropyl alcohol," he says with a heaping helping of derision. "How the hell can you get to your age without knowing that?"

I gulp back any retort, end the call and purchase the clear bottle of magic fluid. It works like a charm, erasing the offending ink blob on the glass.

The fucker doesn't even say thank you.

I fume about Stu the rest of the afternoon. I clock out three minutes early, just because I can't face this asshole again before the end of the day. I've held back smashing his arrogant face in as best as I could, but I'm at my limit.

I take a longer walk than usual. I don't want to deal with the subway in my state of mind. I'm wound tight as a drum. New York City is a great place to get lost among the crowd, to window shop and see how the other half lives, with no interference from strangers who have better things to worry about than some guy they don't even know. I take my time, strolling slow. I pass the jewelry window, full of sparkling diamonds that generate rainbows under the light. I pass the clothing store, with the super thin mannequins, both male and female, shrunken under tiny designer clothes meant to entice the elite.

I just walk on by.

And then it happens. I happen upon a music store. A white baby grand piano sits in the window. It gleams under the spotlight, its keys inviting tender fingers to touch and explore, like a lover. A beautiful, sexy, inviting lover.

I walk inside the store without even realizing it. I'm drawn to that piano. The salesman greets me with a smile. He must think I have enough money to buy anything in his store. He's sadly mistaken, but I don't tell him that just yet.

I have to get closer to that piano.

"Do you play?" he asks as we approach it.

"Some," I say. "I'd love to have one at home so I can learn more."

He nods. "Well, this one is a beauty." He starts to prattle off a ton of specifics that mean nothing to me.

My fingers land on the keys. Music wafts in the air.

By then I know that I'm hopelessly addicted with no possible cure. There's something in me that demands to be expressed. Watching music is a watered-down substitute. I want to create music. I know this the minute I hit that middle C.

When I finally settle on the bus heading home, words clutter my brain, stacking one on top of the other. The words don't fit together at first. I have to rearrange them to convey what I want to say. Aunt Susan's voice keeps whispering in my ear. *"Make it happen."* Make a dream happen. Chase the rainbow. Reach for the stars…it's all trite and derivative, which frustrates me. It's bubbling up in my spirit, uncontained, yet I can't find the proper channels to release it.

If I magically come up with a combination of words I like, I hum a little melody behind them so I won't forget them, singing them over and over in my head. Everyone around me likely thinks I'm nuts, but it's New York, so they're probably used to it.

When I get back to the neighborhood, I can't even go home. I head to my local haunt, Fritz's, for a beer. The cute black waitress is there, as is a heavier girl with a shock of red hair and tattoos along her chest and arms. She wears black-framed glasses, and when she smiles it makes me smile too.

As different as she is from her bartender, I find this other girl just as cute. Of course, that's usually how it is with me. Call me a romantic, but I've always found women fascinating, like mysterious puzzles that are so much fun to unlock. I'm an Italian, for fuck's sake. This is what we do. We appreciate the finer things in life, those beautiful things that make life worth living. For me that has always been wine, women and song.

Like ol' George Thorogood, I like 'em all. Tall girls. Skinny girls. Curvy girls. Blondes, brunettes and redheads, and girls of every race. They can be tattooed or plain, serious or silly, but every single one of them shines like a diamond when they smile, or their eyes flash, or they walk by in a perfume-scented breeze. Their curves invite to be held. Their voices invite to be heard. Their skin begs to be touched. Far too many guys don't get this. They see women as paper dolls to collect, pretty or perfect little badges of honor they wear with pride.

The way I see it, every single woman is pretty if you know where to look, and I don't mind looking. Nothing has ever meant more to me than finding that treasure everyone else forgot. I was the kid who would send anonymous valentine's cards to the girls in my class I knew wouldn't get any otherwise. Their smile was often reward enough. A girl is always prettiest when she knows she's appreciated.

This new girl takes my order as I perch on one of the barstools. I get the feeling she hasn't been appreciated for a long, long time. "You're new here," I say, still wearing my smile from before.

I can tell from the sparkle in her eye that she likes what she sees. "Not so new. It's my dad's bar. He's finally decided I'm old enough to work in it. Happy thirtieth birthday to me."

I laugh as I reach across the bar. "Nice to meet you. I'm Giovanni. Friends call me Vanni."

"Pam," she says. I like the way that sounds. Sweet and simple, like swinging on a hammock on a perfect summer afternoon. "What can I get you?"

I lean forward, my arms crossed over each other. "Let's test your muster behind the bar. Guess."

She laughs. It's a hearty, robust sound. Like music. "Challenge accepted." She turns her back for a moment and then returns with my favorite beer on tap.

I take a sip. It's right on the money. "Okay, I was kidding. How did you do that?"

She shrugs with another smile. "No big deal. That's our most popular beer with the regulars. Local brewery and all that."

"And here I thought you were psychic," I say as I bestow a cocky smirk. "I was going to ask you what to do with my future and everything."

"Oh yeah?" she says as she leans across the bar to face me. "Life got you down, gorgeous?"

I shrug. "Torn by what I want to do and what I need to do."

She laughs. "I know what that's like," she says.

"Oh yeah?" I echo. She nods. I rest my chin on my hand. "So what did little Pam want to be when she grew up?"

She laughs more. I love the sound. It makes me happier just to hear it. "First of all, I've never been little. Secondly, I'm not telling you because it's silly."

"Well, now I gotta hear it." She shakes her head, giggling to herself. "Tell me."

She leans towards me, to whisper as loud as she can over the jukebox in the corner. "Fine. But if you laugh, I'll charge you double." I lock my lips with an imaginary key and toss it over my shoulder. She glances both ways before she leans even closer. She smells like peonies. "I wanted to be a Rockette."

I immediately purse my lips so that I don't laugh. She reaches for her water nozzle and sprays me. I laugh as I reach for a stack of napkins to dry myself.

"Okay, hot shot. What did you want to be?"

I smile. I'm having a good time. The best time I've had in quite a while, in fact. "Guess."

Her big green eyes travel over me. "Well, lemme see. You're dressed like a corporate flunkie, but you have hair straight out of the 1980s. Those soulful brown eyes tell me you're generally up to no good." I can't help but chuckle. "And that mouth is pure sex. I can so see it just behind a microphone."

My eyes widen. "Okay, you're kind of freaking me out a little, Pam."

"Come on, dude. Look at you. Who would you be if it wasn't a rock star?"

I sigh and take another swig of beer. "That's what I keep asking myself."

"So what's stopping you?"

I shake my head. I can't even remember anymore. I open my mouth to talk about my aunt, but I can't yet. The pain is too fresh. "I'm twenty-six. I have a house. I have two jobs. I have a girlfriend."

She nods. She gets it now. "Let me guess. Your girl doesn't want to share you with the world."

"My girl doesn't think I'll get that far."

"Well, that's kind of shitty."

My eyes dart to hers. I'm surprised by her reaction. "She just wants us to be practical. It's really hard to make it. I mean, when did you give up on your dream to be a dancer?"

She shrugs. "I'm not sure that I ever gave it up entirely. It'd be a sad existence if we give up hope in our dreams." I continue to stare at her, waiting for her answer. "I don't know," she finally says. "It just ceased being a priority, I guess. It just fell further and further down the list until it slipped off of it entirely. I don't think I even noticed. In fact, I kind of forgot about it until you asked."

That instantly depresses me to hear it. "So what are you going to do about it?"

"Depends. What are you going to do about it?"

I smile. She reminds me a lot of my aunt, but for once it doesn't hurt. I hold up a finger, indicating I need a minute. I reach into my pocket and pull out some money for the jukebox. She watches as I peruse the selection, and then Queen's ode to fat, luscious bottoms blasts from the speakers. She laughs as she realizes what I pick. I wear a smile as I walk back to the bar, my hand outstretched. "I'm going to ask you to dance."

She only thinks about it for a moment before she wads up her towel and tosses it on the bar. She takes my hand and I lead her to the small, deserted dance floor. I grab her by the waist and lead her through some sexy moves to the pulsating beat. Her hips undulate under my palms to the music with natural grace. How could she ever think her dream was silly? I lean forward to tell her in her ear, "You really can dance."

Her eyebrow cocks. "Can you really sing?"

I hold her close and pick up on the next verse. I can feel her practically swoon against me, which makes me feel like the most powerful man on the planet. That's not a rush I get delivering mail to scowling businessmen in stuffy suits. It emboldens me. She reaches up to say in my ear, "You should never give that up. You have a gift."

God, I hadn't heard that in so long. I realize now it's all I've ever wanted to hear, ever since my aunt passed. "And you shouldn't give up dancing," I tell her. "You can really move."

"For a fat girl," she fills in but I shake my head.

"For anyone." I hold her closer, unafraid of those full curves. They're sensual. Womanly. "You don't see me complaining, do you?"

She shakes her head and laughs, as if I've told her a funny joke. "You are a shameless flirt, Giovanni Carnevale. Maybe you should take some of that charm home for your girlfriend."

I pout. I'm not ready to leave. For the first time in months, I feel like someone actually gets me. But she has a point. The dance and flirting have been fun up till now, but it can't go anywhere.

I'm a lot of things but I'm not a cheat.

After the dance is over, we return to the bar where she tends to more customers. I fish my pen out of my jacket and grab some extra napkins from the tray. I jot down all the lyrics I had memorized on the ride home.

I come up with a solid chorus, which I copy onto another napkin. I take ten dollars out of my wallet and place it on top of the folded napkin. On the top I write, "*See you at Rockefeller Center.*"

The next day I call in sick to work. It's the first time I've done this ever in my working life, but I can't face Stu. I know if he says one nasty thing to me, I'll strangle him with his designer tie. And I've been going non-stop for months. It's time to take a mental health day.

I take my checkbook and head out for one of the most important purchases of my life. I figure it's the only way to get the monkey off my back.

"Why did you get this?" Lori asks me in a small, angry voice as she stares at the second-hand upright piano that I bought. I spent a little money on it, but it was worth it. That wall had never looked complete without Susan's piano, and the new one fits perfectly in the outline on the wallpaper left by the last one. It's like sliding the last piece of the puzzle into place. "You don't even know how to play," she finally says, as if reason or practicality had anything to do with my purchase.

"I'll learn," I say as I pull her to me. "You'll teach me."

She stands rigid in my arms. She's livid. "I thought you gave all this up."

"I did," I reassure. "I do. I just… I just need to do this, Lori."

Her eyes meet mine. "And you didn't think to ask me about it?"

I bristle immediately. It's my money, why can't I spend it on what I want–something I would have never given away in the first place?

More importantly, why is it that ever since I got the house and the savings in my bank account, I immediately went from *me* to *us*? Without even being asked, I had to start thinking for two, which was something I never thought I'd do. Relationships are fun, but I learned my lesson about happy endings when I was just a toddler. I finally shrug at this person I now have to account to, though I'm not entirely sure why. "I knew what you'd say."

"And what does that tell you, Vanni?" She spins away from me. "I told you before. This is our future. Do you think it's easy to take classes all day and work at a stupid bar all night? I'm doing this so that later on, we'll have something solid, something we can count on. Music isn't that, Vanni. And it never will be."

"I just bought a piano," I say, but I know I'm lying. It's more than a piano. It's a sign that I haven't given up yet. It's a sign that there's still a smidgen of that rebel kid left inside of me, the one who used to steal cassette tapes when he couldn't afford to buy a stick of gum, who used to play air guitar until he got dizzy… who learned it was okay to sing and let his voice be heard. (Thank you, Aunt Susan.)

I can still be me, and that's important, isn't it? It feels important. It feels like a goddamned lifeline. Maybe… just maybe… with that piano in the house, I won't be so tempted to walk off the Brooklyn Bridge every week after monotonous, soul-sucking week.

After I get the piano, I blow off the clubs and Cynzia's to practice while Lori works. It has to be while she works, or else she fumes so much I fear she'll set off the smoke detector. And forget sex. Ever since she saw that piano, she has given me the cold shoulder.

Some nights, she doesn't even come home. Her former roommates have rented out her room, but they always open their home for sleepovers.

I welcome the break as I try to recall every single thing Aunt Susan ever taught me about the piano. By the beginning of May, I have written two songs, "*Make it Happen*," for my beloved aunt, and "*Dancer Girl*," for Pam at the bar, who is the only other person on planet Earth that believes I could actually make my dreams come true.

Everything that drives me now is heavily influenced by the idea of following one's dreams. I don't realize until the end of May that the universe is about to test me to see if I really mean it.

CHAPTER SEVEN:

The twenty-fourth of May starts out like any other day. I am in Manhattan by eight o'clock in the morning, my white shirt pressed and my dress pants wrinkle free. I spend most of the morning delivering the mail like I always do, in and out of all the offices of our large conglomerate. By now most people know me by name and greet me. The receptionists in particular wear big smiles when I enter the room. They flirt with me. I flirt back. It's all harmless enough. In fact it breaks up what usually turns out to be a dreary, boring day.

The hours speed by until lunch, where I escape downstairs to one of the restaurants. I don't eat much, but the notebook I carry at my side at all times is filled to overflowing with all kinds of ideas for songs and music. I can't stop thinking about it. It's on my mind during my commutes back and forth to Brooklyn. It's on my mind when I get up, or when I go to sleep.

Sometimes it's even on my mind while I'm making love to Lori. I don't tell her, though. Thanks to her hissy fit over the piano, I realize that my love for music has become like an illicit affair. I can't talk to her about it. I can't share my love or passion of it with her without her feeling insecure, like it jeopardizes everything we have. I have to keep it on the down low, just to keep our relationship intact.

By May, she makes peace with music by viewing it as my hobby. She doesn't like it, but she's accepted it. As long as I show up for work every day at McKinley, Donnelly and Roth like a good boy, she plays the part of doting girlfriend. She still lobbies hard for a college degree. I finally appease her and we visit the local city college, where she pores over brochures to find the right career path for me. To throw me a bone, she adds some music courses in there, telling me that I can work in the industry if I just stay realistic. Maybe I can't be a rock star, but I can find solid, steady work at studios and record labels.

"They have mail rooms too," she says, but it doesn't have the appeal she thinks it does.

Still, part of me wants to give it a try. I want to sing, but I need to eat. Those are just the facts. Maybe I *can* have both if I just play it smart, like Lori and Tony tell me. I look out the windows and see all the young people on campus at the dawn of their adulthood, taking chances, meeting challenges, and there is a part of me that feels like I should be a part of it. I was never the best student, mostly because school bored the shit out of me, but there was something about the idea of actually doing something concrete to shape my future that appeals to me, even if I didn't know what the hell I wanted to be.

Nothing has a stronger appeal than performing, though. Being dream-adjacent isn't quite the same as making my dream come true. Now that I'm writing my own songs, I feel even stronger that this is a legitimate path for me.

Unfortunately, so far only Pam concurs.

The rest of my day ambles by like most Tuesday afternoons. It's still early in the week, with hump day yet to go. In fact the only good thing that can be said for Tuesday is that it was one day beyond Monday. It's still too far away from the weekend for my tastes.

And I hate that. I hate that I have been marching along week after week, trying to get from the doldrums of Monday, to the hopeful hump of Wednesday so that I can race downhill towards Friday.

By now I start to dread Monday morning by Friday night. I only get forty-eight precious hours to myself before I have to head back into the city and rent my life for another week in exchange for a paltry paycheck.

I feel my life literally passing me by, and thirty looms closer on the horizon by the minute. All I have really figured out so far is where I'm going to live and who I will live with.

But even that is up in the air these days. Every time she becomes dour about my music, I feel less and less connected with her. Once upon a time that was a bond we shared. It was how we met. But now she has other priorities.

I find myself at Fritz's nightly. Both Pam and Cheryl keep me smiling. They're cute as hell, not to mention friendly and flirty. And I know that's just part of their job, but it's a hell of a lot more fun than hanging out with the house, being silently punished for wanting more.

Pam provides the strongest voice for following my dreams, which makes her even more appealing. Now my "other woman" (music) actually links me *to* another woman, and I find more and more excuses to see her. I enjoy it. I look forward to it. And Pam generally never lets me down.

When I finally presented her song to her the weekend before, I sang it to her in her car, while she stole away for a break. We do that sometimes, when the bar is loud and we can't really talk otherwise. She listens mostly, while I prattle on about the bands I've seen in the city. Like me, she doesn't see the harm in just seeing where it goes. So I was pleased to perform for her at last, just me, her, and her song. There were tears in her eyes as she listened. She looked so beautiful I had a momentary urge to kiss her. It seemed as natural as breathing. I think I may have even leaned in a bit, but she pulled away before it could go too far.

She's not the kind of girl to break up a relationship. And I'm not the kind of guy to juggle two women.

It just feels so damn good to be around someone who believes in me for a change. It's like a drug. It replaces alcohol, honestly, because I feel better about the "high" I'm getting. And there's no hangover to speak of, unless you count the way I now have to suppress that part of my life to keep the peace at home.

Sometimes I wonder if I'm holding onto Lori because she reminds me of the Vanni I used to know, the one who doted on his aunt and worked a Cynzia's, singing for tips.

Who I am now is still up for debate, with the mutant bizarro Vanni taking up way too much of my creative time as he battles the concrete jungle of New York.

Little do I know that this hazy day at the end of May will force my hand, to decide the kind of Vanni I want to be once and for all.

"Giovanni," Stu barks from his doorway. "I need to speak to you in my office, please."

I fight the urge to roll my eyes. He always makes it sound like such a big deal, but usually it's a dickish power play. It always sounds to the rest of my coworkers like I'm about to be torn a new asshole, which puts me on display for everyone as I cross the crowded floor like I'm heading for the gallows. When I get into his office, however, he usually tells me he wants to trade this color for that in his color-coding system, or something equally as mundane.

But I shut the door behind me and stifle my sigh as I face him. "Yeah, Stu?"

"Take a seat," he says from his seat behind the desk. Another power play. God, he's such an asshole. Still, I do what he says and take my seat. "We're going to be making some changes going forward," he tells me as he pulls out a new employee manual. "We're getting a lot of new clients, and they mean business. They want to work with the best of the best, so we have to prove we're the best on every level."

I nearly bite my tongue in two. He wants me to treat mail delivery like it's some kind of Olympic event. What a joke. A monkey could do my job. Hell, a monkey *is* doing my job. "How does this affect me?"

He pushes the manual across his desk to me. "We're focusing on every single aspect of the company, including the way we present ourselves to the clients. We've decided to change the dress code. Khaki pants. Royal blue shirt and a gold tie. Brown dress shoes. No ostentatious jewelry or visible tattoos. Hair must be kept tidy and trim, with neatly trimmed beards and hair no longer than the collar for all male employees."

I stare at him for a long moment without saying anything. I'm trying to figure out if he's joking, because surely I didn't hear him right. "You want me to cut my hair?"

"By Monday," he says with a nod. "That's when all the changes are being implemented."

"But I'm in the mail room. Nobody really sees me but other employees."

"Clients see you when you're on the upper floors," he assures. "And your image represents all of us."

It's absurd. "And if I don't want to cut my hair?" I ask, because it's the last fucking thing I want to do for a job as shitty as this one.

"Non-compliance with these new employee standards is reason for dismissal."

"So you're saying you'll fire me if I don't cut my hair."

"I don't want to," he asserts, but I know he's full of shit. "This comes from the big bosses upstairs. Way over my head."

I glance at his head, where his thinning hair races away from his pale, drawn face. I see how his eyes twinkle as he watches me, the corner of his mouth itching to curve up into a satisfied smile.

"I have no choice," he says. "And neither do you."

And he's completely right. If I want to keep working at McKinley, Donnelly and Roth, I have to cut my hair. It sounds so simple. So why is it so hard?

"It's just hair," Lori tells me as we share dinner that night in the kitchen. "It'll grow back. Besides, that hair is totally dated anyway. I always thought you'd look so hot with a shorter shag cut," she says as she reaches across the narrow table and musses my hair. "Or maybe just buzz it off. Show 'em that you mean business." It always comes down to that with her. But when do I get to be *me*?

She slips out of her chair and wiggles her way onto my lap, looping her arm around my shoulders. "You have such pretty eyes anyway. Why would you want to keep them all covered up?"

"Because it's part of who I am," I tell her softly. Why doesn't she get that?

"You'll still be you," she tells me with another kiss. "Just with more respectability. People will take you as seriously as you take yourself."

I nudge her off my lap before heading towards the fridge for another beer. "What are you doing, exchanging notes with Tony?"

She leans against the table. "He's right, you know."

I don't say anything. I just stare at her and wonder how we'd grown so far apart in such a short period of time. It dawns on me we've known each other a year, but it feels as if we are total strangers. I lift my beer for a sip before I leave the room.

I don't even care if she hears me tinkering around on the piano. The sands are falling in the hourglass of my dreams. I have until Monday to scrape every last ounce of musical ambition out of my soul.

It's easier said than done.

The rest of the week speeds by like stop-motion animation. I don't get very far from minute to minute, but if I stand back and look at it, hours and days have gone by without my noticing. Before I know it, it's Friday. "Giovanni. My office, please!"

I take a deep breath and count to five before I follow my balding boss into his office. He doesn't even bother to close the door.

"I was kind of hoping you'd have fixed your hair issue by now," he says as he takes his seat on his teeny, tiny throne.

"I haven't decided what I want to do with it yet," I hedge.

"Better make it quick. You're running out of time. If you show up at eight o'clock on Monday with long hair, you're going to get fired. I have no choice."

He repeats that a lot, like it means anything. Regardless of whether it's his choice or not, he's enjoying the hell out of it. And *that's* what makes him a raging asshole. "You know what? You're right," I tell him at last. "You don't have a choice. But I do."

I reach behind my head and pull the elastic band that is holding my thick, long hair in a ponytail. I feel it spill around my shoulders. It feels sensuous, like a lover's hands against my skin. And I love the way it feels. I love the way it looks. I love the image it presents to the world about who I am, which sets me apart from anybody else. "I do a pretty good job around here," I tell him. "I have hardly missed a day of work since I started and I earn every dime twice. And I don't see how my having long hair will make me any better at my job, or any better as a walking, talking billboard to the company."

"That's irrelevant. You work for us, and we set the standard."

"You also knew what I looked like when I got this job."

"As a favor to Mr. Beillo," he points out. "Who is in management now simply because he knows how to pick his battles."

"Oh, I know how to pick my battles, too," I promise. "For five months I've let you keep me under your foot, berate me, insult me, treat me like garbage just because you're a miserable fuck. But if you think I'm going to change who I am to grovel for some $10-an-hour job, you're nuts."

"It's just hair," Stu points out with a sarcastic sneer.

"Exactly," I shoot back. "It's just hair."

He leans back in his chair, his fingers linked together in his lap. "So that's it, then? You're really going to burn a whole bridge over a haircut?"

I only need a second to think about it. "Yes."

"Fine," he says as he sits up to grab his phone. "I'll make sure payroll cuts you your last check by quitting time today."

I'm both terrified and exhilarated. I stood up for what I wanted, but it had cost me dearly. If I'm honest, though, it only costs me the thing that never fit me in the first place, something I never, ever wanted. No kid lies in bed at night dreaming of the day they can work in a freaking mail room.

By the time I make it back to Brooklyn, I'm ready to celebrate. I head straight to Fritz's, which is abuzz courtesy of a new karaoke machine to turn up the volume of 80s night. The bar is so full I can barely squeeze between the bodies. I hold up a finger to Pam, who knows already what I order. She nods and gives me a wink. I turn around to face the happy folks crowded around the tiny stage erected on the limited dance floor. Some woman nearing her 40s is massacring *"Open Arms"* by Journey. I grimace through it, while everyone else claps and encourages her on. They're all happily under the influence, which I presume makes it easier to enjoy the show.

Pam appears like an angel beside me, offering me a frosty mug of beer. I lean down so she can hear me. "When did you decide to go karaoke?"

She laughs. "This is the first weekend. It's sort of a trial run." We glance around the crowded bar, which is more business than this neighborhood haunt has seen in quite a while.

"Looks like it was a successful experiment," I say.

She shrugs. Her lovely apple cheeks flush with a faint hint of pink I can still detect under the colorful lights. "It was my idea," she says. "Confession, you kind of inspired it."

"Oh, yeah?"

She nods. "Yeah." Her bright eyes sparkle up at me. "You should totally go up there. Show them how it's done."

"You think?"

"I know," she says. "You'll have them eating out of the palm of your hand, Vanni."

With a shrug, I figure what the hell? I get in line and set up my song. I dig back a little deeper in time and pick *"Time of the Season"* by the Zombies, because I've always thought it a sexy song. A sexy song deserves a sexy delivery, and I'm more than ready to shed that rat race idiot who used to work at McKinley, Donnelly and Roth. I toss my hair with my fingers, and I untuck my dress shirt, which I unbutton halfway down my chest. I almost wish I could shed it completely, but that seems too much.

Maybe one day...

As soon as I hit the stage, it's as natural as breathing. I look out at the expectant faces in the crowd, like a lion surveys a pack of juicy wildebeests. The girls in particular are ripe for the picking. They brazenly scope me up and down, sending me suggestive smiles as they stare up at me.

Well, what do you know? The girls I love actually love me back. They're not looking down their noses at me like Stu. They're not rolling their eyes at me like Lori. They look at me like I'm interesting, fascinating, appealing, and all I had to do was step on this stage. How fucking wonderful is that?

The minute the song starts, I'm somebody else. Only this somebody isn't some pathetic little automaton punching a time card. I wield power like a magician, and the microphone is my wand. I hear my voice through the speakers. It doesn't even sound like me. It sounds better than me.

It's *him*, the New Vanni who has finally given his last fuck.

The girls come apart as I sing the lyrics to them. They turn into instant groupies. It blows my mind. I open my mouth, and they rush to the stage. They can't seem to get close enough. I relish in their attention, getting grittier with every verse. I pull one of the girls onstage with me to dance during the music solo. When I begin to sing to her, she practically melts at my feet.

This is so much better than some florescent-lit hellhole in the basement of a skyscraper.

Pam cheers the loudest as I finish and hop down off the stage. Everyone chants my name, which makes my blood pump in my veins.

"Didn't I tell you?" she says as I reach her. "Palm of your hand. You're a natural, Vanni. You're going to be headlining sell-out venues one day. I know it."

"I have a long way to go still," I tell her. "I have hardly any experience and zero opportunity."

"I don't know about that," she says as she heads back to the bar. There are a stack of free magazines for the NYC music scene. She opens it to the back where there are tons of classified ads. "There's your opportunity, honey," she says. She points to her stage. "There's your experience. I mean, you're going to be here anyway, right? Hone your skills where you can. Before you know it, you'll have mastered something great."

I can't resist. I pull her into a hug and hold her tight. She feels warm and comfortable in my arms, like a plush teddy bear. It feels so good that I don't want to let go, so I don't for a long moment. I just relish every inch of her. She clears her throat and pulls back. I know she's still keeping her distance because of Lori. Frankly, that only makes me like her more.

I don't tell Lori about my karaoke success that night when she comes home from the club. I don't tell her about quitting, either. While she's at work all that weekend, I'm practicing my new skill as a singer in front of the mirror at the house, and then on that tiny stage at the bar. When several girls hit on me, asking to take me home, I figure I'm doing something right.

Or at least, *he* is.

I like this new guy a lot more than the other one. He's got confidence and swagger. I almost believe him when he struts across that tiny stage and drives all the girls crazy. I make up for the lackluster rendition of *"Open Arms"* on Saturday night, where no fewer than five girls fall head over heels in love with me.

It's empowering. That night, when Lori gets home from work, I practically pounce her from the front door. We make love in the living room, then again in the kitchen, and finally in the bedroom.

I borrow some of the new guy's swagger to make her come until she nearly passes out. I figure everything is fine until Sunday afternoon, when she finally asks. "When are you going to get your hair cut, Vanni? The weekend is nearly over."

I grin at her. "I didn't hear any complaints last night when you grabbed it and told me to fuck you harder," I growl as I pull her into my lap. She turns away from my kiss.

"Vanni. I'm not kidding around. You know you have to cut your hair."

I sigh. "If I want to keep that job, then yes. I have to cut my hair."

"What do you mean if?" she says at once.

"I mean if, Lori. Jesus." I know I'm just putting off the inevitable, but I can't yet utter the words. I have to push her out of my lap and turn away so she can't see my face.

"Vanni."

I take a breath and just go for it. "Fine. I quit my job."

Her eyes are lethal. "When?"

I rip the bandage all the way off. The word lands like a hand grenade. "Friday."

She immediately flies off the bed. "What the hell were you thinking? How could you quit? Do you know how hard Tony had to fight for them to hire you?"

I stand to face her, by now just as angry as she is. "And just how much of my life do I have to give up in exchange for that generous gesture, Lori? A year? Five years? Fifty?"

"It was a chance to build a career," she starts, but I'm over it.

"It was a shitty no-where job and you know it."

"It didn't have to be. You are the one not trying hard enough. You can go to school. You can cut your hair–"

"Oh, right. Just change everything about myself to make everyone else happy. Sometimes I feel like I died with Susan that day. I haven't recognized myself since she's been gone."

"Look, I'm sorry your aunt died, Vanni. But you would have had to grow up either way. You're twenty-six years old. You're a man. If you want to be taken seriously–"

I scoff. "You keep saying that to me, but I'm starting to think the only person not taking me seriously is you."

We stare at each other for a long, hard minute before she finally grabs her clothes that are slung over a chair next to the bed. "You're such an asshole," she grits between her teeth as she slips into her jeans. "I gave up everything for you. I gave up my apartment, my friends, my life. I moved in here and helped keep you together every day since your aunt died. And all I get from you is grief. You want to play around like a kid and I'm the big mean meanie who is trying to turn you into a man."

"Fuck you," I spit.

"You'd like that, wouldn't you?" she retorts. "Get me in bed, keep me distracted. Anything to keep from facing reality."

"And what reality is that?" I ask. I can't seem to stop myself.

Her eyes meet mine. "You don't have what it takes to make it, Vanni. You're 100-percent dreamer with zero discipline. You have a little talent, sure, but no skill, and certainly no patience to develop any. You want to be a star, but have you ever thought about what kind of hard work it takes to really do the job well?"

Immediately I want to bring up all the practice that I've been doing, playing until my fingers cramped, learning what songs I could, and writing new songs along the way. I'm pretty proud of how far I've come. I know it's useless. She sees music as a hobby. "I've got an idea," is all I say in answer to her question.

"Yeah, well if you think I'm going to work my ass to pay the bills while you go off and play, you've got another thing coming, Vanni. I want a partner, someone who knows where he's going and knows what it takes to get there."

"You're just assuming I don't because I want to pursue music."

It's her turn to scoff. "You don't want to pursue music, Vanni. You want to be famous. You want to live the high-flying life of a celebrity. But when it comes to working at something, at anything, you suck."

I follow her through the house as she heads for the front door. "So you're just leaving?"

She whips around to face me. "I'd stay forever if you could just get your head on straight." She waits for a moment, as if she expects me to grovel and beg for her to stay, to promise her that I'd do whatever she wanted to make her happy.

Only I tried that, and I was the miserable one.

"I've got to do this," I tell her. "I know you don't understand. But it's just something I need to do for me. If I fail, I fail. But at least I'll know that I tried."

"Fine. You do what you need to do. Just don't expect me to watch you blow through Susan's inheritance on a pipe dream."

She slams out the door.

I can't wait to get to Fritz's that night. There I'm not derided like a child for believing in my dreams. I'm celebrated for being good at something I only dreamed I could be good at. There's a glimmer of hope there that pumps into my veins like heroin.

There's also Pam, who has never criticized me for who I am or what I want to do. When she looks at me, she really sees me. And that person really matters to her, with all his silly hopes and dreams. I realize that is what I've been missing most all this time.

Suddenly I want to see her more than anything.

As I drive up in the parking lot, however, I see Pam standing outside the main entrance, in the arms of another man. He's a little older than me, with dark, short hair, wire-framed glasses and a slight paunch. He looks like some kind of nerd, but Pam doesn't seem to care. She reaches up for a kiss and the lucky sonofabitch obliges.

I remain in my car until he leaves. The longer I have to wait, the more I fume. Every single time we managed to get close, she used Lori as her excuse to break out of any embrace. Has she been hiding this jerkoff the whole time?

I'm still mad when I enter the bar, where she tends to customers, wearing that same jovial smile. Our eyes meet. I know I'm not the only one who feels it sizzle down to my toes. I motion for my beer and she nods, before she quickly looks away.

I know now that's guilt she wears.

She avoids me through much of the night. It's as if she knows I know. Finally I grab her wrist as she deposits drink #4. "We need to talk."

She relents with a small nod, motioning to Cheryl that she's taking a break. She allows me to pull her around the bar and off towards the parking lot, where she lets me into her car. "What's up?" she says, once we finally get settled.

"Lori left me," I tell her. Her eyes widen as she stares up at me.

"I'm so sorry," she starts, but I don't let her finish. Instead I cup my hand around her neck and pull her towards me, crushing her full, sexy mouth under mine for a demanding kiss. It's like I want to erase any trace of any other man's lips there, because they don't belong. She's so stunned her lips part in a gasp, and I deepen the kiss immediately. From the way she swoons against me, I can't imagine that dork would have anything on me. I moan into her mouth as she kisses me back, just for an instant. Then suddenly she pushes against my chest, pulling away.

"Vanni, I can't."

My eyes drill into hers "Why not?"

She sighs. "I'm... I've been seeing someone."

It's a guilty admission, as though she'd been caught cheating. Like she has to answer to me. And right now, she does. "Since when?"

She struggles for the words. "Since... since forever I guess. I mean, he's an old family friend. He's known my dad for ages. They invited him for Christmas dinner, and, I don't know. I guess we just thought we'd see where things would go."

I grasp her arm with my fingers. She's being seeing this fuckwad since *Christmas*? Is she fucking kidding me? "I see. And you never thought to bring it up?"

"Why would I? You had someone. We were just... I dunno. Funning around."

"I'm pretty serious now," I tell her, leaning so close I could kiss her again. And God knows I want to, even though she just shakes her head.

"Vanni," she says. "Look at you. You could have any girl in this bar."

I know that's true. It's not conceit. I've sung in front of these girls all weekend, which comes with a lot of extra attention even when I'm not behind a microphone. They shove folded napkins with their numbers on it in my pockets, some even copping a feel as they pull away.

Had I been a different sort of man, I could have had any number of them.

But none of that excite me more than Pam does. She is so different from Lori in every way, from her crazy red hair and her tattoos, to that luscious hour-glass figure that feels soft and full, like an angel in my arms. Her rose is in full bloom. And goddamn if I don't want to caress each and every sensual petal. "What if I said I wanted you?"

She touches my face with her hand. "I'd say I'm flattered… but I'm also realistic. You are on the cusp of something amazing. I know it way down deep in my soul. There's no room there for… for ordinary," she says, struggling for words. Is that how she really sees herself? "I'm sorry Lori left. Really. But you won't need her where you're going. You won't even need me." She reaches up leave a sweet peck upon my lips. "You surpassed ordinary from the very first song you wrote. And that's just the way it is."

She holds me in her arms, a strong hug meant to reassure me. I let my hands slip easily over her back, relishing in how she feels under my fingers. Despite my passion for all women, and my experiences thus far, I've never really been with a voluptuous woman before, and I find that her womanly figure is inviting and luxurious to the touch. I just want to lose myself inside of her and never find my way back out again.

She pulls away from me suddenly, as if she senses how my cock jumps at the thought. From the flush creeping up her neck and into her face, I know I tempt her every bit as much as she's tempting me.

"I gotta go back to the bar," she says. I do not stop her. Instead we exit the car and walk wordlessly back into inside. I then head to the stage where, if nowhere else, I'm the star. More girls pile around me, and I'm tempted to take one back to my now-empty home.

Instead I stop at a liquor store on the way home and buy a couple of bottles of whiskey. It's going to be a long night, and I need the comfort of a couple old friends.

Later, while I'm sitting in bed and killing bottle #2, I prowl through the want ads in the back of the music magazine Pam had given me. I don't know what I'm looking for until I find it. It's a small ad, but my eyes zero in on it all the same... as if it had been waiting just for me. And maybe it was.

NEW BAND SEAKING LEAD SINGER. MUST KNOW 80s-90s ROCK. SOME SONGWRITING SKILL PERFERRED BUT NOT REQUIRED. INQUIRE WITH YAEL SATTERLEE.

I don't even think twice as I reach for the phone.

CHAPTER EIGHT:

Instead of going to McKinley, Donnelly and Roth Monday morning, I head over to SoHo's Cast Iron District where Yael has a loft. The old building is huge and private, which explains why I practically hear Yael playing all the way to the street. But there's no one around to complain.

He answers the door, wearing jeans and an old rock T-shirt, his jet black hair tied back away from his face. Though I sense he doesn't do it often, he smiles immediately. He offers his hand. "Hey, man. Glad you could make it."

"My pleasure," I tell him as I follow him inside. "Great place."

"Thanks. I think I've driven away every last neighbor but it's been worth it. Come on, I want you to meet the guys."

We turn the corner to a large living space. It's a studio apartment, so Yael's bedroom, such as it is, is secured behind an Oriental room divider in the corner. There's a kitchen on the opposite wall, and a door for what presumably is a bathroom in the corner. At least a dozen guitars line the walls. He plucks one down as we pass. "Hey, guys. This is Vanni."

A man in shorts, tank top and flip flops rises through a dense cloud of smoke as he stands up from the thread-bare sofa. "Hey, how's it going?"

I nod and shake his hand as Yael makes the introductions. "This is Felix Soto. He's our drummer."

"It's really nice to meet you," I say. He looks every inch a California stoner, but I can tell by his biceps that he is not afraid of intense work.

The bathroom door opens and another, younger guy emerges. His hair is black as night, much like Yael's, but his eyes are a pale blue, made even lighter by his thick dark lashes. He looks like he just stepped off the cover of a magazine. "And this is Bobby Rocco. He's our bass player."

I shake his hand. "Vanni. Nice to meet you."

We all sit around the large coffee table, overflowing with cigarette butts, marijuana paraphernalia and sheet music, some printed, some done by hand. "So tell us what kind of experience you have," Yael says.

"Right now, karaoke," I say, which makes Bobby chortle openly.

"So no band experience?" Felix asks.

"Some," I say with more confidence than I feel. Right now I feel like a kindergartener who just got caught picking his nose. "Years ago. Garage bands when I was a kid, mostly, but we never really went anywhere. Wanted to pursue music full-time but any job I got as a singer usually didn't pay shit. A boy's gotta eat," I finish with a cheeky grin.

"But you write music," Yael persists. I shrug.

"I doodle," I say as I pull the folded piece of paper from my pocket and hand it to him. He opens it to skim over "*Make it Happen.*"

"You play piano?" he asks.

"A little," I confess. I know that any other singer would bullshit his way into the band, but I want to start on the right foot. I motion to the piano sitting in the corner. "May I?"

Yael nods and I head over to the baby grand that barely fits where a dining room table is supposed to go. I turn on the microphone on the mic stand, which sends feedback throughout the room. I don't even need the sheet music as I begin to play. "*Havin' a dream, but going nowhere. Punch that clock, cut my hair. Waiting for permission to start my ignition. Just a regular Joe, still I know if I want something I have to make it happen. No excuses, no regrets. Make it happen. Raise my voice, learn the steps. Make it happen, grab that rope before I fall. I gotta make it happen, or it won't happen at all.*"

As I sing, Yael fiddles around on his guitar to accompany me. Following his lead, both Bobby and Felix jump on their instruments. Music swells in the large, open space. What started as an idea, explored with simple notes and futile words to express it, has now become *music*.

I damn near cry it so fucking beautiful.

After I'm done with my song, Yael jumps into a cover of "*Livin' on a Prayer.*" I take the microphone and walk over to the band where they sit in a circle overlooking the window, where I get into the character of the song without holding anything back. I don't miss a beat when he segues into "*Man in the Box,*" slowing it down for "*Creep,*" and then finally "*Patience.*"

No one says anything as we plow from song to song. They're completely in sync with each other, clearly these are familiar staples of their current set lists. And I step easily and quickly into place. I don't need the sheet music for the songs that they play. Every single selection is right in my wheelhouse, songs I've been singing since I was a kid. The music from the last note finally dies out, echoing through the vaulted ceilings.

No one is laughing anymore. In fact, they all glance between each other, silently communicating about what they've seen and heard.

Finally Yael breaks the silence. "Think you'd be up to testing onstage in front of an audience?"

"Whatever, whenever," I say at once.

"We have a gig this Friday. Seedlings, where we met," he adds, to remind me.

My eyes meet his. That's where Lori works. If she sees me perform with a band, I know it'll be the last nail in the coffin of our relationship.

But I can't think of anything better to show her how fucking serious I really am.

Yael hands me the flier, which gives all the details on the gig. "*The Yael Satterlee Experiment: Featuring guest singer*," it says. I cock an eyebrow.

"Auditions haven't been going all that well," he tells me with a cockeyed grin. "But we have some friends that aren't really up for a full-time music gig. They fill in when we need them," he said. "We're still trying to find the right fit for us."

My eyes meet his. I know I'm what they're looking for; I could hear it when we performed. It was completely natural from the start. "I'll be there."

That week drags no matter what I do to pass the time. I go shopping for some new clothes, to wear in front of a band. This includes a tight pair of black jeans which fit like they were made for my body. Every chance I get, I sing every single song on that set list. I even attempt to learn them on piano, not because I think I need to but to further my own education as a songwriter. I love picking apart the notes and learning the chords. Nothing is more rewarding when, after frustrating minutes of floundering, I finally hit the right keys. I end up playing more by ear than by sheet music.

I work at Cynzia's part-time during the week like I had been. Everyone there thinks I'm still working for the consulting firm. Little do they know I'm working even harder trying to crush the material given to me for the next step in my audition process.

The only thing I don't do is call Lori. She's not calling me either, so I know this is probably just a power play, to see which one caves first. I hate games like this. I thought she was above it.

The more I think of how she hadn't really supported my dreams, even before Susan died, I can't really deny that I have been unhappy with things between us for a long, long time. Worse, she never seemed to care. Almost from the moment Susan was buried, Lori has been single-minded in our pursuit to "make it better." We renovated the house, we upgraded our jobs, and she tried her best to get me involved in higher education.

If that had been the life I wanted, it all would have been a dream.

I thought about that moment in the loft in SoHo, when the guys virtually wrote my backup music to my song, fleshing it out into a living thing I could hear outside my own head. From that moment I knew that I would never be content with her dream.

My only hope now was that she'd see how hard I had been working. Then maybe she'd know that I really do have what it takes to make this work, at least enough to give it a real shot.

I realize of course this hard work has more to do than just getting into a band. I have something to prove, to the guys in Yael's band, to Lori… and to myself.

I decide to work out my act at Fritz's. We don't mention that kiss in her car, or her new man, when I ask Pam if I might use the small stage to hone my performance. I could have done it at home, of course, but I gravitate there because of anyone I know, she is the only one who don't treat my dream to be a singer like it's some kind of joke. And I need her voice in my ear to drown out all the naysayers who have planted their nuggets of negativity for months.

Like I suspected, when I tell her what kind of chance I have, she wants to help. Maybe she still feels guilty about that kiss, or that she never told me about her other guy. Either way, though technically the karaoke is only utilized on the weekends, she opens the bar early to me every single day so that I can work out a stage routine while they prep for the night ahead.

Pam makes a great groupie. Her face is so expressive when I target her from the stage that it becomes a challenge to see how far I can go. I can't help but wonder what it might look like if I actually fucked her. I don't know why the thought jumps in my brain, but I can't get it out once it's in there. And knowing that she's off limits only makes it hotter for me. Since we both know nothing can happen, I indulge it during the performance, doing my best to make her blush as I openly seduce her from the stage, like mental foreplay.

By Friday morning, I'm worked up in more ways than one.

I catch a cab into town, where I meet up with the guys at Yael's loft. Everyone is in great spirits, though I'm pretty sure that both Felix and Bobby are chemically enhanced. Yael is a straight-edge vegan, so I know his head is clear.

When Bobby offers me a drink, and Felix offers me a puff, I turn them down. I want my mind just as clear when I take that stage.

We get to Seedlings at ten before ten that night. We go onstage at midnight, but Yael wants to see how the crowd is reacting to the other bands in the lineup. It's essentially a local music night. Seedlings is great about cultivating raw, untapped talent, giving them a place to play so they can turn into polished performers, hence the name. It's where amateurs like me pay their dues.

Getting there so early doesn't really help my nerves. I feel like a stallion locked up in the starting gate. I really want a drink to steady my nerves, but I know better. I head to the bar to order a bottle of water instead. "Hey, Micah," I say to the familiar bartender.

"Vanni," he says with a smile. "What brings you to the city?"

I'm with the band. "I thought I'd check out the new music," I say. "Is Lori here? I haven't seen her."

"She's around here someplace. Check the parking lot. She's been taking her breaks out there lately."

I nod, take my bottle of water and head out to the private parking lot for the staff and talent out back. I spot her car easily. For some reason it makes me think of sitting in Pam's car, particularly the night I stole a kiss that wasn't mine to take. She was right to pull away. Things are so complicated, and I'm not really free. I do owe Lori something for all she has done for me since Susan died. So what if she hasn't called me since she left? We mattered to each other for all this time, there has to be something left.

I start to take one step towards it and then decide I better not. Instead of telling her, yet again, what this dream means to me, I'd rather show her. I honestly can't wait to see her surprised face when I take the stage. I'm glad she's getting her break out of the way early. Now I know she won't miss it.

But just as I turn back to the bar I realize that the obscured car on the other side of hers is rocking.

My brow creases as I snake my way through the cramped parking lot towards the red compact car Lori purchased to get her back and forth to Brooklyn. The closer I get, the more detail I can make out about the car parked right next to it. The black sports car is brand new, with dealer tags still on the back, and it has a large figure sitting in the driver's seat, which I can barely make out through the foggy windows.

Everything sets off warning bells. Is this some big, rich muscle-head dude jacking off while watching my girl listen to music? Weirder things have happened in New York. Maybe she was nice to him in the club and he followed her out to the car. I'll fucking kill him if he even thinks about touching her.

Of course, the closer I get, the more I can see that it's not just one person sitting in the driver's seat, it's two. The couple is clearly fucking, with the smaller of the two, presumably the female, riding the person sitting in the driver's seat.

That's not the most shocking discovery I make. As I round Lori's car, I spot the familiar parking permit hanging from the rearview mirror, one specifically made for McKinley, Donnelly and Roth. It sways back and forth with their zesty lovemaking, no doubt a quickie before she has to rush back inside to finish her shift.

I hear the woman's screams, which sound so goddamned familiar it cracks my heart before I can make out the detail through the fogged glass. My good-girl Lori, who had always pushed me away whenever I tried to cop a feel or steal a kiss anywhere near her job, now calls out the name of another man. "Fuck me, Tony!"

I stumble backwards, backing right into another car. I can't look away, even if I want to. My girl straddles my best friend, giving him the fucking of a lifetime right in the parking lot where she works like some common whore.

I gulp hard as my water bottle drops to the asphalt. I'm rooted to the spot as the details in the car become clearer. I'm unable to tear my eyes away as he grabs one of her tits and makes her cry out even more. I feel like I'm having some demented out of body experience.

I want to wrench the door open and pull them both out by the pubic hair, but I can't move. I stay there until they are finished. I watch them kiss deep, and I know immediately it's not just sex. There's true intimacy there.

There's familiarity.

I watch as she slides off of his lap into the passenger seat, where she puts on any clothes that were discarded. Almost simultaneously, they both exit the car and turn back towards the club, where they spot me at the same time.

I will give it to Lori. She actually has the decency to look guilty. "Vanni," she says, but it tapers out with her breath. "What are you doing here?"

"Watching the show," I grit between clenched teeth. "Wanna tell me what the goddamned *fuck* is going on here?"

Tony doesn't look ashamed. He tips his chin and rounds the car so that he can stand between us, as if I would pose a threat to a woman. "Listen, Vanni. We didn't want you to find out this way."

"How did you want me to find out?" I snap. "Did you rent some fucking billboard in Time Square?"

"This isn't what it looks like, man," he says, holding up a hand.

"Funny because it looks like you were fucking my girl. Or was she just fucking my best friend?"

He sighs, but he doesn't apologize. Instead, he says something much worse. "I love her."

"What the fuck?!" I explode.

"It happened a few months ago," she confesses softly.

"Before my aunt Susan died? Or after?" I glare at Tony. I remember how he had been such a mensch and driven her home Christmas Eve. "Maybe during?"

"We didn't mean for it to happen, bro."

"What *did* you mean to happen, '*bro*?'"

"It's just been so difficult," she tries to explain. "I was under so much pressure–"

I can't even let her finish. "*You've* been under pressure?! Are you fucking kidding me?"

"This is part of the problem, Vanni," Tony says. I turn on him with pure venom. "You can't see past your own selfish nose anymore. It's all about what you want, what you think you deserve.

Look, I'm sorry your aunt died, but shit happens, man. We just have to do the best we can to get through it."

"All you want to do is play," she spits at me. "Who gets to be the adult now that Susan is gone?"

I cross the feet between us, coming nose to nose with Tony, who won't let me anywhere near Lori. "Get the fuck out of my way."

"No," he says with a shake of his head. "You've hurt her enough."

"Hurt *her*?" I repeat, incredulous. "How the fuck did I hurt her? I just wanted to fucking sing. It's not the end of the goddamn world, for crissakes." I can't stop the obscenities, even if I wanted to. But I think finding out your best buddy is screwing your old lady is the best reason to curse if there ever was one.

"It's a dead-end road and you know it. You really think people are going to pay money to see some part-time pizza cook sing?"

My fist clenches so tight that my short nails carve into the palms of my hands. I want to punch him so bad I can taste it. I want to crack his head onto the concrete like an egg. I want to knee him right in his balls, which are probably still sticky with my girlfriend's cum. Tony doesn't even flinch. He's waiting for it. I realize then that he's *been* waiting for it.

I shake my head with a snarl I can't contain. "Fuck you," I tell him. I look at her. "And fuck you. You both deserve each other."

I spin on my heel and stalk back to the bar. I can still see them in my mind's eye, fucking in that front seat, her shirt over her tits, her skirt likely over her ass as she rides him. His hands cupping and squeezing her ass as he pumps himself into her, like he owns her. Like she's his.

And it's been going on for months.

I head straight for the bar and order a shot of whiskey. Bobby idles up next to me. "So the man does party after all," he says as he motions to the bartender for another round. "Maybe I was wrong about you, Carnevale. Maybe you will fit in just fine."

After the bartender brings the shots, Bobby lifts his glass to me. "To a great show."

I spot Lori off in the corner, clocking back in for her late shift as a cocktail waitress. Her skirt is short, and her top is a button-down shirt that she has tied at the waist. Yet all I can see now is her naked body straddling his.

Bobby's gaze follows mine. "She's cute," he says.

"She's a whore," I spit.

"Aren't they all?" he wonders as he orders yet another round. "Don't let 'em get you down, man. There's always another one willing to take their place." My eyes meet his. "In fact, I'd wager that you'll probably get at least five drinks and ten phone numbers after we perform tonight. And groupie sex is fucking crazy. They'll do anything you want. Do you know how much anal I've gotten just from being in a band? It's unreal," he says with a satisfied chuckle.

By the time we get on the stage, I'm buzzing pretty good. I'm also pretty pissed. When we launch into our rock act, I have no problem getting into the character of a bad boy. I make sure Lori's watching as I swivel my hips towards the crowd of girls down front. I run my hand down my body, towards the bulge in my tight pants. I'm no porn star by far, but I've never had any complaints. The screaming girls in the front row certainly don't have any.

We perform our set of about five songs. When I step off stage, there are a group of girls waiting for me, some holding out drinks to me. I smile as I take them one by one, chugging them all down like a champ, and feeling a little less pain as I do so. The ego-stroking doesn't hurt, either.

"Oh my God! You're awesome!"

"You should totally be famous."

"If you're not busy tonight, maybe you could head uptown with my friend and me. I know this great club!"

They're so forward and direct it kind of takes my breath away. I feel hands on my body, even sliding down towards my ass, and dangerously near my crotch.

I herd them towards the bar, where I order a round for all of my new fans. This endears me to them even more. It's a pricy bar tab, but I figure I'm not saving for a future anymore. Bobby joins me, with an armful of girls himself. "To a great show," he toasts, and all our new fans agree.

I glare at Lori as she focuses on her work, but she's all thumbs as she tries to serve drinks. She can't keep her eyes off of me and the crowd I've attracted.

That's right, I think to myself. *See what you threw away for something ordinary, you stupid bitch.*

I put an arm around the two girls flanking me on either side. They're cute... I think. By now I'm fairly drunk, so details are beyond me. All I know is they're warm and willing and pressing up against me, their hands drifting lower to cup my ass shamelessly.

I use all my functioning brainpower to will Lori to look our direction as I plant an open-mouthed kiss on one of them. She's a redhead with full, pouty lips. "What's your name?" I ask.

"Madison," she says.

I look down at her hands, searching for that tale-tell X that would let me know if she is underage. There's no X. There are also no rings. "I'm pretty drunk. I think I need someone to take me home and put me to bed." She cuddles up against me with a wide smile. "You wanna get out of here, Madison?" I say in a low voice, near her ear.

She nods and I grab her hand in mine, pulling her through the crowd towards the entrance. We push past Lori, whose face screws up in a scowl. She's got a lot of nerve to be pissed. Fuck her. I can't believe I ever spent as much time as I did with her, trying to become some corporate clone to make her happy.

That's over. I swear right then and there I'll never sacrifice myself to make anyone happy again. They can accept me as is, or they can find the door.

I hail a cab and then pull Madison inside with me. She practically climbs right into my lap, laying a kiss right on my parted lips. I let my hand roam down her back and over the sweet curve of her ass. I cup her face in one hand as I part her lips with my tongue.

There's no call for romance here. She's not someone I may marry someday. She's a girl who clearly knows the score. She wants to fuck a singer, and right at that moment, I want to fuck a groupie. We're just two consenting adults. Who gives a shit what the world might have to say about it?

I'm still partially drunk when we reach the house in Bensonhurst. I pull out a bottle of booze from the kitchen cupboard before I take her upstairs to my old room. Lori had changed it into a sitting room, where she used to like to escape to read on a futon bed we got from a second-hand store. This was her space when she lived in this house, and a fitting place for the exorcism I knew needed to be performed.

I collapse onto the futon, and Madison follows me down. She's as hot for me as I am for her. Correction, she's hotter for me than I am for her, which means I'm the boss. She's eager and enthusiastic, so much so that she slides down my body all the way to my lap, where she unfastens my jeans.

I guzzle more booze as she takes me into her warm, wet mouth. God, the sensations are fucking fantastic. Her tongue swirls around my hardening shaft like a snake. I wind my hand into her curly red hair, pushing her down, forcing her to take more. "You like that, don't you, girl?" I murmur. It's been a while since I've been with someone who likes it.

I wonder if Lori likes to suck Tony's dick more than she liked to suck mine.

I push Madison's head further down. "Take it all, baby," I command.

She expertly sucks me off until I'm grunting like a caveman. I marvel that not only does she take it all, she swallows, too. It was so sexy and so dirty and so naughty–it was nothing like the Old Vanni who used to inhabit this room.

That guy's officially gone. He went up in smoke the minute he saw his girlfriend fucking his best friend.

That means Good Boy Vanni is gone. Corporate Lackey Vanni is gone. Now there's only this guy, who is getting his dick sucked by an actual groupie after singing to her during a live gig.

This was never really a part of my dream, but I'll take it.

I pull her up across my lap, discarding her clothes like an afterthought. She arches her back to force her firm tits into my hand and towards my mouth. I oblige her, making her crazy as she gyrates against me. "You were so sexy tonight when you sang," she tells me as she nibbles at my ear. "It made me so wet for you."

"Oh yeah?" I ask as my hand slithers between her legs to see if she's telling the truth.

"Yeah," she breathes as I torment her throbbing clit between two fingers. "I knew I wanted to fuck you the minute you stepped out on that stage."

I drive her crazy with my fingers as I nuzzle her sweet-smelling neck. She whispers such dirty things in my ear that it doesn't take very long for me to grow hard again. It's like a scene straight from a porn movie. No muss, no fuss. I wanted, I took. And she's thrashing on top of me, screaming for me to fuck her. I fish a condom from my old nightstand. I slide it on before I shove myself up inside her and watch her face as she rides me.

Only I don't see her face. I see Lori's face; the same face that she wore when she had Tony's dick stuffed up her cheating twat. I grimace as I hold Madison in place, bucking up inside of her to thrust away every last memory.

She never knows how she's being used. She doesn't even care. She climaxes hard all over me, screaming out my name. Honestly, it's never sounded so sweet. It's like she is introducing me to someone I've never met.

"That's right, baby," I tell her. "Say it!"

"Vanni," she screams again before she collapses against my shoulder.

I don't even think about Lori as I come. I simply pass out on that futon in a whiskey-soaked daze, clutching a naked stranger against me.

CHAPTER NINE:

I wake up the next day with a throbbing headache and a sore dick. We haven't moved from the futon, and her long limbs are wrapped around me, holding me in place. Memories of the night before fire to life in my brain. I disengage myself gently, which causes her to stir. Her blue eyes peel apart and then she smiles as she runs her hand along my body. "Morning," she murmurs.

All I want to do is get rid of her. I know it's a shitty thought, especially after the night I gave her. But I know that's all I can give her. I'm still completely wrecked over what Lori has done, and I know this by the way my heart sinks when I wake to find a strange woman in my bed instead of my girlfriend.

I'm not sure I'll ever recover. How can I trust anyone again? All these months she'd been pretending to be the perfect girlfriend, being there for me after Susan died, helping me rearrange my life into something that looked like the life she wanted, my own feelings in the matter be damned. Meanwhile she's been screwing Tony on the side, keeping an ace in her pocket in case I can't pull it together. And it becomes clear to me now that she never thought I could.

It's all been a big game. And I hate games.

Yet now I'm a player too, and this beautiful, naked girl beside me is a stark reminder of that.

Her tiny hand finds my swollen cock. I grimace as I attempt to pull away. "Didn't you get enough last night, sweetheart?" I use a term of endearment. I have to. I don't remember her name.

"Nuh uh," she says with a grin as she kisses her way up my chest, over my shoulder, along my neck.

Somehow she kisses away each regret, at least for Little Vanni, who stands tall and proud in her hand, ready for more action. Still, I push her hand away. "Sorry, babe. I have a full schedule today." She pouts, so I kiss her protruding bottom lip gently. "But it was fun. I'll never forget it."

It's a promise I know I can keep. Thanks to Lori ripping out my heart and stomping all over my ego, I know memories of my first official gig couldn't be sandblasted off of my brain.

I slide back into my jeans. I know my hard-on tempts her. Frankly it tempts me too. But I wasn't lying. I do have a lot of things to do today, the most important of which is finding out if my final "audition" for Yael sealed the deal.

It takes some work but I finally convince her to leave. I give her money for the cab and an orgasm for the road, rubbing her off as I hold her pinned against the door, making her scream again. I figure it's the gentlemanly thing to do. I had just used her like a dish rag, after all. This new Vanni definitely takes what he wants, but I figure he doesn't have to be a *complete* dick about it.

After I watch her cab pull away, I reach for my phone. Yael answers on the second ring. "Hey, man. What happened to you last night?"

"Met up with an old friend," I grumble before I change the subject. "So what's the word?"

"I have to say it. The crowd loved you. I got booked for three other gigs. I really think we've got something here. The job is yours if you want it."

Despite everything else, my spirit swells with joy. I know in an instant this is what I've been waiting for. It's worth everything, even losing Lori–one of my last real connections to the old Vanni.

I head back to SoHo, where we all brainstorm what kind of new sets to perform. Bobby and I lean towards sex-driven material. Yael relents and Felix just smokes a joint as he lets us hash out the details. Felix is so easy-going that he doesn't give a shit what he plays, just that he plays.

I don't leave that loft again till close to midnight, and I know right where I want to go.

The party is still in full swing as I arrive at Fritz's. Drunk patrons screech through the karaoke playlist, while Pam and Cheryl navigate the jam-packed bar. It wasn't dancing, but I suspect the success she'd made of Fritz's in the short time she's been managing it makes Pam a happy, happy girl. She has a wide smile for everyone she sees.

I realize then that I love those full lips. My cock jumps just thinking about it.

The Old Vanni accepted it when she pushed me away. What will this new Vanni do? I hold up my hand till she sees it. She nods with a smile. She knows just what I want. I then disappear into one of the VIP booths which has clearly been reserved with a placard on the table.

I don't care. I plop down on the cushioned seat anyway.

Pam personally brings me my beer. I give her a sly smirk as she shakes her head. "I have a party coming in any minute for this table," she says as she places the beer in front of me.

"I won't be here long," I tell her as I grab her hand. "Let's dance." I don't even wait for her to say yes. I pull her towards the dance floor.

"Vanni, I'm working," she protests.

"You're on a break," I tell her as I pull her into my arms. How she fills them immediately turns me on. I don't care about the tempo of the song playing. I crush her curves to me anyway. "Guess what?"

She gives me a suspicious side-eye glare. "What?"

I lean down to whisper in her ear. "You are looking at the new lead singer of *The Yael Satterlee Experiment*, featuring me."

Her eyes pop open wide. "Oh, Vanni!" she cries as she wraps her arms around me and hugs me. "Didn't I tell you something big was about to happen?"

I squeeze her tight. She feels like heaven in my arms. It's like comfort food for the soul. "You did. You're the only one who did."

"I don't see how anyone can hear you sing and think otherwise," she says.

"Lori thought otherwise." My tone sharpens as I say, "She wanted that button-down corporate raider so much she started to see my best friend on the sly. *Former* best friend," I amend.

"Oh, Vanni."

Her hand feels like silk against my forearm. I hated the pity in her eyes but relished the warmth of her touch. "Yeah, found 'em fucking in his car in the parking lot of where she works, where I just so happened to be performing. I thought I was going to show her. Little did I know she had something to show me."

"How long has it been going on?"

"Months," I say as my eyes meet hers. I trust her enough to show her that pain.

She reaches up to hug me again. "Fuck her," she says. "You're too good for her anyway."

I hold her tight. "I'd rather fuck you," I say against her ear. She tries to pull away but I hold her fast. "The song isn't over."

She relents, but remains stiff in my arms. I know she can feel the promise of my hard body. She struggles to keep control of herself. It only makes me hotter for her.

"Come home with me," I murmur into her ear. "I'll buy us a bottle of champagne. Let's celebrate dreams coming true."

She chuckles softly. "I'm no Rockette."

"I'd pay to see you dance. My private dancer," I add with a smirk, before I launch into the Tina Turner classic.

"You're a sweet talker, Giovanni Carnevale, but I ain't buying it. Now please. I have to get back to the bar."

"Fine. Then meet me after the bar closes."

"Vanni," she trails off.

"Why not? One night, toasting a friend's success. What's wrong with that?"

"I already have plans."

From the way she looks away from me, I know she means that she's got plans with that other man. Why does that only make me want her more? Unlike Lori, who clearly had chosen Tony over me, I know that Pam wants me most. I can feel it in the way she fights the attraction between us. She didn't choose someone else to trade up from me. She is with that man because she thinks she can't have me. But she can have me. I hold her close so she can feel me harden against her to show her that.

She trembles in my arms. I want to kiss her, right there in the middle of that tiny dance floor. I want to crush my mouth on hers, forcing her lips apart with my tongue and make her melt against me, forgetting all about whatshisname. My cock jumps. Her wide eyes dart to mine, but all I can do is stare at that mouth and think of what it would taste like, and what it would look like wrapped around my dick. I bend my head closer until I hover just a breath above her, torturing her with the sweet anticipation of a kiss, rather than the kiss itself.

She wants time? I'll give it to her. But I'm damned sure going to show her what she's missing.

"Rain check, then," I say softly. Without another word I release her. I fish money out of my pocket for the beer I won't even drink, and then head for home.

Alone.

I don't have much time to hang out at Fritz's the weeks that follow. We have another gig, so we are hard at work trying to polish our stage show. Bobby suggests that we make the set list sexier, with naughty songs to get all the girls hot. Yael rolls his eyes. I know he wants to keep our musical integrity the focus of the band, hence the name. Bobby is a tried and true salesman, who just wants us to get more gigs. Plus he's a total dog, who is out to bone as many hot young chicks as possible like any hot-blooded American male in his early twenties. "Now that we have this sexy piece of man meat," he'd tease, referring to me, "we might as well take advantage of it."

We add *"Feel Like Making Love"* and *"Fat Bottomed Girls"* to the set list, with only two weeks to learn and perfect them by our next show. I suggest *"Loving, Touching, Squeezing."* Unfortunately it has personal meaning to me now, but also because it challenges me to learn the piano part, since I'm the only one besides Yael who can play.

And I like that challenge almost as much as I like the challenge of matching Steve Perry's killer vocals.

We're at Yael's loft more often than not, and I'm usually with Bobby whenever we have any free time at all.

He decides I need a fashion overhaul. We find a shop in the Village that sells vintage clothes, where he flirts shamelessly with the cute salesgirl who assists us. "How old are you?" he asks as his eyes make that familiar trail over her figure.

"Nineteen," she answers. Her eyes dart away from his, shy and embarrassed.

Bobby steps closer to her, wrapping his arm around her shoulders as they face me. "How would you dress him to make him sexy?"

A flush rises in her cheeks as she looks me over. "He's already sexy."

Bobby flashes a smile. "Good answer. But seriously, what could he wear that would make those panties of yours melt right off?"

"Come on, man," I say. My aunt Susan would have beat me with a yardstick if I were shamelessly preying on someone that young.

But the salesgirl seems to like it. "I've got some stuff," she says.

"You're going to get arrested, Bobby," I tell him as soon as she's out of earshot. He just shakes his head as he watches her ass while she walks away.

"She's all woman from where I'm standing." He turns back to me. "The young ones are a lot of fun. What they lack in experience they make up for with enthusiasm." He punctuates his sentence with an obscene wiggle of his tongue.

I think about the groupie I had taken home from the first gig, who did, indeed, have a shitload of enthusiasm. I kept expecting her to show up on my doorstep, begging another night of uninhibited sex. So far, she had disappeared into the night, filing me away as a nice memory and nothing more.

I don't know how I feel about that yet. On one hand, I'm certainly not looking for anything, so it is revelatory to find a girl who is all about the sexual gratification of a conquest, same as me. On the other hand, that big ol bed gets lonely without another person to share it with. There are nights I'd reach for Lori out of impulse, disappointed to find she is no longer there.

Then the heartache would bubble up all over again.

I haven't talked to Lori or to Tony since that night. There is no point. They made their choices. If I'm honest with myself, I've made mine too. Despite how lonely it gets in that old brownstone, I'd rather have this life now rather than the life I had tried to live for the both of them. I haven't missed McKinley, Donnelly and Roth or Stu one iota since the day I quit. I'd rather spend sixteen hours rehearsing with the band than eight hours racing around like a nitwit under banks of harsh florescent lighting.

The only thing I do miss is a regular paycheck. We don't get paid by the hour, we get paid by the gig. This means I'm dipping more and more into the tiny, but precious, nest egg that Aunt Susan left me.

Thanks to the long hours I'm keeping with the band, I have to let the job at Cynzia's go as well. No more hairnets, but no more tips, either.

I'm hesitant to buy much of anything for my new wardrobe, but I know that each gig is vital to booking the next. When the salesgirl returns with a selection of clothes, I pick out the ones that will make me the most appealing to the crowd. "You remind me of Jim Morrison," she says as she holds up a shirt button-down shirt. "You should definitely wear this opened."

"How do you know who Jim Morrison is, baby girl?" Bobby asks her with a grin.

"I love all kinds of music," she says as she grabs some ripped jeans and a black cotton shirt.

"You should come see us play. I can get you on the list."

She offers yet another shy smile. "Sure. Can I bring some friends?"

He leans forward. "Do they look like you?"

"Some," she says. "Some are hotter."

He grins at me. "Then by all means. The least we can do for your help turning this guy into a rock star."

She's sweet as she turns to me. "He was already a rock star." She looks away quickly.

Bobby nudges my arm with his. He knows this juicy little berry is ripe for the picking.

We spend about an hour in that shop, where she dresses me pretty much head to toe. She adds a host of accessories to my base wardrobe of pants and a shirt. She finds cool belts, either in snakeskin or made of metal, she secures studded cuffs on my wrists and silver rings for several fingers. "Do you wear polish?" she asks.

"I never have," I answer.

She disappears behind the counter to withdraw a bottle of black nail polish. "Put it on a few days before the gig, so they're kind of rough and chipped by the time you perform. It'll make you look edgier."

"She's right," Bobby says. "I wear it when I play."

In the end, I purchase all the things she's selected for me. "I hope you get paid by commission," I tease.

She laughs. "No, but that's okay. It'll be worth it when I see you play."

Her eyes are hopeful as she stares up at me. God, she's sexy as hell. Nineteen, though. That's young, even for me.

Bobby doesn't seem to care. He flirts all the way till the moment we leave, and the minute we're out the door, he's fantasizing about the conquest he predicts will happen about an hour after the show. "We should get a hotel room in the city," he says. "VIPs only."

Now that I've changed into my new wardrobe, we decide to scope out the venue, to see how the crowd responds to different acts. The minute we get there, Bobby befriends the bouncers and bartenders. The venue is bigger than Seedlings, so it draws a bigger crowd. They're young and fairly hip, with a definite edge. The band onstage is alt-rock, which is a big hit.

"Hey, sugar," a voice says near my ear. I turn to the person speaking. It's an older woman in her 40s, with dark brown hair and bright brown eyes the color of cognac. "Care to dance?"

I glance her over. She's tall, about 5'8, which is still fairly short in comparison to my height. She wears a leopard print dress, cinched at the waist, and black platform pumps. I'm pretty sure the gold she wears around her neck, wrists and fingers is pure, and that her diamonds are real. I smell the money all over her. "Sure," I say, before I take her hand and lead her to the dance floor. She's in my arms before I can turn around.

She links her hands behind my neck, sliding up my body like a snake climbing a tree. This is a woman on the make. I grin. "Awesome band," I say, referring to the group onstage.

She doesn't look away. Instead she shrugs and says, "Call me old fashioned, but I prefer classic rock."

"Yeah?"

Her smile widens. "Yeah."

I hold her a little tighter. "You should come back next week, then."

"Is that so?" she asks and I nod. "What's so special about next week?"

"I hear the band scheduled to perform is really good. Good old, honest-to-goodness rock and roll."

She presses her breasts against my chest. "Sounds hot. Will you be there?"

"You never know," I tease. My arm circles her waist and I grind up against her to the beat. She licks her lips as her hands slide down my back towards my ass.

I decide then and there she has a lot more to show me than some nineteen-year-old. I'm feeling pretty proud of myself as the dance ends. I wrap my arm around her shoulders and guide her back to the bar. "Let me buy you a drink," I say.

She shakes her head. "I've got to go. Rain check," she offers, which reminds me of my frustrating encounter with Pam.

Bobby catches up to me almost immediately after she leaves. "That's fucking brilliant, man!"

I'm puzzled as I look at him. "What?"

"Oh, come on! You know who that is, right?" I continue to stare at him blankly. "You really don't know?"

I shake my head. "As far as I know, she's just some woman who asked me to dance. Why? Who is she?"

"Ever heard of the name Tina Nunes?"

At first I shake my head, but then something about that last name sticks. "Wait. Doesn't Julio Nunes run Sedução?" I ask, referring to a popular basement nightclub on the lower east side.

"Used to," Bobby clarified, "until he had to fork it over to his ex-model wife *Tina* in the divorce."

My eyes widen. She owns one of the most prominent music clubs in the city, where producers regularly scour for new talent, and I just invited her to watch us perform. Either I'm the luckiest asshole in the world, or Bobby is pulling my leg. "Are you shitting me?"

"Man. When you reel in a big fish, you really reel in a big fish, don't you? Do you know what that kind of exposure could mean?"

I nod slowly. Of course I know what it could mean.

Bobby grabs me by the chin and kisses me soundly on the cheek. "God, I knew that this face would be our golden ticket!" He orders another round. "You do whatever you need to do to make her happy. She could open so many doors for us." He laughs. "Fortunately for you, she's good looking. And you know the best thing about those rich, older chicks. No baby mama drama."

I gape at him. "You want me to sleep with her?" I mean, I was planning to do that anyway, but not for a cost.

Bobby stands straighter and leans close. "No sleeping involved, amigo. I want you to fuck her and fuck her well. It's all about relationships in this business. And she has zeroed in on *you*. You can't squander that opportunity. I mean, it's not like you're cheating on anyone," he points out. "You're a single, good-looking guy. Get your kicks while you're still young enough to get 'em. Hell, if it were me, I'd have left with her tonight." He winks at a cocktail waitress who squeezes past. "On to Plan B," he says before he chases after the cute brunette balancing a heavy tray on her arm.

That night I return to the brownstone alone. I head straight to the bedroom, where I shrug off my shirt and hang it over a chair that Lori had handpicked. I fucking hate that chair. Every time I look at it, all I can see is her straddling Tony, naked and screwing in my aunt's old room.

Who knows if they did? Apparently there was a lot going on between them that I didn't know. Did they sleep together in my bed? Did they bathe together in my tub? Did he fuck her on the kitchen table like I had so many months before?

And when the hell will I stop obsessing over every single painful detail like some heartbroken wuss? Fuck 'em. I'm better off without both of them.

The New Vanni would never put up with any of that shit. Hit it and quit it, that's his game. No one has time for feelings in this uphill climb towards the top. And now one of the most influential club owners in town slithered up on my hook without my even knowing, in a textbook case of serendipity.

Old Vanni would never barter his body for his career. Susan, who had come *thisclose* to becoming a nun, would never have allowed it, and she was his guiding moral compass.

The New Vanni had no such compass. It was broken under the weight of crushing betrayal, from the two people he had trusted the most, including a "good girl" girlfriend, who had made him wait for months before he could even get in her pants.

How long did it take Tony to get into them? The New Vanni doesn't have to give a shit. He's got one priority: to break into this business and make a living doing what he loves. And right now he's got too much to do to get ready for the gig of his life to worry about what used to be or what might have been.

I am going to make quite an impression on Tina Nunes, and I don't give a fuck what anyone else might have to say about it.

CHAPTER TEN:

The next week leading up to our gig, I am a man on a mission. I drive rehearsals every bit as hard as Yael, who is equally excited about Tina catching our band. Sedução is a star-making club, which plucks acts from the underground music scene and plops them into the mainstream. It's an express lane for success. For us to have this opportunity so early in the history of the band is a really big deal.

And *she* came to *me*. Before she even heard me sing, or knew I was a singer, she wanted *me*. The New Vanni knows just what to do with that. The girls think I'm sexy? The girls want to fuck me?

Just wait till they hear me sing.

I polish this new persona all week long, both with the guys and at home. I'm liberated to be that guy I never would have dreamed to be otherwise. I'm not a playa. I'm not a womanizer. My aunt raised me to be a good boy and an even better man.

But on stage I could be anybody, that's the beauty of it. From song to song, it's a role to play. And if seducing the ladies sells tickets, then where's the harm in that?

Now that I have plenty of time without a "real" job, I focus on my physique. I've always had energy that I had to burn off, so exercise has always come easy to me. Only now I know I'm sculpting myself into a product to sell. I start doing incline sit-ups, as many as I can stand. I chip away further at my precious nest egg and turn one of the upstairs bedrooms, Mama's old room, into a gym courtesy of a weight bench, free weights and a line of mirrors against once wall. I also install a stereo system so that I can internalize these songs till I till I know them backwards and forwards.

Bigger and better, that's my plan.

I know I can't work miracles in a week, but it gives me something to fill the time now that I'm single. I get to Manhattan early every day so I can jog in the park. That's the exercise I like best. Central Park is one of my favorite places in the city. You get to see something new every day. It's never mundane or boring or predictable. I download all the songs from our set and listen to them, in order, as I mentally prepare each and every performance where I can own each song as if it is mine.

And, late at night when I can't sleep–or face that big platform bed alone–I work on my own stuff. I even write a song for Tina, about the sexy older woman I know can teach me a thing or two. I know we won't be able to perform it now, but I've always dreamed bigger than the now anyway.

By Saturday I'm amped up like a prizefighter.

I arrive at the venue before anyone else. I scope the crowd, to see how they respond to the opening bands. We don't headline, not yet, and the only way we ever will is if I learn how to play these crowds just like a fiddle. The girls will be easy. They're all buzzing thanks to a busy bar churning out gallons of colorful, fruity drinks. But I want to get the guys too, and I know the best way to do that is by the music. I watch how the frontmen lead their bands, taking mental notes on what I can add with our own set.

When it's our turn to perform, I'm ready to strike. I hit that stage with a newfound aggression. I stalk that tiny space, boldly interacting with the crowd right in the front row. Fortunately for me, this includes the cute little salesgirl and several of her equally sexy friends. Since I already know her, and I know how she reacts to me, she's an easy target. The New Vanni sinks his seductive claws into her and won't let go throughout the set.

I have to have some outlet for the energy, considering I don't see Tina anywhere.

I don't drop the persona, though. The flood lights keep me blinded to the rest of the crowd just beyond the edge of the stage. I shake my ass for all of them. You never know who's out there in the audience. I'm not just performing for this crowd, I'm selling us for future gigs and I know it.

I seduce very girl in the front row, as if I have any intention of getting them all into bed. They're putty in my hands, figuratively speaking. In fact, it's working so well the men scatter from the stage, intimidated or turned off by my seductive onslaught.

I surprise Yael when I turn the spotlight on him during one of the guitar solos. I know he's not about the fame or attention. He just wants to play. But he's so kickass he deserves the attention whether he wants it or not. "On lead guitar, ladies and gentlemen, the one, the only, Yael Satterlee!"

What few men there are down front throw up the horns while Yael loses himself in his solo. It draws more men to the stage to listen to the band. I smile to myself how well it's all working. Sometimes it's just too easy.

When we finally take our bow, the crowd is clamoring for more. While the guys load out their equipment, I head straight for the bar. I'm mobbed almost immediately by a horde of girls, all of whom want to buy me a drink.

Since I'm a gentleman, I let them.

My eyes still scan the dimly lit bar for any sign of Tina. Surely if she sees how well we did and how well the audience responded, she'll book us for her club in a heartbeat. That's what this week has been about, and I have absolutely no doubt that's exactly how it will go.

Only she's not there. I'm surrounded by sexy, beautiful women, but none of them happen to own the biggest underground clubs in the city. The realization of this is like a pinprick in my overfilled balloon. As successful as the gig has been, I feel like I have failed to do what I set out to do–namely launch our new band into the stratosphere with one kickass performance.

Did I really think it would be that easy?

Apparently the New Vanni did.

"Hey," I hear a female voice say right next to me. I turn to see the nineteen-year-old sales clerk, hooked arm and arm with a tall blonde. "You were great up there! And you looked so hot."

I smile for her. I had used her shamelessly throughout the set so I figure I can't blow her off now, even though I know better than to be interested. She's way too young. "I followed all your advice," I say with a smirk I've come to perfect, as I hold up my chipped, black nails to prove my point.

She laughs. "This is my bestie, Jena," she says as she introduces her friend.

"We loved the show," the blonde tells me, her blue eyes sparkling with similar interest. "You're really good."

"Our Vanni is great at everything," Bobby says as he comes up behind the girls. He recognizes the salesgirl, so he has made a beeline for us the second he gets his equipment put away. "Would you both like to join us for an exclusive after-party at the hotel down the street?"

As young as she is, the salesgirl doesn't miss a beat. Her smile widens and she nods her head, grasping her equally enthusiastic friend's hand in hers. "We'd love it!"

"Great," Bobby beams. He hands her a card from the hotel, with the room number written on the back. "We have to finish up here, but you both can head on over. The party is already in progress."

He takes my arm and withdraws me from their circle. He has other girls to parade me around in front of, to make a similar offer with similar cards.

"What are you doing?" I ask.

"You, my good man, are going to celebrate your success in style. I already have a buddy of mine over there setting things up. By the time we get there, you'll have your pick of VIP guests who are just dying to show you how much they appreciated your performance."

I scowl immediately. "Not everyone will be there. Tina is M.I.A."

He shrugs it off. "There will be other nights. It's not like we're going to get worse, you know what I mean?"

I shrug. I suppose he's right.

We meet up with Yael, who is as beside himself as a stoic Emo like him could be. We've booked more gigs, including a couple more performances right here in this club. "It's not headlining yet," he says. "But we're on our way."

It's a small victory, much smaller than the target for which I was aiming, but I'll take it.

I decide to accompany Bobby and the rest of the guys to the party at the hotel.

We've rented a suite, all part of the cost of doing business. There's enough booze and "party favors" around that everyone is in high spirits, no pun intended. Felix immediately joins the group of weed enthusiasts on the balcony, to get high as they marvel at the lights of the city and contemplate the wonder of the cosmos.

There are some guys present, who immediately corner Yael to discuss things like guitars and music theory.

Bobby steers me over to the bevy of beautiful girls–arguably the most beautiful from the crowd at the club–all of whom eye me like a rib eye steak about to be thrown on the grill.

Bobby has no qualms about doing just that. "Here's the man of the hour, ladies," he says with that cheesy, shit-eating grin.

Immediately the salesgirl appears at my side, with her blonde friend flanking me on the other. Everyone wants to get me a drink, and graciously I accept. Within a half-hour I'm raging drunk, but so is everyone else in the hotel suite, except maybe Yael and his music nerd posse.

As the booze slows down my brain, the more hedonistic New Vanni takes over. There are more girls present than can possibly fill my arms, but each one of them tries to have a go at it, as much as my predatory little salesgirl will allow. She may be young, but she knows what she wants. I kind of dig that about her.

And God, she's cute. Short dark hair, that tapers down to her slender neck. She's petite, but the short skirt she's wearing makes her tanned legs appear even longer, especially tucked one under the other as she pastes herself to my side.

With her more revealing club wear, I can see now that she sports some ink on her chest, a dragonfly with wings right across the tops of her breast, its body dipping low between. Her nose is pierced, as is her tongue, which sends electricity right down to my groin. She wears chains and leather, suggesting that she isn't as vanilla as most nineteen-year-olds I've met, which, admittedly, aren't many. Even when I was nineteen, I had my eye on older women, thanks to the sexy cougar who took my virginity when I was a teen. I figured older women knew a thing or two more than the silly girls who went to my high school.

But this girl has a few secrets of her own, I can tell by the familiar way she cozies up to her friend, who has me equally pinned on the other side.

I have to wonder. Have they been in my web? Or am I in theirs?

This is a new experience for me, and I can't say it's necessarily unpleasant. I've worked myself up for a week straight to seduce Tina Nunes, with nowhere to spend this energy except my pseudo-gym at the house. The promise of these two soft, curvy girls at my side is a lot more enticing than 100 extra sit-ups. We're talking two women at once. Isn't that every guy's fantasy deep down?

I watch Bobby interact with a couple of girls who want to know all about the bass. Actually they don't give a shit about the bass; they just want to get closer to the hot musician in the band. With a smile on his face, he closes an arm around either of them, practically pulling both into his lap. He sends me a victorious smile and a wink before he starts making out with the both of them right in the middle of the party. Their hands immediately roam over his body. They don't care they're in a room full of people. They're going to go after what they want... and what they want is the unfulfilled promise of sex we subconsciously (or, in my case, purposefully) made when we played.

Still, as fun as it is, I haven't crossed the line yet. There's still time to head any potential problems off at the pass.

I pull the salesgirl close. "You should probably get home, girl. Isn't it past your curfew?"

She captures a lock of my hair in her fingers. "Do you want me to go?"

That's a loaded question. No, in fact. I do not want her to go. But I know she should. I know that's what Aunt Susan would tell the both of us, after she whipped us raw with her yardstick.

Aunt Susan's not here, I remind myself. Mama's not here. Tony and Lori aren't here. And truthfully, the Old Vanni who needed all of them to tell him how to be a good boy isn't here either.

I shake my head slowly as I snake a hand around her neck to cup the back of her head and draw her closer. Her lips cover mine like she's been waiting to kiss me for a week.

Maybe she has. The thought stokes the fire within. Maybe Tina Nunes found some other boy toy to play with, but this girl has probably been thinking of me every single night this week, unable to resist the chance to get closer to me... so that I can give her the night of her dreams.

What kind of jerk would I be if I denied her that one simple wish?

I force her mouth open with my tongue, claiming her kiss immediately. I feel her tongue stud, which is hot as hell. She moans against me as she presses more into my arms.

Since I am a polite host, I can't forget her friend, who is plastered to my other side. I close my arm around her shoulders and pull her in as well, breaking the kiss with my salesgirl to seek out the lips of the blonde next to me.

Suddenly their hands are all over my body. My cock springs to attention. He's literally such a hedonistic prick, but I can't blame him for responding. I've had some fun in my day, but I've never had an armful of two girls ready to do anything and everything I want to please me.

When the salesgirl whispers, "Let's go to the bedroom," it's like finding a winning lottery ticket. I can hardly decline.

At least, the New Vanni can't, especially after he sees that Bobby has already taken his armful of women to one of the two bedrooms in the suite.

"Let's go," I tell my salesgirl.

I haven't even gotten her name, but she doesn't seem to care. She drags me by the hand towards the unoccupied room, with Jena trotting happily behind.

I barely get the door shut behind us before the salesgirl rips off her top, revealing her naked torso to me before she practically launches into my arms. I don't even have enough time to properly inspect her tattoo. Her mouth opens under me for another blazing kiss, as Jena kneels down beside me, unfastening my jeans and peeling them down from my body. My cock is so hard it springs free almost immediately from its restraints. Hands and lips are all over my body, and I'm just drunk enough to mentally float away on that cloud of sensory overload.

Jena makes fast work of my clothing, until I'm standing naked in front of her. She runs her fingers along my shaft. "You're so big," she murmurs. It only makes me harder.

"What are you going to do with it?" I ask as I run my hand through her soft, sunny hair.

Without missing a beat she takes me into her mouth. What do you know? She has a tongue stud too. I shudder hard before I reach again for my salesgirl. She rubs her small tits against my chest as she kisses me hard and deep. The sexy songs I've been singing blare in my head as fireworks explode in my brain. What a crazy fucking finale to my week. Is this what it means to be a rock star? Whatever I want, whenever I want it? No questions asked?

It's a whole new world as I disentangle myself from the girls and drag them to the bed. On the nightstand there are condoms and lotions next to a bucket of champagne, ready and waiting for a night of debauchery. We fall together, with them on either side of me. There are lips and hands and naked skin everywhere. As Jena crawls up my body to capture a scorching kiss, my salesgirl goes down on me with experience belied by her young age. My head tilts back as I groan, my fingers tangled in her short hair. Normally I would call her by her name as I urged her on, but we seemed to have skipped over that part. I'm operating by new rules now, rules that give me the right to take both of these women at the same time with no regret or remorse.

My hand disappears between Jena's legs and she gasps into my mouth as I find that tiny, hard little nub at the center of her pleasure core. She shudders against me as she kisses me harder. My cock jumps in the salesgirl's mouth, so big it will hardly fit in her throat. She lifts away to work my shaft with her hand. The cold air makes me strain for her even more. I fumble for the nightstand, where I grab the box of condoms. I toss one towards the salesgirl. As I feel the cool sensation of latex slide down around my dick, I position Jena to straddle my face, where I happily dive in to replace my fingers with my tongue.

Likewise, my other sexy playmate straddles my hips. Before I know it, I'm inside my nameless salesgirl. She sinks down on top of me, soft and sure. She's so tight I can't believe it. I feel her conform to the curve of my cock as I snake my tongue inside of Jena. We've all got a similar rhythm now. My hands are on Jena's full ass, holding her open as I alternately spear her with my tongue and lick circles around her clit. She's trembling over me. After working her up all night, I know she's on the edge.

The salesgirl grinds down on top of me, squeezing me tight inside of her. I disengaged one of my hands from Jena to slide down my body and between the salesgirl and me, to fiddle her clit until she's exploding around me with a loud scream. After she's collapsed on top of me, I tap out of our current position.

I want to see what's going on.

The salesgirl lands on her back, with Jena on all fours in front of her. She dives in between her friend's legs while I enter her from behind, sinking into her deep and true. I hold her hips as I stare down at the sexy scene in front of me. The salesgirl grabs one of her tits in her hands, squeezing the nipple and crying out from the intense pleasure her friend is giving her, all the while looking me straight in the eye.

It's more than I can stand. I pummel Jena, who slams back against me with each stroke. Polite romance flies right out the window. This is dirty, raunchy *fucking*. Everything I was on that stage, I am on this bed. There are no complaints, there are no expectations, there's just the sound of primal animal sex rising in the air. It's so hot I can barely keep it together long enough to get her off. Jena comes just a hair before I do. I'm breathless as I collapse between them. They curl up on either side, their hands in my long, damp hair as they plant tiny kisses against my sweaty body.

Yeah. This is so much better than delivering the mail.

It's a fucking fantasy come true, and I didn't even know it was mine until it happened. Now I want more. I don't know how long we have that room, but I'm determined to get the most of it. I'm in no hurry to head back to that brownstone in Brooklyn where all my ghosts linger–including the ghost of my cheating ex-girlfriend.

With a growl I pull one of my new lovers up for a punishing kiss. Let Lori fuck the every dick in New York for all I care. There is a line of women to take her place.

And with any luck, I'll fuck 'em all before I ever have to see Lori's hateful, two-timing face ever again.

The hotel room is trashed the next morning, when both Bobby and I emerge from our respective bedrooms. Felix and his buddies are strewn about the sitting room in various cannabis-induced comas. Yael has split, but that's not surprising considering this isn't his scene. He's all about the music, not the fringe benefits.

"I'm so fucking sore, man," Bobby confides with a happy smile, rearranging himself in his jeans with one hand. "I hope your night went as well as mine did."

"No complaints," I say with my own shit-eating smile. It was my first threesome, and I knew it wouldn't be my last. I still hadn't gotten the salesgirl's name, but none of that seemed to matter. As young as she was, she knew the score going in. She got what she wanted every bit as I got what I wanted. It was a tidy little arrangement.

Hell, I'm sorry I didn't get her phone number so that we could hang out again sometime.

It's even worth the cost of the VIP after-party, which sucks all my personal profit for the gig *and* taps into my savings. The room itself was hundreds of dollars per night, not to mention all the refreshments and party favors. We also take care of our guests, particularly the female ones. We hire a limo to take them whenever they need to go, to give them the red carpet treatment all the way to the end.

It's exorbitant, but Bobby insists that we have an image to maintain now. The bigger we make ourselves, the more we will attract to us. "No one knows you're a star until you show them," he reasons. "Dress for the job you want, not the job you have."

Following his logic, I figure no one has to know the truth, that we're living hand to mouth–or in my case, losing money on my rock-n-roll lifestyle. As long as I look like a star and act like a star, no one is none the wiser.

"All they'll know is that they got one fantastic night with a star on the rise," he tells me as we step into the elevator. "They'll tell all their friends, and the next show will sell even more tickets. All the little girls want what the other girls have."

I don't know about all that. I don't really care. It was a helluva night, with another gig booked for that weekend.

Maybe this time I can convince Tina Nunes to come down for the show. The New Vanni has a few things to show that sexy cougar. After the night I've had, I'm more confidence than ever. I've never really had any trouble getting a girl into bed eventually, but it was a shot to the old ego that I only needed to snap my fingers and I could have my pick of any number of girls, who would do whatever I wanted just to make me happy.

By the time I get to the brownstone, I don't feel like the poor street kid from Philly, or the pizza slinger from Cynzia's. I don't feel like the loser whose girlfriend was screwing his best friend under his nose. For the first time ever, I feel like *a somebody*.

Bobby is right. It's time I let the whole world know it.

CHAPTER ELEVEN:

It is with my newfound confidence that I head to Sedução the very next night. I'm feeling pretty good about myself, I can't lie. Every time my thoughts return to that sexy threesome the night before, I feel like god. Those girls worshipped me in the best possible way. With every command they were ready to do whatever I wanted to make me happy, any position, any sexual fantasy or kink I may have wanted.

Of course that makes me feel like a king. I am a hot-blooded Italian after all. When I walk through the dark hallway leading me downstairs to Sedução, there's a strut in my walk. Tina may not have shown up the night before, but I know for a fact that she wants me. If she won't come to me, I'll go to her… this once anyway.

I know I have what it takes to keep her coming back for more, no matter how she wants to use me.

I amble to the bar, where I order a beer. While I wait for my order, I glance out over the venue. It's a large, sprawling joint, the basement of a repurposed industrial warehouse. Everything gleams steely gray, lit with neon blue racing along the top of every wall. The ceiling is mirrored, with various lighting contraptions to keep the room swirling with vibrant color. The black-tiled floor sparkles with shimmering multicolored glitter so it looks like you're walking on diamonds.

The stage is located in the other end of the room, and it's larger than anything we've played so far. My mouth curves into an absent smile as I imagine what it will be like to perform there. This is a high-end crowd. I should know by how much I had to shell out for a cover.

It is clear that Sedução misses no details. Everything is perfection, right down to the patrons themselves. The women are flawless. The men are wealthy. This is the best of New York. That demands the best in return.

I can't wait to play here.

"Here's your beer," the bartender tells me. I throw a fifty at her, to cover the beer and a very generous tip. Her eyebrow arches as she looks me over.

"Want me to open a tab?" she asks.

I lean closer. I love the way her pupils dilate with interest. This is going to be easier than I thought. "Consider it a bribe."

Her mouth curves into a smile. "A bribe for what?"

"To get me a little closer to your boss, Tina Nunes," I admit openly with no shame.

She chuckles. "You're going to need a little more than that, hot shot," she tells me as she starts to turn away.

"How much?" I ask, making her turn back. One of the swirling lights overhead glints off my money clip as I withdraw it from my back pocket, making sure she catches a glimpse of the bulge in my pants. A flush immediately creeps into her neck. Two birds, one stone.

I release the bills from the money clip and flash a handful of fifties and hundreds. I withdrew way more than I needed to make this statement, but I figured I'd borrow from Bobby's playbook and make myself bigger and more appealing to the fancy Sedução crowd.

The bartender leans forward. "What's your name?"

"Giovanni Carnevale," I tell her, as if I'm somebody important, as if she should know, as if she should remember.

"And how would Ms. Nunes know you?" she asks.

I give the young bartender my best smirk as I hand her a hundred dollar bill. "We like the same music."

She takes the bill and folds it, then slides it in her shirt, presumably towards her bra. "Wait here," she tells me.

She's only gone for five minutes. When she returns, Tina is nowhere to be found. "She'll be with you in minute," she tells me. I glance to her tag. I might as well get her name.

"Thanks, Sasha," I say as I withdraw another fifty. "I'll take a shot of your best whiskey while I wait."

It's crazy to be throwing around money like I can afford to lose it, but I tell myself I'm dressing for the job I want, not the job I have.

I'm on my second beer and my third shot by the time Tina finally joins me. "Mr. Carnevale," she says as she extends a graceful hand adorned by expensive, sparkling jewelry.

"Ms. Nunes," I say as I lift her hand to my lips. "Nice to see you again."

Her eyebrow arches. "We've met?"

My eyes narrow as study her. Is she feigning ignorance or does she really not remember me?

I'm a little offended if the latter is true.

I mention the name of the other venue. "I invited you to catch our show when we played there last night."

She nods as if she suddenly remembers, and in the same moment remembers exactly why she had forgotten. "I'm sorry. I was busy. I'm still busy, actually. What was it you wanted?"

For a moment I'm flummoxed. "I wanted to speak to you about booking your club."

She chuckles. "I'm sorry. You'll have to go through my talent acquisitions director. Call back on Monday."

She turns to leave but I grab her arm to pull her back. Her dark eyes harden as she glances from my hand and back up to my face, as if I'd just committed a grievous faux pas. "I'm sorry. Maybe I was mistaken. I could have sworn we had a connection when we danced last week."

"We probably did," she shrugs. "But that was last week. You should really learn how to take advantage of opportunities that are handed to you, Mr. Carnevale. Some won't come around a second time."

I stand facing her in shock. She pulls away from me and starts to walk away, but turns back.

"Oh, and I have to tell you that in order to play Sedução, you need to be a polished professional. Flashing money around here like you know what to do with it, only to waste it on a bartender, is an amateur play." I get angrier as she talks, but she doesn't seem to care. "If you want to make it in this business, you need to learn how to take what you want with authority. No apologies." She looks me up and down and says, "Come back and see me when you've gotten some swagger."

She spins on one of her expensive, crystal-studded high heels and stalks off into the crowd of people who could buy and sell me if they wanted.

I turn back to Sasha, who offers a helpless shrug of her shoulder before she turns back to her other customers at the bar.

What a waste of $500.

I'm in a sour mood as I head back to Brooklyn. I stop in at Fritz's because I'm not ready to go back to the house alone. The blue-collar crowd is lively as they karaoke their drunken little brains out. Fuck Sedução. These are my people.

Pam isn't behind the bar, which is unusual. I park myself in front of Cheryl, who has already poured a glass of my usual beer. "Hey, sexy," she says with that bright, wide smile. "Didn't expect to see you here tonight. I thought you had a gig."

"That was yesterday," I tell her.

She leans on the counter. "So how'd it go?"

"Great," I tell her. And it was great. I was just in a sour mood because of that elitist bitch, Tina Nunes. "We've got at least four more shows booked."

"See? We told you things were going to start happening for you."

"Thanks, Cheryl," I say. "Maybe we should book this place."

She laughs. "Maybe. You'd have to talk to the boss about it, though."

"Where is Pam?" I finally ask.

Cheryl is quiet for a moment. Finally she says. "She's in Vegas."

My brow furrows. "Vegas? Why?"

Cheryl clears her throat as she leans close. "She's getting married, Vanni."

My mouth drops open. "What?"

She nods. "Yeah, she and Doug decided to elope. They left this morning."

Doug? What kind of a boring fucking name is *that*? "I don't understand. I knew she was dating but I had no idea it was this serious."

She shrugs. "They've been friends forever. I know that her father has been on her case about settling down. He wants to retire and he wants to leave the bar to her, but he's afraid that she'll wind up alone if she doesn't marry first. So they've spent a lot of time together, especially with the family."

I'm dumbfounded. "But if she wanted to marry for her family, why would she elope to Vegas?"

"Dunno," she says as she motions to someone at the other end of the bar. "Took me by surprise too. But the heart wants what the heart wants, I guess." Her eyes narrow. "Are you okay?"

I nod. I'm fine... except I'm not. I realize I have been harboring the fantasy of making love to Pam as if I could one day make that happen. It wasn't just flirty, I really wanted to feel her in my arms, to kiss those pouty, sexy lips and sink into her like a dream come true.

Only now I can't. I would never fuck another man's wife. I'm not that far gone.

It's crazy but I wish I could call her, to ask her why, to talk her out of something that just feels so wrong. No doubt someone named Doug is walking her down the aisle to some tacky Elvis impersonator. Did she even have time to get a dress? Or was she in some sweat pants, getting married through a drive-thru?

Vegas? Doug? None of it makes any goddamned sense no matter how many times I run it through my head.

I sit on that stool all the way to closing time, trying to wrap my mind around it. I've had quite a few beers and quite a few shots by then. Cheryl wants to call a cab, but I assure her I can walk. "You're more than welcome to join me, though," I slur.

"Go on, now," she says with a wave of her hand. "You know I would rip your shit in half."

"And I'd die with a smile on my face," I grin. But she ain't having it.

"Go home. Get some sleep. You're going to need all the energy you can get to be a world-famous rock star."

"All the more reason for you to sleep with me now, so you'll have a story for all your grandkids."

She laughs. "I already told you, I don't date white boys."

"Fine," I say as I pull out my money clip. "But you'll regret it one day."

Her eyes widen when she sees the stash of cash in my hand. She bends closer with a harsh reprimand. "About as much as you'll regret waving all that cash around. Are you nuts?"

I shrug. I don't care. After the day I've had, money means nothing to me.

At least I think it means nothing until I realize after about two blocks that I'm being followed by a couple of young, rowdy punks from the bar. I walk a little faster, and they keep a steady pace to catch up to me. Within minutes they're both on either side, and they crowd me towards a dark alley.

"Give me your money," one of them says, the minute they have me obscured from the street.

"Fuck you," I slur. Like I'm going to give my Aunt Susan's money to a couple of meatheads in wife-beaters and camo pants.

The other guy delivers a punch I'm not expecting, right to my abdomen, till I bend over at the waist. Before I can stand upright, the other guy elbows me on my back, dropping me to the ground. Both of them deliver kick after kick until I'm broken and bleeding and wholly unable to stop them from pulling out the money clip.

I hear them laugh as they take off down the alley. This isn't the first time I've been mugged, but it's the first time it really hurts, since they've taken off with nearly a thousand dollars I can't afford to lose.

All because I wanted to be a big man for Tina Nunes. I'm such a fucking idiot.

I moan as I roll onto my back and look up at the night sky. I can just picture Aunt Susan looking down on me from heaven, shaking her head in disappointment. "Yeah, I know," I murmur into the night air, to no one in particular.

Whether I'm Old Vanni or New Vanni, I know I'm a mess. Did I really think I could have any kind of instant success?

I deserve to be in the gutter precisely where I lie.

CHAPTER TWELVE:

I don't go back to Fritz's for the entire summer. At first, I'm too embarrassed to show my face after the mugging incident that left me with a couple of broken ribs and a black eye. After the visible injuries heal, I realize that my ego is still smarting. I know I can't bear to see Pam again. If I see that wedding ring on her finger, or, God forbid, meet Mr. Doug himself, I might just pop a vein. The more I think of how she married somebody out of the blue, the angrier I get. We had flirted almost non-stop for months, but she never bothered to tell me that she was seriously involved with someone else? Here I was thinking she was the anti-Lori, but she had been harboring secrets of her own. She made it sound like they were just trying out a relationship. Now she is bonded to him for life, and that's what marriage is to me. A lifelong, sacred bond.

I know what happens when a spouse skips out of the relationship. I saw what happened to my mother when my dad split. I heard her crying herself to sleep every night, even years after he'd left. It made me hate the bastard more than I ever thought possible. I hated my absent father from the time I was five years old, and I realized that I didn't have a daddy like everyone else in my school.

He left Mama. He left me.

How do you do that after you promise someone forever?

And how could she promise *anyone* forever? If she is truly in love with this guy, how come I could see the longing in her eyes the last time I held her in my arms? I felt her body yield to me. I knew then it was just a matter of time. Now I'm being denied something, something that I really didn't know how much I wanted until it was taken away.

She's playing a game with a big risk. One thing I do know about this New Vanni. He doesn't like being denied.

He hasn't been able to get Tina Nunes out of his head either, although that obsession isn't just about sex. Who the hell did she think she was to tell me about swagger?

After the next gig, I single out a couple of twins to take back to our hotel. It's another steep price tag to portray the status of rock star, but it's easy to forget those minor details while I'm fucking two gorgeous sisters at the same time.

They think I have swagger.

They think I'm worth a good fucking, no matter who they have waiting at home.

By now I know better than to ask.

It's easy to work out my frustrations with them. They're down for anything, and the more depraved we get, the more vindicated I feel. So what if Tina thinks I have no swagger? She's not the only club in Manhattan.

By the end of August, we've performed at nearly a dozen clubs, several more than once. The groupies multiply by the dozen at each new show. Yael has been working the Internet angle, finding a bit of a following thanks to the music and videos that he has posted on his official music website and social media.

I let him handle all the online stuff. I'm much better face to face. Both Bobby and I are the hound dogs of the band. We romance the groupies at each and every show, with a special VIP party at whatever hotel is nearest to the venue when we're done.

After four months, my savings account has shrunk by half. I'm paying more money than I have coming in. I know that if something doesn't change soon, I'll need to go back to Cynzia's just to stem the bleeding.

It only strengthens my grudge against Tina Nunes, which I take out on every single wide-eyed groupie who waits back stage just to see if she can get some time with her favorite new rock star.

I realize at this point that I've become a total manwhore, but I'm okay with it. I'm in the prime of my youth, and what is that for if it's not to sow some wild oats? No one is getting hurt in the equation. I give them the time of their life and they polish my ego like a freshly minted penny.

Everyone's happy. No one is playing games. It's just good old fashioned casual sex: all the orgasms, none of the guilt.

Bobby makes a hell of a wingman, and together we rack up the conquests left and right. After a while I know that the money we invest into the VIP rock star experience has dick to do with building our brand. We are getting our rocks off with good looking girls who dream about fucking guys in a band.

But like I said, no one is playing games. We never even make it past the hotel bedroom. We offer a night of raunchy sex and that's it. No phone numbers, no last names… no expectations, no disappointments.

It keeps my mind off Pam for the most part. The girls Bobby handpicks for our hedonistic orgies tend to fit a specific type, so none of them have the voluptuous curves, which still makes me hard as a rock whenever I think them. They're all young, anywhere between 18-22. They're all gorgeous, the kind of beauty that would stop traffic. And they all want one thing and one thing only: they want a guy who knows how to fuck them.

Who better than members of a naughty rock band?

I've dusted off more sexually charged covers to include in the set. The crowd really gets into them, especially when I shed my shirt or bring girls on stage to dance with us while we perform.

The dancing is critical, because that's how Bobby makes the final cut for our VIP party. If they're willing to jump on stage and show us their moves, we know that they'll be game for a more intimate setting. Most times we're right.

I've only been wrong once, with a tall redhead who wanted a more one-on-one encounter. She tried to get me to her private hotel suite, but that's not how this game is played. We play on my home turf or not at all. It's just easier.

Honestly I prefer the easy conquests. They've helped me heal from the sting of Pam's unexpected elopement.

Yet there are nights when I lie in my bed at the brownstone, staring at that ugly chair that Lori bought for the house. I have to admit that I had planned on making love to Pam in that chair. It was only fitting. The lying bitch who never believed me had left behind a memento of her tired, ordinary tastes. I needed to cleanse it with an enthusiastic tussle with a woman who had, essentially, inspired me to chase after my dreams and make them a reality.

Somehow I must be holding onto hope that I'll get Pam into that chair in the end, otherwise I would have turned it to kindling by now.

Every time I stare at it and I get angry all over again. I become confused all over again. I wonder, over and over again, who am I going to get to fuck me in that chair now?

I end up throwing a lot of angst into my songwriting. We've got a few of my songs in the set, but most of the original stuff is Yael's and it's heavily instrumental.

If Yael has a problem with my horn dog behavior, he hasn't said anything. Most of our expenses have been out of pocket, rather than robbing the band, which had been his problem with the last guy. The music is more important to me than the sex, which I prove to him every single time we rehearse or write songs together.

All our current bookings are in the more modest, mid-range clubs as a result. I have no idea how to fix it, or even if it's my place to do so. This has always been Yael's baby, so I defer to him constantly.

That changes the first week of September 2005, when we face enough invitations to perform outside of Manhattan that we must think about transportation for the band.

Bobby finds the perfect solution, an old RV that looks like a relic from the 1970s. It looks like shit but the price is right.

So right, in fact, that I have just enough money left in my savings to cover it.

"I can't ask you to spend your last dime on this," Yael says as he looks over the vehicle. We need it, or something like it, to hit venues outside the city. Not only does it have enough room for all of us and our equipment, it gives us room to grow. We can go coast to coast in this dream machine, which is what I instantly dub her.

"Maybe not if I'm just a hired singer for the band," I say, letting the implication hang there in the air for a bit. His eyes finally meet mine. "I do this, we become partners. I think you know we have something special here. And it's not a one-man show anymore. We have a kickass band and I want to see where we can take it. As brothers, and equals."

I hold out my hand. Yael stares at it for a long moment before he brushes past me and stalks away.

"Let him mull it over," Bobby tells me. "I'm sure he'll come around."

It takes our first gig to Boston, where we use every last nickel we make to pay for rental van hauling everyone to and from, when he finally concedes.

I write the check to the dealer, leaving less than a thousand dollars in my account. The situation is critical, and now that the band is half mine, I know it's up to me to do something about it.

I head to Fritz's for the first time in months, to talk to Pam about booking a show.

At least, that's what I tell myself. The minute I walk into the door that deceptively sunny October afternoon, I know that I've been waiting for the excuse to come back, to see her again–to have a reason to interact with her.

She has her back to me as I approach the bar. She's talking to one of her distributors, placing her order for the booze she'll need. A plain gold band adorns her left ring finger. It doesn't hurt as much as I think it will. It might have, had it been loaded with diamonds. Then I'd probably feel like a second-rate shit who couldn't shine Doug's fancy shoes.

At this rate, I see him the same way I see Tony. He's playing with the toy I wanted, so clearly he's worthy of my envy as much as my disdain. Since I don't know the guy at all, it makes it easy for me to twist him into whatever pathetic caricature happens to bring me the most satisfaction at the time.

Knowing he could only give her some tacky Vegas wedding and a cheap, bargain-basement wedding ring makes me feel superior, even though I couldn't give her any better even if I wanted to.

I say nothing as I sit on the stool at the end of the bar. I wait patiently as she conducts her business. Her voice coats my tense nerves. I realize I am nervous to see her again. When was the last time that had happened? When she turns to face me, our eyes meet and I swear I feel lightning shoot to my core. God, does she have to be so beautiful?

She gulps hard before she walks to the end of the bar where I sit. "Vanni," she says softly. Every nerve ending jumps in response.

"Pam," I greet in return. "Or is it Mrs. Doug now?"

She sighs deeply as she reaches me. "I'm sorry you had to find out that way."

"Me, too. You could have told me that it was even a possibility. Then I would have left you alone."

"Would you?" she challenges. Then she shakes her head. "Look. It doesn't matter."

"It matters to me," I murmur. "Why'd you do it?"

She swallows hard. "I love him."

"Bullshit," I say. Her eyes dart to mine. "You wanted me. I know it. You know it."

"That has nothing to do with me and him," she tells me, but she won't look me in the eye. I know she's lying.

"Are you pregnant?" I ask softly. It's the only other thing that makes sense.

"What? No!" She's clearly flustered. "Why does it matter where or when?"

"I just want to know when you knew. One night you're dancing in my arms. The next you're flying off to Vegas to marry some family friend."

"I just knew, okay, Vanni? Can we just... can we just start over as friends or something?"

I stare at her until she takes a step back and drops her eyes. "I think you know the answer to that." I watch the flush rise up her neck and into her face. "But you'll be happy to know I'm not here for that."

Her voice trembles when she speaks. My dick twitches as I watch her mouth, that sexy, beautiful mouth with those full, tantalizing lips. "Why are you here?"

"I'd like to book my band here." *Yeah, I said it. It's my band. I did it, lady. I made my dream a reality. Suck on that.*

She scoffs immediately. "We barely even have a stage."

"I've watched entire bachelorette parties get on stage and sing the numbers from the *Rocky Horror Picture Show*. We can make it work." She takes a deep breath. I know she's running through every excuse in the book to turn me down. "You can bill it as a Bensonhurst boy does good. It'll give me much needed exposure and it'll fill your bar to capacity." *You'll also get to see how many girls I can get every time I open my mouth to sing. Think about that next time you climb into bed next to whatshisname.* "I plan on getting local press to promote it. Everyone in the neighborhood knew my Aunt Susan, and she's a huge part of the reason I'm even in a band." *As are you.* "It's a win/win for both of us."

"I don't know," she stalls.

"Do you have to run it by your husband?" I ask, purposefully spiteful.

She glares at me. "No."

"So what's the problem?" I reach out for her left hand, which is on the bar in front of me. I hold it up to inspect the plain gold band on her finger. "Afraid you'll realize you've chosen the consolation prize?"

She yanks her hand back. "Do you have to be such a dick?"

"I'm not trying to be a dick." *Yes, I am.* "I just need exposure and I thought who else would I turn to, except the person who started me down this path in the first place?"

From the look on her face, I know I've just sunk the basket. Fuck Tina Nunes. I have plenty of fucking swagger. It helps me negotiate a deal like I've been doing it all along, rather than leaving it to Yael. It was his band before. It's our band now. I start my negotiations high, which she counters with something more modest.

It's almost a sexual act getting us on the same page, figuring on fair compensation, though it's less than what we ordinarily pull in.

I figure a gig is a gig, and any amount is better than zero. At least that's how I plan to pitch it to Yael and the guys.

I don't leave the bar until we settle on a date. One: I'm not going to let her blow me off. Two: It makes me ridiculously happy just to be with her again. I can see in her eyes that, married or not, she still wants me. This is good news for New Vanni, who is all about gratification. It gives me a couple of months to perfect this new persona, the one that will make Pam second-guess jumping into a marriage with whatshisname.

I want to punish her even more after spending the afternoon with her. If that means I have to keep putting myself in her face, to remind her of what she gave up, then that's what I'll do.

I know that doesn't make me a nice guy, but I'm beginning suspect that nice is not on the short list of the New Vanni's qualities. He's got determination, ambition and a healthy ego, and, frankly speaking, nice isn't always compatible with those things.

Old Vanni was a nice guy. He was raised to be a nice guy. And where did that get him? He ended up alone while his "nice" girlfriend screwed his best friend behind his back for months, right when he needed her the most.

Old Vanni or New, I wasn't going to make *that* mistake again. Love is for suckers.

Hell, I think I've found the title to a new song. I work on it as I hop over to Manhattan to let the guys know the big news.

"You did what?" Yael asks.

"I got us a gig. It's at my neighborhood bar."

He scoffs as he returns to his guitar, tweaking notes for a new original song. "First stop, Bensonhurst. Next stop, the Cleveland. Maybe Sandusky. I know. Cucamonga."

"That neighborhood is invested in me. What better way to sell out a venue?"

"Of what? Thirty?"

"One hundred and fifty, actually," I say, suddenly annoyed. "And since when are we pickers and choosers where we book?"

"I'm trying to get our foot in the door. You do that in the city, where people are constantly scouting out new bands–bands that have already worked their way up to play there."

I chuckle. "You're such an elitist, Yael. Learn that at Julliard, did you?"

Yael sighs as he looks up at me. "It's nothing personal, Vanni. It's just that… we've played those gigs already."

"Really?" I shoot back. "I haven't."

Our gaze holds for a moment. "Look, man. If you have something that you want to prove—"

"I do," I say as I cut him off. "Not just to the people in the neighborhood, but to you too, I guess."

"Vanni," he starts but I'm ready to dig my heels in.

"So here's the deal. I get us a gig in the city, a big one, and you do my show in the sticks."

He cocks an eyebrow. "And where is that?"

"Sedução."

He laughs the minute I say it. "Do you know how hard it is to get booked there without some kind of connection?"

"Oh, I have a connection."

"And who is that?"

"Tina Nunes."

Again he chuckles. And each time he does, it only solidifies my resolve even more. "Sure," he finally says, and I know now it's a challenge. "You get us into Sedução and I'll play your neighborhood dive."

"Deal," I say as I spin on my heel and stalk out his front door. I have no idea how I'm going to make this happen, but I've got two months to figure it out.

CHAPTER THIRTEEN:

Because I no longer have any money to wave at Sedução, and it really didn't work when I did, I know I have to plan another type of attack in order to get Tina's attention. I enlist the aid of my favorite salesgirl as I stop at the vintage shop to boost my wardrobe. Thankfully she wears a nametag, so I don't have to confess that I never got her name in the first place. "Hey, Chelsea," I say with my best smirk. She blushes almost immediately.

"Hey, Vanni," she says. And she didn't even need a nametag to do it. "What are you doing here?"

I run a finger along one of the shirts near where she's standing. "Does a guy need a reason to see his favorite shop girl?"

She giggles and looks away. She seems so young, like a schoolgirl. It's hard to believe she's the same girl who practically jumped me in a sexy ménage a trois with her best friend. "So how's Jena?" I ask, patting myself on the back that I remembered at least one of their names.

You should always remember your first threesome. It's just good manners.

"Good," she says. "We thought about seeing another show, but a lot of your venues are 21 and over."

I stand a little closer, hovering over her, practically inhaling her sweet scent. "There are ways around that," I tell her.

Her hopeful eyes widen. "Oh yeah?"

I smile a little wider. "Yeah. I could put you on the crew to get you into the club. They'll just mark an X on your hand so you can't get drinks at the bar. It's no big deal."

"Yeah, but, what can I do?"

I run a finger down her arm, bared by the sleeveless top she's wearing. "You can dress me," I tell her in a lower voice. I clasp her hands in mine and guide her back to the dressing room, which is concealed by clattering beads and panels funky, multi-colored fabric.

I barely get the door closed as I lift her up against me. She's so small it makes me feel like a giant. Her arms lock around my neck and she kisses me back as hard I kiss her.

I didn't necessarily mean to seduce her in that small cubicle, but seeing our reflection in the mirror make it a temptation impossible to deny. My hands spread large against her tiny frame, molding her to my body, which isn't looking too shabby given how much time I spend in my makeshift gym at the house. I've already outgrown most of my shirts as a result. I watch as she peels my shirt from my torso, discarding it into a heap in the corner. "I know what you need," she says before she disappears from the cubicle. She comes back with a black shirt that is a size too small. Funny, six months ago it was my regular size. The shirt hugs every contour of my chest as she pulls it down. I reach for her again, but she shakes her head with another grin. She escapes one more time to fetch a pair of scissors.

She cuts a small spot in the top of the shirt, then uses her fingers to tear it open, like she can't wait to see what's underneath. I lift her up until her legs lock around my waist. She's wearing shorts, which makes fucking her a little more difficult. Instead I just grind against her, so she can feel how hard I am. She moans against me before inspiration hits.

"I've got an idea," she says as she practically jumps from my arms. When she returns, she's carrying motorcycle jeans made of black leather. Before I can say anything, she's unfastening my denim and peeling it from my body. "Every bad boy needs some leather," she says as she kneels in front of me.

I feel like a bad boy as I stand in front of her, which I can see at every angle thanks to the mirrors. There's a smile on my face as I step out of the jeans and into the pants. She bites her lip as she eases the tight jeans up my muscled thighs and around my ass. There's no hope of fastening them, not in my current aroused state.

"I don't think it'll fit," she teases.

"Not yet," I tell her as I cup the back of her head with my hand. She easily pulls my cock free and I watch her in the mirror as she blows me. God, she's good at this. "How did a young thing like you get so good?"

She moans against me, and I'm putty in her hands.

I stare at my reflection and the New Vanni comes more clearly into view. There's no trace of a nice guy in that small cubicle, getting blown by a virtual teenager, out in public where anyone could walk in, including her associate minding the cash register some thirty feet away. And he's not sorry, not in the least little bit. He's given himself permission to take what he wants.

If only Tina could see me now.

Like I promised, I get Chelsea into the next gig that weekend. She brings a new friend with her this time around, someone over twenty-one. I wear the outfit she's chosen for me, and all I can think about is how hot she looked going down on me in that public dressing room. It lights such a fuse to my performance, even I wouldn't deny how I crushed it. I nailed the vocals, and I could tell by every sexy girl in the front row that I have made each and every one of them fall in love with me.

By the time we head to the VIP party after the show, the crowd has doubled. It's almost impossible to get one of the rooms for myself so that I can treat Chelsea to another magical night. She surprises me again by dragging at least two other girls with her.

The only girl who gets my number at the end is Chelsea.

By the end of the week, she's truly part of the crew, dressing everyone so that we look like we actually belong together. She's also been by the house a few times to overhaul my wardrobe. I finally fuck in Lori's chair, but it's still missing something.

I've got bigger fish to fry.

I finally head to Sedução that Saturday night. The joint is hopping, with more beautiful VIPs than I've ever seen gathered in one place. A guest band performs, so I can see just what kind of talent Ms. Nunes is seeking.

I have to admit, they're pretty good. They have a chick for a lead singer, and she's exotic as hell. Tall and statuesque, with dark skin and short cropped hair. She wears a white leather mini skirt and go-go boots, which gleam under the black light. Her body undulates like a snake as she sings about love, loss and heartbreak.

"Enjoying the show?"

I turn my head towards the female voice. It's the bartender I had bribed to get close to Tina. I smile at her, thankful that she, too, wears a nametag. "Tremendously. How about you, Sasha?"

"I enjoy all the bands that come through here," she tells me as she pours me a drink. It's what I had ordered the last time. Clearly she's gunning for the same kind of tips I left before.

I simply tip her with a smile. "Too bad you're missing one of the hottest up-and-coming bands in Manhattan."

"Yeah? Who's that?"

My mouth hangs open as I contemplate the answer. I want to answer the question, but saying *The Yael Satterlee Experiment: Featuring Giovanni Carnevale* is a bit of a mouthful. "It's a secret," I tell her instead.

She grins as she leans across the bar. "Is that so?"

I nod. "I had to take a blood oath. It was pretty serious."

She looks me over. I'm wearing that torn black shirt and my leather jeans. Chelsea has started teasing my long, straight hair so that it frames my face with tousled curls. I stopped just short of wearing sunglasses. The dimly lit club is hard enough to navigate as it is, and despite the New Vanni's newfound arrogant-assery, even I find that to be too much of a dick move.

For now.

I trail my finger along her forearm. "But everything has its price. Under the right duress, I might be persuaded to let my tongue slip." I run tongue around my shit-eating grin just to make my point.

"And what's your price, hot shot?"

"A drink," I announce.

"I'm working," she says.

"After you get off," I suggest. "Or before. Or during."

She chuckles. "If this has anything to do with Tina," she starts, but I cut her off.

"Fuck Tina."

Her eyebrow arches. "If that's what you're after, hon, I should tell you I'm not the way to get it. You want her, you go get her. I'm nobody's stepstool."

"I get that," I tell her, while mentally erasing Plan A from the blackboard in my brain. "I'm just coming on to a beautiful woman. No crime in that, is there?"

She eyes me carefully. "I suppose not."

"Good," I say as I withdraw a pen. I nab a napkin from the stack right next to her and jot down the address for our next gig. "You show up there. Drink's on me. No Tina. No problem. What do you say?"

She glances down at the napkin. "I'd say that I'm working that night."

"That does present a problem," I agree. "I just hope you're well enough to work the rest of the week. Terrible flu going around. I mean it's the 24-hour kind, so you should be fine if you take one personal day to yourself."

I take her hand in mine, and bend to kiss each finger. I can feel her tremble. She knows she should pull away but I know she can't. With a smile, I flip her hand over to kiss her palm, darting my tongue in a small, discreet circle until she shudders against me. I toss a twenty on the bar to pay for my drink, then I leave without even touching it.

CHAPTER FOURTEEN:

I don't know if Sasha will show up until I see her face in the crowd. By then I know I have her, and I didn't even have to sing one word. Not only did she ditch work to catch my show, she's dressed in a short skirt and a halter top, which suggests she's either on the hunt or wants to be hunted.

The palm trick works every time.

I give the performance of a lifetime, singing almost exclusively to her from the stage. During an INXS cover, I shed my shirt and toss it to the crowd. Sasha doesn't lunge for it like the rest of the girls. She can't keep her eyes off my chest.

The feeling is more than mutual. She's got spectacular cleavage from where I'm standing, creamy tantalizing breasts that invite me to explore with my fingers and my mouth. When she bites her lip, I know she can read my thoughts. But what else was she expecting, really?

I link my thumb in my front pants pocket, drawing attention to what she's doing to me.

Chelsea is nearby, which makes things a little awkward, but it's not like she's opposed to sharing. She's young but she knows the score. That makes things easier considering the New Vanni has got a full agenda. I have less than seven weeks to book Sedução. Assuaging hurt feelings doesn't quite make the list.

When I exit the stage, I worm my way through the excited crowd, mostly female, all of whom want to congratulate me for my killer set. I really don't have to head to the bar if I don't want to; several girls have purchased drinks for me, from bottles of water to bottles of beer, which they try to hand to me as I pass by. I wave them away with a smile, making a beeline for the bar anyway. I don't look around for Sasha. Instead I flirt with the girls who surround me. They giggle and blush as they try to wedge themselves even closer to me. I indulge them happily. It is one of the perks of New Vanni's new life, I can't lie.

I scan the crowd, where I spot Sasha easily. She stands near a tall table near the stage. She's trying her best not to look my direction. My face cracks apart in a self-satisfied smile before I turn to the bartender. "What's she drinking?" I ask, pointing towards Sasha.

The bartender grins at me before he fills another glass and hands it to me. I toss some bills on the bar before I disengage from the girls crowding me to make my way towards Sasha. "Give me a minute, ladies," I say.

Bobby, my ever-present wingman, wrangles them with the lure of the VIP after-party experience, which allows me a smooth escape.

Sasha doesn't even look at me when I approach from behind and set the drink on her table. "Sasha," I greet warmly. "I didn't think you were going to come."

"Bullshit," she chuckles.

"Okay, I was hopeful," I confess with a grin of my own. "So what'd you think?"

She nods. "It was good. You all have a really great sound. And you have a hot look."

My eyes meet hers. "Hot enough for Sedução?"

She laughs again. "So that's the reason you invited me," she says. "I was wondering."

"Part of it," I shamelessly admit as I glance down her shirt. Up close the view is breathtaking.

She glances towards the bar. "It isn't because you're lacking female companionship, that's for sure."

I shrug. "What can I say? I get by with a little help from my friends." I stand a little closer. "Would you like to be my friend, Sasha?"

She shudders. I try not to gloat. "You're really cute," she says. "But I'm not exactly the kind of girl who chases after rock stars. If that was what I was after, I wouldn't need to leave Sedução."

I trail a finger along her neckline, stopping just short of the silky, creamy skin of her breast. "Interesting choice of shirt for someone who isn't out to fuck a rock star."

Her eyes never leave mine. "You're assuming I wore it for you. Maybe, just maybe, I wore it for me."

I have to laugh. I like this girl already. "Touché," I acknowledge. I look around the crowd. "Let's get out of here."

Her eyebrow arches. "And go where?"

I lean forward, almost till our noses touch. "It's a surprise."

And indeed she is surprised the minute we walk into the dimly lit dining room at Cynzia's. She laughs as I pull her to one of the booths. "Hey, Santino!" I holler from the counter. "House special, extra large, extra cheese, extra fast."

"You'll get it when you get it, Joe," Santino grumbles.

Sasha grins at me. "Joe?"

I shrug it off. "He hasn't gotten that right since I started working for him six years ago."

"You work here?"

"Used to," I admit. "Might again if things don't turn around soon."

"Tell that to someone who didn't see that crowd tonight."

"It's good," I concede. "But it's not where I want to be. Not by a long shot."

"Hey, Vanni," Alicia says as she stops by our table to pour a couple of glasses of water. Her eyes are still so hopeful as she looks at me, like one day I'm going to whisk her right out of that tiny dining room and off into the sunset like some adolescent fairy tale. "Did you want some wine?"

I look at Sasha, who nods. "Just a couple of glasses of house wine," I tell Alicia, who nods and exits the table.

I turn back to Sasha. "So let me guess," she says. "You want to be at Sedução."

"To start," I reply. "I want to perform every big venue from Madison Square Garden to the Hollywood Bowl. I want to sing the National Anthem at Yankee fucking Stadium and have my own show during half-time at the Super Bowl."

Her brown eyes are thoughtful. "Small town boy with big dreams?"

"Anything wrong with that?" I ask with a raised eyebrow.

"No," she says. "Dreamers change the world."

"Is that what you want to do?" I ask. It occurs to me suddenly that I'm interested in the answer. It seems like it's been forever since I've actually *talked* to a woman.

She takes a deep breath. "That's a loaded question."

I sit back in the booth. "I've got nowhere to be."

She eyes me carefully before she admits, "Well, I do."

I sit up straighter now. "Husband?" I ask. It hadn't even occurred to me.

She shakes her head. "Not anymore."

"I'm sorry," I say. And I mean it.

She shrugs. "Shit happens, what can I say? Anyway, he gets to go have a party and I get to raise a couple of kids. Seems fair." She tips a glass to her lips and takes a long drink without looking at me.

In the space of a second, the Old Vanni erupts from my core and I feel like a giant shit. "You certainly shouldn't have skipped a shift for me."

She laughs. "I didn't," she confesses with an embarrassed grin. "I had the night off anyway. I was lying because I just didn't want to spend it in another bar. I already work at two."

I eye her thoughtfully. She's a pretty girl, with brown hair and dark eyes. Only she isn't really a 'girl' at all. Now that we're in a restaurant instead of a bar, I can see the faint lines around the corner of her eyes. She's not some young groupie like the girls at the club. It hits me suddenly that she had been absolutely sincere before. She isn't wearing hot clothes for me at all. She is taking a break from laundry and cleaning and runny noses, and needs to feel like a sexy woman for *herself*.

It honestly makes her even sexier.

Knowing she works two jobs to support her kids reminds me instantly of Mama. I can see the same strain in her shoulders and around her neck. She's carrying the world on her shoulders, and here I was, about to use her as some trampoline into Sedução. God, I can be such an asshole sometimes. I immediately switch gears as I lean forward on my forearms. "How many kids do you have?"

"Two," she says as she reaches for a breadstick. "A five-year-old boy named Hugo and a three-year-old girl named Imogen." Off my look she screws her face into a wry smile. "My ex and I were pretentious hipsters, as you can tell."

I laugh. "No, I dig it. I'm partial to people with unusual names, particularly children."

"Nice to know, Joe," she says with a smirk that instantly makes me like her more.

I chuckle. "So when does the carriage turn back into a pumpkin?"

She glances at her watch. "About an hour. You better work fast."

I can't stop my smile if I wanted to. She could have been anywhere in the city tonight, and she's with me, eating pizza and drinking wine. That counts as progress in my book. "I already did."

The arrival of our pizza interrupts our conversation. I dive right in, suddenly ravenous. She digs into her own piece and murmurs her approval. Alicia fills both of our glasses with more wine as Sasha and I sit in comfortable silence.

She finally places what crust is left of her slice onto her plate and folds her hands on top of each other on the table. "That was good. The wine is top-notch. The company is interesting."

"So glad you think so."

"Where is this heading, Vanni? Do you want me to fuck you or do you want me to book you?"

I wipe my hands on my napkin. "Is it too much to ask for both?"

She chuckles again. It's a nice, lilting sound. "Yes," she finally answers, definitively but with a smile. I just look at her and wait. "My life is complicated enough already. I don't need to add some crazy rock star to the mix. I'm just looking for friends, now. Nothing more. And really, there's nothing I can do for you at Sedução. Tina picks every single band. She keeps everything very hands-on."

"Fair enough," I nod. "But you did say you worked at two clubs, did you not?" She purses her lips. I reel her in. "You know my band has something special, Sasha. We just need a chance." I take her hand in mine. "Be a friend?"

She hesitates a long moment before she finally says, "No promises, but I'll see what I can do." Another glance at her watch. "I really should go."

I nod and stand, and she follows as I lead her towards the entrance. We step outside and I hail her a cab to take her back home to Queens. I open my arms for a hug, and she doesn't deny me. I close my arms around her soft body and squeeze her tight, just for a second, just so she can feel how much I've enjoyed our time together.

Most of my female interactions these days have been one-night-stands. Fun but usually forgettable, especially since there have been so many.

I realize then that New Vanni could use a friend, and Sasha is easy to like.

That night when I head to bed, I don't even look at the chair.

The next week we work hard on our gig the following weekend. Each and every week we grow more cohesive, and act more and more like a band. I perfect my stage persona, with a little help from Chelsea, my favorite shop girl. Since she works in a vintage store, they get a lot of clothes in every week that she gets to prowl through to find the right look for me.

She doesn't ask me about Sasha, which I like. With her being so young, I was worried she'd get a little too attached, like Alicia at Cynzia's. But it doesn't seem to bother her to let me go on my way when all my needs are met. I wonder sometimes about the life she's living. I figure with her being in college, especially around so many of her uninhibited friends, she's got an active social life all of her own.

I don't begrudge her at all. You're only nineteen once, might as well enjoy it.

By that following Friday night, we hit the stage like cannon fire. We're on a list with five other bands, and we land somewhere around the ten o'clock hour. The crowds are good, the groupies are smoking hot, but Sasha is nowhere to be found.

Neither is Chelsea, which is unusual. I'm left oddly out of sorts. Part of that is probably because it's our first performance where we don't host an after-party, but most of the groupies are new and don't really expect one. Plus, it's a bit like shooting fish in a barrel. I could already see which girl would be willing to do which naughty sex act just by the way they sidle up to me at the bar. Thanks to my peculiar funk, I'm just not in the mood, no matter how sexy they are.

After the band loads out, I turn to Bobby. "Hey, I have an idea. Let's head to Sedução."

Bobby toasts me with his full glass of beer, which he chugs and drains, all in one gulp.

We make it to Sedução just before midnight. They have a full roster as well, although their bands are obviously more well-known than the ones that played with us. It stands to reason, since Tina only books the best talent, usually on the cusp of nationwide exposure and success.

That's why it's more important than ever for me to secure us a place there.

I spot Sasha right away, but she's too busy tending bar to notice. I don't say anything to Bobby. When it comes to women, he has one primary goal: get them into bed. He has a very short list of turn-offs, but one of which is mama drama. "They take half your money, want half your time and, let's face it. Their bodies never go back to the way they used to be. Get 'em young, while they're still down for anything and aren't carrying a lot of extra baggage."

For most of the summer, that was just what we had done. The girls who paraded through our various hotel suites all fit the criteria. They wanted a night with a sexy rock star, and we wanted lots of sex with a variety of partners, no strings attached. It'd been mutually fulfilling up until now.

But the girls who had been taking up space in my head weren't really sex objects at all, even though I probably would fuck them if given half the chance.

There was Tina, of course. I wanted to get her attention, and I was ready to make her pay for saying that we weren't polished professionals and I had no swagger.

There is Pam, who is likely spending her waning days of summer with the hubby, Mr. Doug. Every time I think of him my mouth curves into a snarl. There was a sweet way in how she cared about me, how she pushed me to follow my dreams and encouraged me when I was down. It was so nice to have that again after losing Aunt Susan, that I could still see remnants of the Old Vanni whenever I looked into her eyes.

I like that. When I'm with her, I feel more *me*. And now she'll always belong to someone else, which puts her off limits for me no matter how much I want her. The only thing worse would be if she got pregnant, which I expect to happen any day. That's the way it works, right? First comes love, then comes marriage. Then comes Pam with a baby carriage.

I still have my doubts that she actually loves this fucker, not in the same way she could love me. That's the one shred of hope I have left that it's not over between us. But I know if she ever gets pregnant, that will sever every last tie. Even if she gets her head out of her ass and realizes that it's me she really wants, I would never break up a family. I could never be that heartless and self-serving where an innocent child is concerned.

And then there's Sasha, the woman juggling a dozen drink orders behind the bar in front of me. I have to admit, learning she was a single mom actually added to her appeal for me. It reminds me so much of Mama, that I find myself wondering what her children look like. *Hugo and Imogen.* I remember their names, which is very unusual for me. But then again, Hugo and Imogen are two unusual names.

I like the way I feel when I'm with her, too. She reminds me that I'm still a good guy deep down, and I need to be reminded sometimes.

I tug Bobby's sleeve and guide him over to the bar. "What do you know, Joe?" she greets with a grin when I finally wedge myself in between the patrons at the bar to stand in front of her.

"Joe?" Bobby repeats, his eyebrow arched.

"Long story," I say. "Bobby, this is Sasha. Sasha, our bassist, Bobby Rocco."

She reaches for a handshake. "I remember. I saw you guys play last week. You were really good."

"Thanks," he says with his best flirty smile, but I know he's not interested in her. Like I said, his tastes are pretty exclusive. Even if her hint of crow's feet didn't put him off, finding out she had a couple of kids would send him packing.

"So what's new around here?" I ask as I survey the scene. Another killer band wows the crowd. Tina knows what she is doing, that much is clear. What is even clearer is that we have every right to be on that stage, too. And I don't plan to stop until we get there.

An effervescent blonde with bouncy curls and a bodacious smile squeezes herself between me and another guy at the bar. "Hey, hon," she calls Sasha, with one of the most adorable accents I've ever heard. "Can I get another Manhattan and Long Island Iced tea?"

I grin down at her. She's plastered to me, I can feel every luscious curve. "Those are some pretty Yankee drinks for a girl with such a sweet southern accent."

She looks me up and down with sparkling blue eyes. Her smile widens. "I can handle it."

"I bet you can. Where are you from?"

"Tennessee," she says. It drips like brandy from her lips. "How 'bout you?"

"Brooklyn," I say with pride, but she shakes her head.

"Before that," she says.

My eyebrow arches. That's talent. Makes me wonder what else she can do. "Good ear." She waits expectantly so I finally supply an answer to her question. "Philadelphia, born and bred."

"The City of Brotherly Love," she says and I nod. "Ever been?"

She shakes her head and those curls bounce over her slender, bared shoulders. "Not yet. It's on the list, though."

"So how did you know I was from Philadelphia?"

She crinkles her nose. It's adorable. "Don't laugh, but, I took an improv class when I first came to New York."

"Not laughing," I say as I glance her over again. In fact, I find her fascinating. It's not common for me to meet women nearer my own age, especially one who has no reason at all to impress the likes of me, some average Joe in a dimly lit nightclub. I hold out my hand. "Vanni."

She chuckles, a warm, deep sound. "Seriously? That's your name?"

I shrug with a grin. "Short for Giovanni." I lean closer. "It's Italian."

She eyes me playfully. She's wise to my game. Her whiskey-dripped voice pours over my senses as she closes a soft hand around mine. "Iris."

I pull her even closer and bend down to say closer to her ear, "Nice to meet you, Iris." I refer to my friend, who is scoping out a young hottie at the end of the bar. "This is my friend, Bobby." They shake hands, but he's no more interested in her than Sasha, who arrives with her drinks. "So are you here for a hot date? If so, he's a shit for not buying these overpriced cocktails for you. I say you should drop him entirely and join us."

Again she chuckles. "It's a hot date with an old friend." She points at a table, where another woman sits by a flickering flameless candle. She's a Rubenesque beauty with dark brown hair highlighted with funky blonde chunks, all swept up tight in a neat ponytail. With her black-framed glasses and minimal makeup, she looks like a hot, smart nerd. Even from twenty-five feet away, I can see there is much more than meets the eye.

"Invite her," I say. "Two of you. Two of us. We're evenly matched. It's kismet."

"Well, normally I'd love to but she's only in town for a short time." She looks me up and down again. "It's been fun and you're real cute, but I have to get back to my friend."

"Let me carry your drinks at least," I say. I'm not ready to give up yet. I'm Giovanni Carnevale, for crissakes. Seducing more than one woman at a time is sort of my thing now.

I don't even give her a chance to decline. I take the drinks from the bar and make a beeline for the sexy friend at the table, nodding to Bobby to follow along.

Before I can reach the table, however, I hear another female voice behind me. It's not a southern accent. It's spiced with sensual Portuguese. "Mr. Carnevale."

I know it's Tina before I even turn around. "Tina," the blonde says, which surprises me further. How does this country girl know one of the most influential people in Manhattan?

"Iris," she says as they share a half-hug and a side-kiss. "They're taking care of you, I trust?"

"It's been lovely, thank you."

"Least I can do," Tina purrs with a smile, and I realize that Iris didn't have to pay for her drinks. She's a guest, which makes her even more interesting to me.

"Andy will get you a copy of her review by the time she heads back to Tennessee tomorrow. I'm sure it's going to be quite favorable."

"Good to hear," Tina says before she turns to Bobby and me. "And how about you boys? Enjoying Sedução?"

Bobby nods his head. He may not be into older ladies, and who can blame him, when he's barely twenty-three himself? But he knows the kind of power Tina wields in this town, and like he said when we first saw Tina, she's hot. "It's an amazing club, Ms. Nunes," he says. "Maybe one day we'll even have the honor of playing here."

Tina slides her dark gaze from his face to mine, where she shamelessly inspects the "new" look head to toe. "Maybe," she finally says.

I think my heart stops beating for a minute as I stare down at her. Iris uses this opportunity to take her drinks from my hand and slip away to her friend at the table ten feet from where we're standing, but I've already forgotten all about them. When Tina turns back towards the bar, I change direction to follow her.

She wants me to take what I want? She's about to get exactly what she asked for.

Bobby follows as well, but I nod my head in the direction of the young hottie in the skin-tight red dress showing more T&A than a beer commercial. "I got this," I tell him.

He's uncertain for a moment but finally relents. I step behind Tina at the bar. Since she's only five-foot-eight, (over six

150

feet if you count her stiletto heels,) I can shadow her almost entirely with my lanky frame. I know she can feel my body heat as we stand a breath apart.

I take a silky lock of her hair in between my forefinger and my thumb as she motions to Sasha, who places a bottle of expensive champagne and two flutes on the bar in front of her.

Without even looking my direction, Tina walks away, leaving her drink order behind. I glance at Sasha, who looks down at the champagne in front of me before nodding off to the dark corner where Tina strides.

I grab the bottle with one hand and the glasses in the other as I push through the crowd to follow behind.

I disappear down the mirrored hallway, with plush velvet seating next to the bathrooms and "employees only" doors. I head down another corridor, passing two big guards dressed all in black, who stand on either side, hands clasped and faces stoic. One glance to the champagne in my hand and they nod me through.

I walk all the way to the end of the corridor until I reach a door made of black glass. I tuck the bottle in between my bicep and my side to open it and walk inside.

The room is even more dimly lit than the bar. I can hear the music thunder through the walls, which are made of mirror and glass. There's plenty of plush seating and another bar, although this one isn't tended by an employee.

Tina stands behind the leather bar, putting ice in a silver ice bucket. I don't say a word as I nestle the champagne bottle in the ice. I set the glasses down. "So is this where I audition?"

She offers a smile. "In a manner of speaking." She walks around the bar and heads straight towards the white circular seating in the middle of the room that surrounds a smaller stage. With a click of the remote control, a sexy house beat fills the cozy space and multi-colored lights flicker off of the reflective glass on every wall and on the ceiling.

She crosses one bare leg over the other and her short white skirt slides up her lusciously tanned skin. I set the bucket next to her, cross over her and sit on her other side. "So what song would you like me to sing?" I ask as I lean closer to her.

"You still don't get it," she chuckles. "This isn't about singing. This is about image," she says as she trails a finger down my chiseled chest. It makes all those upside down sit-ups worth the trouble.

My voice is soft as I drill my gaze right into hers. "And do you like what you see?"

Her finger trails all the way down my chest and across my stomach, stopping just short of the bulge in my pants. "I'd say you have a great deal of potential. That's what I saw that first night. Otherwise I never would have asked you to dance."

It's my turn to chuckle. "You didn't even know I was in a band."

"It's so cute that you don't think so," she says. She leans back against the cushion, propped against one arm, her chin resting in her hands as she looks down her reclining, sexy body at me. "Do you honestly think I'd waste my time on you simply because you're cute? Schnauzers are cute. I'm a business woman, and making money is never far from my mind."

I lean across her to take the champagne out of the bottle and pop the cork. I pour her a glass and then I pour myself one. "So how are we going to make a lot of money?" I ask, plain and direct.

She sips her champagne. "You've got a good look. Really retro and nostalgic. Kind of like the reincarnation of Jim Morrison or Michael Hutchence. You just need to work on your sex appeal."

I can't stop the laughter even if I want to. "Apparently you've never seen the crowd of girls I pull in after every show."

"Keyword: girls," she says as she sits up. "I cater to the strictly VIP set, Mr. Carnevale. Celebrities. Debutantes. Socialites. We're talking Manhattan royalty. Rich and powerful people, especially the women. They have caviar tastes and platinum standards, so they like their men to be self-assured and masculine. Emotionally you're still a boy chasing your dick around."

My eyes narrow on her as I swallow the bubbly, expensive liquid in a loud gulp. This bitch has a lot of nerve. "Is that a fact?"

"Don't pout, Vanni. It's not attractive." She kills one drink and holds the glass up for more. I hesitate only a moment before I fill it. "Like I said, you have potential. And I have no problem signing your band to perform in my club. *Once* you're ready," she adds when my eyes widen.

I set my glass and the bottle on the floor. "So is this where I take what I want and fuck you in your secret party room?"

"I don't fuck in my bar," she tells me as she drains another glass. "I've actually got a business proposition for you." My eyebrow arches and she continues. "Sedução is hosting a special event next Friday. Dreadfully boring thing, to benefit by my ex-husband's foundation for the under-privileged. And I, as the charitable ex-wife, will be all smiles as I greet all the two-faced backstabbers who have chosen to give their allegiance to my cheating ex-husband instead of me in the wake of my well-publicized divorce."

My brow knits with confusion. "So what does any of that have to do with me?"

Her gaze traipses lazily across my body. "I've been looking for a musical act to entertain our guests for the event."

Have I missed something? Was she trying to book us for a gig? "But you don't even know if I can sing."

"It's so cute that you think I don't," she says again as she reaches for the champagne bottle herself. "I'm going to be honest with you, Vanni. I could book any number of acts in this city, many of whom would waive any payment just to give back to a worthy cause. I have the biggest names in music–hell, in entertainment– who are just a phone call away to do any favor I ask. I've done that for years and years and frankly, I'm over it. I want to show those two-faced busybodies something new. Something," she says as she leans forward, close enough I can smell the perfume from her neck, "that they've never seen before."

I lean back. It's rather cute that *she* doesn't think I've done my homework. "And this has nothing to do with the fact that I'm exactly the same age as the model who will be hanging off your Julio's arm, I guess."

She chuckles. "Now see? That is swagger. You're a smart boy, Vanni. You know what I'm offering. It doesn't really matter why as long as you get your foot in the door, now does it?"

"I'll have to talk it over with the guys," I bluff.

"Why?" she asks. "I'm not booking them."

My eyes shoot back to hers. "What?"

She leans closer. "Just you. One night. Show me what you can do and then we'll talk about all the rest." Her eyes devour me. "It's quite simple, really. You get the opportunity of a lifetime, and I get the hottest guy in the room on my arm. What have you got to lose?"

I shrug away and stand to my feet. "Look, I don't know what you think you're buying here," I start, but she cuts me off.

"I'm not buying anything, sweetheart. I'm investing." She stands as well. "Do I look like a stupid woman to you, Vanni?"

I look her over. I concede after a moment with a slight shake of my head that she doesn't.

"There's a reason so many of my acts go national after being featured on my stage, honey. I know what I'm doing. I can take you and your little dive-bar band and make you all stars like that," she says as she snaps her fingers. "But I didn't get to where I am giving away favors. It's tit for tat in this business. You want me to give you your big break? You have to ask yourself, what are you willing to do for me?"

She steps closer, running her hand along my abdomen and up my chest. "One night. One performance. One chance. It's more than I'm willing to give anyone else. If you don't think you deserve that chance, tell me now. Because if there's one thing I hate, it's wasting my time."

I contemplate my choices. Doing a solo gig feels like a betrayal to my boys. But if I don't do this gig, we may never get another shot to play at Sedução again, at least until we've broken into the big leagues, and who knows how long that will take? At this rate, I'm weeks away from going back to Cynzia's just for a paycheck.

Besides this was part of my big plan, isn't it? I had sworn to Yael I could book Sedução, and here I was, with the opportunity quite literally being handed to me. One week, one little old week, and I could secure the first major step for the band.

I grab her hand as it slides down my rock hard stomach, stopping her just before she reaches my cock. She's not the only one who can put a carrot on a stick. "So how much does this little event of yours pay?" I ask with a slightly raised eyebrow.

"Don't you want to donate your fees for charity?" she asks with an innocent pout.

"Charity starts at home," I tell her.

She chuckles again. "Atta boy," she says. She names a price, and I can only hope my eyes don't widen with shock. "So what do you say, Vanni?" she asks as her dark brown eyes meet mine.

I lean down, my mouth hovering over hers in an almost-kiss. I don't say a word until her breath hitches. "I say you've got yourself a date."

CHAPTER FIFTEEN:

That Monday I begin leading a double life out of necessity. I can't say anything to my band about what I'm going to do, simply because I don't want to get their hopes up of booking Sedução. After all the games she's played thus far, I don't trust Tina quite yet. I have no guarantee she's not going to flake out on the second, less guaranteed part of her offer and book our band after she's done using me like a dish rag on Friday.

I'm no idiot. I know she only wants to parade me around under her ex's nose as her new boy toy, in revenge for his latest arm candy. Recent tabloid articles had been floating the idea this new girl's been spotted with a baby bump. Considering old Julio left Tina for her, that news must be really hard to swallow, especially in front of all their friends and the press this event will generate.

And Tina is completely right. She didn't get to the top by giving out favors. I know I'm going to have to work my ass off to secure that gig for the rest of us, and that's my most important job come Monday morning.

Unfortunately for me, we also have a gig on Saturday, and Yael's rehearsal schedule is just as intensive as Tina's. It is the first of many lies when I tell him that I've had to take some shifts at Cynzia's during the day, pushing our band rehearsals to later at night.

I arrive at Sedução by ten o'clock, and more burly bouncers let me in. Tina waits for me at one of the tables. She's dressed in a black pencil skirt and heels, with a silk, sleeveless blouse in blue, and looks just as sexy as she does showing a lot more skin. It's just in the way she carries herself. She's impeccable head to toe.

I sit at the table without being asked. She barely looks up from her paperwork. "First order of business, we have to work on your image."

I immediately bristle. "My image?"

"You look every inch of what you are: a singer in a bar."

"Correct me if I'm wrong, but isn't that the look that drew you to me?"

She chuckles as she spares me a glance. "I didn't pick you based on how you are, honey. I picked you based on how you could be." She looks over her shoulder towards the darkened bar, where I see that some employees have already begun setting up for the day. At least one employee in particular.

"Sasha, can you buzz our friends in? They should be here by now."

Sasha nods and picks up the phone.

"Friends?" I ask.

"I called in a few favors," she tells me as she shoves her paperwork into a folder and stands.

Within a minute, a group of people flood the empty bar. Leading the charge is a woman with a bright pink pixie cut, who has clearly come from an alternate dimension sometime in the 1950s. Her black Capri pants are covered in bold, white polka dots. She wears platform pumps with a peekaboo toe, revealing her equally pink toenails. Her white button-up shirt is tied at the middle, and a large bold pendant rests between her unnaturally cone-shaped breasts. She looks like someone took Lucille Ball and Madonna and threw them both in a psychedelic blender.

Tina makes the necessary introductions. "This is Frankie Fleck, stylist extraordinaire."

The unusual woman holds out a hand, which I shake.

"This is Giovanni Carnevale," Tina tells Frankie, who begins a slow circle around me where I stand, looking me up and down. She lifts up a lock of hair, brushing it away from my face.

"You dress much too small for that name that big." She turns back to Tina. "So what were you thinking?"

Tina starts to circle me now too. "He's got a great body. We can show it off."

"Slowly," Frankie agrees with a smile.

"Don't take him too far from his blue-collar, Brooklyn roots, but add a little Manhattan flair. Product for the hair; styled, of course. Maybe some blond highlights. Lighten it up. Give it dimension. Better material," she sneers as she fingers the fabric of my vintage shirt. "Retro but not second-hand. Edgy, but still trendy."

They both stop in front of me, staring into my face. "Makeup?" Tina asks. There's only a split second before they both say, "Eyeliner," in unison.

"Needs more bling," Frankie decides and Tina nods.

Frankie finally looks at me. It's the first time they've included me in this little discussion, and I've been too stunned to notice otherwise. "How's the chest?"

I don't bother hiding my smirk as I peel up my shirt to reveal upper body, chiseled hard from all the workouts I've been doing all summer. I'm gratified by the slow smiles that appear on both of their faces.

"I like it. Enough hair that he's got that aura of rugged masculinity," Frankie starts.

"But not so much he's the missing link," Tina agrees.

Just when I start to wonder if I should be offended of how they're examining me like some cut of beef, Frankie's gaze drops downward toward my crotch. "My, my, my. I bet you don't even have to fluff, do you?"

"What can I say?" I quip back. "I'm Italian."

She stands back and takes it all in. "Yes, you are. All right," she decides suddenly. "I think I'm ready."

She turns on her heel and struts for the entrance. She doesn't turn around until she gets there. "You coming?"

I turn to Tina, who nods Frankie's direction. "I thought I was supposed to be rehearsing," I try to remind her.

"There's time for that," she tells me, crossing her arms across her chest. "Unless you're not as confident you can impress me as you think you are."

I stare her down for only a moment before I stalk off after Frankie.

Frankie and her crew head straight for a waiting limo, where my pink-haired hostess plies me with champagne to keep me compliant. We end up in a high-end spa for men, where I get my first mani/pedi, my first facial, a body scrub, and my first spray-tan.

By the time she's done with Phase One, as she calls it, I'm racing to SoHo for rehearsals with the guys.

Having never been plucked and pampered before, I felt like a stranger in my own skin all the while we play. I screw up more than I have in a long while, forgetting lyrics and missing pitch. They throw me completely off-center when I have to explain the tan. "Just trying something new. A friend had a gift certificate and I thought what the hell?"

Just another lie on top of many.

The next morning, Frankie is already there when I get there. Like the day before, she whisks me away without my singing a note. She spends Tuesday getting my hair styled, yet another thing I have to explain away to the guys. I start crafting my story as I sit in a chair, tin foil all over my head, praying for the end of Phase Two.

They layer my long hair, teasing it to look a lot wavier than it usually is. It's now chestnut with honey highlights, or so the stylist tells Frankie. To me it looks brown and a little less brown. They pluck and shape my eyebrows and I get my first straight razor shave.

Wednesday follows the same pattern. When I get to Sedução, Tina is nowhere in sight. It's just Frankie, and this time she's ready to overhaul my wardrobe.

By Phase Three, I'm fairly frustrated. My performance is in two days and I haven't rehearsed once. I can only hope our shopping excursion won't take up all of our afternoon.

Sadly, Frankie has other ideas. She drags me through every funky, trendy boutique in the city. By the time we're done she's dropped thousands of dollars and fills the limo with bags and bags of clothes, shoes, accessories, including jewelry, and a crap load of cosmetics to maintain this high dollar makeover for more than a week.

When we return to the club, there's not enough time for us to take all my new belongings back to Brooklyn before I have to head over to my other rehearsal.

"No problem. Drop them off at my place," Tina decides. She turns to me. "You can pick them up after rehearsal is done. Just tell me where to send the car."

At first I want to decline. I'm exhausted after a week of running around. But I really want to get to bottom of her master plot. She's hired me for a gig to win over the jet-setting Manhattan crowd, but has systematically prevented me from preparing for it.

I need to know why.

I'm so out of sorts, I'm still struggling through our rehearsals for the weekend. I try to figure out what the hell I'm going to do, my mind racing so much it won't slow down even with a hit or two from Felix's sweet-smelling blunt, or with an entire six-pack of Bobby's beer. I'm still amped up when Tina's car comes for me at the deli down the street from Yael's loft.

It takes me to a swanky high-rise apartment building on Park Avenue, where the car pulls to the curb to let me out. A doorman greets me. "Mr. Carnevale?"

I nod and he escorts me inside the large arched glass doorway into the impressive lobby. The floors are marble, as well as the archways and stately fireplaces. The doorman walks to the elevator bank and summons the car. I step inside. He reaches around to push the button for the penthouse. "Have a good night, sir," he bids as the elevator doors close.

The elevator zips me up to the 51st floor, where the elevator spills out into the foyer of a private residence.

The décor is a neutral beige and bone, with gleaming chrome accents. There's a large charcoal drawing in a chrome and glass frame right in front of me. Expensive cut flowers fill a large crystal vase just under the portrait, which keeps drawing my eye.

"That's Klimt, sir," says a male voice that is suddenly at my side.

I turn to find a uniformed valet. Young, like me, clean-cut, unlike me. I stammer as I say, "Pardon?"

He nods towards the print. "The artist, sir. Gustav Klimt. *The Study for the Figure of "Lasciviousness." Beethoven Frieze*, to be exact. Dated 1901."

I study the impish, beautiful woman in the drawing. She looks lascivious indeed. In fact, I can barely take my eyes off of her.

The valet clears his throat and I tear my eyes away to follow him where the hallway spills into the living room. There are large spectacular windows on every wall of the spacious room, one of which clearly faces out towards Central Park, and all the beautiful lights of the city that surround it. Soothing Latin instrumental music pipes through the speakers around the room, which helps set the mood.

"Champagne, sir?" the valet asks.

Champagne. It is quickly becoming the drink of choice in this bizarre new life of mine. "Yes, thank you," I say, feeling utterly ridiculous and out of place.

I walk around the richly decorated room, with cold marble flooring stretching throughout the entire first level. The walls are beige, the furniture stark white. Chandeliers float down from the ceiling in cascading glass bubbles, creating star burst of light around the room and the three, count 'em, three different seating areas.

I head straight for the window facing the Park. I don't even want to know how much she pays for this view. It's like sitting on top of the world.

I guess for people like Tina, that's exactly what it is.

The valet arrives before Tina. He places a silver tray on the large oval coffee table made of glass. I see he has brought a caviar plate in addition to the champagne. I round the large coffee table to take my seat on the cushy beige sofa. As he takes a match book from the crystal dish near a large humidor and lights the taper candles that sit in tall silver candlesticks, I have to wonder how many times he has set the mood in his mistress's web for her.

"Thank you, Bertram," Tina says as she enters. She wears high heels, full makeup and a silk robe. The air is immediately charged with intimacy.

Bertram nods his head and takes his leave, while Tina joins me on the sofa. I notice she doesn't look out the window once.

"Good rehearsal?" she asks. She gently scoops the caviar onto a toast point.

"Not bad," I say as I pour our champagne. "It's kind of hard to concentrate on things since I have no idea what the fuck I'm doing for you yet."

She chuckles as she sips her drink. "Of course you know what you're going to do. You're going to impress me. Isn't that the plan?"

"Is making it harder for me to do so a part of yours?"

She leans back against the sofa. "The way I see it you have two alternatives in this life. Look at everything as a problem, or look at everything as a challenge. If you see problems, then everything that stands in your way turns you into a victim of your own life. But if you see challenges, then every step forward, even the little, incremental ones, are victories."

I look around her extravagant home. "You should know."

"And that's Lesson Number One. So glad you've already learned it."

I lean back on the sofa. "So what's next? Why am I here?"

"Convenience," she said as she leaned back as well. "There's no sense dragging yourself back and forth to Brooklyn every day when I have five extra bedrooms here. You'll be perfectly cozy."

My eyebrow cocks. "You want me to stay?"

"Is that a problem?"

I look around the palatial room again, clearly furnished with finest of everything. She can have anything she wants in the world. And she wants *me*.

A smile tugs at my lips. "Not at all," I say as I put my glass back on the table and slide closer to where she sits on the sofa, in her silk robe, as if she's been waiting for me. If this is my invitation, then I'm taking it. She allows me to crowd her back against the sofa, my eyes dark and hooded as I focus on her succulent lips. I bend for a kiss. Before my mouth can land on hers, however, she halts me with one finger.

"I said that you could stay in one of the bedrooms, but I haven't offered you mine."

My frustration rises. What kind of fucking game is she playing now? "So what am I doing here?"

"You," she says as she reaches for another toast point and scoops some caviar onto it, "are getting a glimpse at the good life." She hands me the toast.

I tentatively take the bite. I've never had caviar before, because the idea of eating a clump of fish eggs had never done much to turn me on. The little black pearls are even less appetizing in person, but I figure what the hell? It is slightly salty as it pops on my tongue, and I try to hide my distaste. I wash away the sweet fishy taste with my full flute of champagne.

She chuckles. "Don't worry. You'll get used to it. Trust me."

"How can I trust you when you're trying so hard to sabotage me? You want me to perform on Friday night and you haven't let me on your stage once."

She shrugs. "You're getting plenty of rehearsal with your band."

"That's not the same and you know it."

"Are you a professional or not?" she asks.

"I'm professional enough to know that I need to test the sound system and choreograph the lighting, and study the sheet music and perform with my accompanying musicians to perfect the set that is oh so important to your event. Do you want me to impress these people or not?"

She chuckles again as she touches my face. "Oh, Vanni. So close and yet so far." She stands. "You can select whichever bedroom you wish, but for your convenience I've put your things in the blue room on the second floor, since it's the biggest guest room I have."

"Blue's my favorite color," I murmur. She just grins.

"Of course it is." She fills her glass one last time. "Goodnight, Vanni."

I sit there for long minutes afterwards, blinking in confusion as I try to process this unusual string of events. How the fuck has this become my life? I'm sitting in an opulent, Park Avenue penthouse, with one of the most powerful women in Manhattan just right upstairs, locked tight in her bedroom while I twist in the wind regarding the show she hired me to perform. I've got a chance to make it or break it in less than two days, with no idea how I'm going to make it all work.

I finally climb the spiral staircase. The blue bedroom is on the opposite corner of what clearly has to be the master suite. It's the only one with a closed door.

A man's robe hangs on the back of the door in the guest room, clearly waiting for a new occupant. I place the bucket of champagne on the nightstand next to me as I flop down on the mattress.

I don't bother to undress until the next morning, when the sunrise pierces through the sheer drapes covering the large window across from the bed. According to the clock on the nightstand, it's a little after eight o'clock on the morning.

I shuffle across the floor to the private adjoining bathroom, where I shed my second-hand clothes that Chelsea had hand-picked for me. I step into the large shower with etched glass doors, and a window that points straight out over the city, including Central Park. The products they had purchased the day before sit along the ledge, unpacked and ready for me to use.

It takes me about an hour to duplicate the hair and the clothes the way that Frankie had suggested.

By the time I head back downstairs, I'm wearing camel-colored leather pants, an open shirt made of natural, breezy fabric, with leather on each wrist and silver rings on each hand. My hair is styled, brushing against the back of my neck and over my shoulders.

I pad barefoot into the formal dining room, which has its own wall of windows with yet another amazing view of the Park. Tina sits at an enormous glass and chrome table, with two place settings prepared out of the dozen that could probably fit there. She eats fresh fruit for breakfast as she reads the paper.

"Morning," I say before I take my seat in front of the other place setting, right next to her. Bertram appears immediately, placing a full breakfast of steak, eggs, toast and hash browns, in front of me.

Tina's eyes scope over me thoughtfully. Finally she smiles. "Now that's more like it," she says as she toasts me with her mimosa.

We arrive at Sedução by nine-thirty, before anyone else. I sit at the bar, drinking some coffee, when Sasha arrives for her shift. "How's it going, Joe?" she asks as she puts her purse away under the counter.

"Fantastic. I've got the dream gig, didn't you hear?"

"I did," she says. She glances down at my coffee. "Didn't anyone ever tell you that you shouldn't drink caffeine if you're going to perform?" She turns away to get the pitcher of hot water, which she pours into a cup. She cuts her first lemon to add it to my drink, along with some honey, before pushing it across the bar to me.

"I don't have to worry about that, apparently. Since I have no idea when I'm going to get on that stage to rehearse."

She leans across the bar. "Always be prepared, Vanni. Rule one in this business."

I rub my tired eyes with one hand. "Is that the rule is this week? I can't keep track."

As it turns out, Sasha is absolutely right. Frankie is replaced by Arturo, the music director. He pulls me onto the stage, where he sits at the piano and I stand next to him. We talk about what kind of music he wants to do and what kind of music I like to do, to find a nice middle ground for my set. He pulls almost all of his inspiration from my new look. "I see you more retro," he says. "Like the dirty rocker boys of days gone by. A virile and unapologetic rule-breaker."

I nod. Sounds good to me.

We finally select five songs for my set, two of which I routinely perform with Yael and the guys. I spend the rest of the afternoon familiarizing myself with the other two. I keep an eye out for Tina, but she's otherwise occupied. It makes it easier to get frustrated when I can't ace the new songs like I'd like. After a couple of restarts, Arturo holds up a hand. "Hold on. I have an idea."

He hops off the stage and walks to the bar, where Sasha prepares the cash drawers. She can barely put them up before he drags her down center stage, where she faces me. He grabs a chair for her to perch upon before he hops back up onto the stage and back to his piano. "Sing it to her," Arturo instructs.

I glance down at Sasha, my unwitting audience of one. The song, like all the songs in my set, is overtly sexual, about a boy's first time with a woman. It's old, originally released in 1982, so I haven't yet memorized the lyrics, which I think is way more important than learning how to sing it to anyone in particular.

Arturo doesn't seem to care. "Come on, man," he says. "Get into character. Do your thing."

I sigh and he begins to play. I try to remember the words and I mess up more than once. Arturo finally sighs in exasperation.

"Don't look at the sheet music. Look at her. *Feel* it. The words will come."

"Fine," I grumble as I sit on the edge of the stage. I look at her. She's looking at me. I try to imagine what it would be like to be alone with her, in a hotel room, where I could take her into my arms and do what I've been learning to do so well: seducing a sexy girl to sleep with me. If we were alone, it would be no problem. I've practically done that in my sleep over the last few months.

I take a breath, shake my head to clear the cobwebs and start again.

Strangely, Arturo is right. The more she responds to me, the more I'm pulled into the song. I ease right into the scene, where I can sing every word like I mean it. It affects her. I can see it in her slightly widened eyes. It only empowers me. I hop down off the stage and walk over to her, slithering around her like a snake, singing into her ear, watching how her pulse races in her neck, and her cheeks flush rosy read. I miss some words, but I don't stumble.

And at last we get through the song all the way through.

The second time it's easier, and the third is even easier still. When I look up and see Tina watching me from the other side of the room, I feel victorious indeed.

Finally I check my watch. It's time to go. The driver waits for me just outside the club, but I have him drop me off a few blocks from Yael's. I'm not ready yet to tell them what's going on.

Unfortunately Bobby is through waiting for me to come clean. He corners me in the kitchen as I warm water for my throat. "What's the deal, dude? You come in every day, looking more and more made over from the day before. If this is some new dress code at that pizza place, I'm not buying it."

I sigh as I cut up a lemon for my water. "Fine. I'll tell you but you can't tell anyone else."

"Who am I going to tell?"

I glance both ways before I reveal my secret at last. "I'm pretty close to getting us a gig with Sedução."

His brows lift in surprise. "Get the fuck out of here."

"No shit," I confirm with a curt nod. "She evidently saw something she liked the other night. She's just polishing my image, to make sure I can cut it on her stage."

"Sweet!" he exclaims as he claps me on the back. He does that a lot, like his personal high-five. "But why keep it secret?"

"Because there are no guarantees. Because I don't want to get the guys' hopes up. Because I'm not completely sure if I trust her yet." I lean a little closer. "Essentially she's using me for arm candy to get back at her ex. I agreed, because she dangled booking the band in front of me."

A slow smile crosses his face. "So what do you know? Giovanni Carnevale has crossed over to the dark side. Never pictured you as the type to play escort, but to each his own."

"I'd sell my soul to the devil to get us away from playing dive bars for peanuts. If I have to go back to Cynzia's, I'll cut my wrists. Besides, it's just sex. Look at what we do at our after parties. At least this has a point."

"They all have a point, buddy boy," Bobby says with a grin. "But good on ya, man. If you have to prostitute yourself out to make it, there are worse options. At least she's hot, for an older chick."

I think about how cool and collected she is, so in charge of every little thing in her world. You bet your ass she's hot.

And I plan to learn a lot from her. Just look at how I've transformed this far.

Oddly, telling Bobby about the truth of what is happening at Sedução is quite liberating. I guess I didn't realize what kind of burden I was carrying around with the lies. I no longer feel guilty as we part that night, when I hop in the hired car to head back to a swanky penthouse on Park Avenue.

"Hey, Bertram," I say to the valet as I enter.

"Sir," he says, very polite and proper.

"Is Tina home yet?"

"She's already retired to her quarters, sir. She asked me to inform you that there is a light supper prepared in the kitchen if you are hungry."

"Fantastic. Thanks, Bertie," I say before I make my way to the enormous gourmet kitchen.

I spend most of the night prowling the house, acclimating myself to my temporary quarters. There's a grand piano in the living room, which I finally get to play. I don't expect to stay here long, not much longer than tomorrow night anyway, so I figure I'll enjoy it what limited time I have left as a guest.

It looks like a place right out of a magazine. Each and every bedroom has its own color scheme. Mine is blue, one is crimson, another is yellow, all deep reach colors offset by ivory crown molding and shelving in each room.

As I wander from one room to the other, I start to wonder what color Tina's bedroom is.

I steal along the carpet down the hallway towards the master suites. There is more art on the wall, and sculptures sitting beside and on top of tables, making the long hallway look less like a home and more like an gallery. It doesn't take long to realize that everything has a sensual theme. There are nudes, both male and female, as well as abstracts that resemble parts of the human anatomy.

Finally I come to a stop in front of the double doors leading into her private suite. I lift my hand to knock, but decide against it at the very last second.

Instead I head downstairs to the private outdoor garden just off of the living room. The balcony is spacious, with stone flooring and bubbling fountains. The sounds of the city below rise like music in the air, so when I spot the hot tub tucked away in a private corner, there's only one thing left to do. The night air crawls along my bared skin like invisible fingers when I strip to nothing and let the stress of my busy week ebb away under the pulsating spray of hot water.

I'm practically asleep when I hear her voice. "You had better to get to bed. We have an early day tomorrow."

I open an eye and spot her where she stands just outside the doorway. She wears no robe this time, only a mint green negligee made of silk. Her dark hair spills over one shoulder and her light brown eyes track me like a cheetah on a prowl.

"I thought you were already in bed," I say as I close my eyes and rest my head.

"You didn't come looking for me, so I was forced to come looking for you."

My eyes snap open and dart back over to her.

She heaves a dramatic sigh. "But I guess if you weren't going to make your move the other night, you're not going to make your move."

I close my eyes again. Another game. I had made my move and she shut me down. "I figured if that was what you wanted, you'd tell me."

"Do you always have to wait for permission?"

"I was raised to respect women," I say. "Your house, your rules."

"That's good news at least. I'll meet you in your bedroom in ten minutes. No need to dress," she adds before she disappears.

I stare after her for a long minute. Surely this is yet another game, but damned if I don't want to play it.

Following her suggestion, I wrap a towel around my waist after I dry myself off, then I take the steps two at a time around the winding staircase towards my room. I don't really expect to find her there when I enter, especially on the bed waiting for me. Yet there she is as she pours yet another glass of champagne.

I start that direction but she shakes her head. "I'd like to see what you've decided to wear for the gala tomorrow. You have at least three wardrobe changes, I trust?"

I can't help but stammer. This crazy broad has me completely off center. "I think so."

"You'll want one or two for the performance, of course. Then one for our arrivals. I expect quite a bit of press there to cover the proceedings. Go on," she says, nodding her head towards the armoire behind me. "Show me what you've got."

I eye her thoughtfully for a moment before I undo my towel and let it slide to the floor. Her eyes are riveted to my body, which brings out my best smirk. I saunter easily over to the armoire, where I withdraw some formal wear for the arrivals. It's a form-fitting tux, but Frankie has already showed me how to make it a lot less stuffy when I put it on. I ditch the tie and leave the matching black silky shirt unbuttoned down my chest. The royal blue pocket square gives it a punch of color. I dress slowly, relishing how her eyes inhale every detail. This was what she was paying the big bucks for, so I figure I'll give her a show. That it's a reverse striptease only makes it sexier.

And since she had done everything in her power to avoid hearing me sing all week, I start singing the song I had practiced all afternoon with Sasha. Tina can't keep her eyes off of me, and for the first time since I met her, I feel like I'm back in control.

Even a fancy woman like Tina Nunes wants to be fucked, and I know just how to give her wants she wants.

About halfway through the song, I start shedding the clothes I had just put on, until I'm once again naked by the armoire. I pull out another set of clothes for my performance, which we plan to keep sultry and sexy all the way through the set. These songs, a Bad Company hit about making love, and a Journey hit about a cheater getting her just desserts, are ones I can sing in my sleep. I've performed them all summer with my band.

The final song, a NIN song where I can be as dirty as I want to be, is still relatively new to me, but I give it my best effort as I try on yet another outfit for her perusal.

This performance I take right to the bed where she sits. I dance to the accompanying music I hear in my head as I use the lyrics to promise her the fucking her of her life. It's a promise I intend to keep as I crawl my way up her body, inhaling her scent, a classic smell of vanilla. I can't wait for a taste.

When I reach her mouth though, she uses that perfectly manicured finger to halt me once again. "Save it for the stage," she says with a satisfied smile all her own. Just like that, the ball is back in her court. She slips away from me and out of the bedroom, leaving me to fall over onto my back and wonder, again, just what the hell I'm doing.

As hard as I am, though, I decide to follow her advice and save it for the stage. Tomorrow is going to be the most important night of my career yet. Sex can wait.

For now.

CHAPTER SIXTEEN:

The next morning, the sun finally rouses me from my fitful sleep. I'm out of bed by seven o'clock, ready to go. A hearty breakfast awaits me downstairs, but I'm too nervous to eat. I drink water instead of the mimosa that sits beside my meal. I'm ready to climb out of my skin I'm so freaking hyped.

Tina joins me for breakfast. Her meal is limited to some fresh berries drizzled with sugar, along with some dry toast and coffee. No wonder she's so thin. The woman never eats. As far as I can tell, she lives off of champagne.

She does take her time with her breakfast, however. She reads the paper thoroughly as she picks at her food. Long minutes tick by and I practically tap my heel into the floor, but she doesn't look up through the duration of her meal.

"Shall we go?" I suggest, simply because I can't take it any longer.

"Oh, I'm not going in today. I have appointments all morning. Hair. The spa. That sort of thing. You go ahead and I'll meet you back here by four o'clock."

She doesn't even have to finish talking before I fly out of the dining room. The hired car takes me to club, where I lug my wardrobe changes in to set up in my dressing room.

I feel pretty sure of myself until I walk in to find another singer already rehearsing with the band. And it's not just some singer, either. It's a famous singer I recognize, one with a lot more star power than I could possibly have. I make a detour to the bar to corner Sasha. "What the hell is going on?"

She sighs, and I know the news is not good. "Tina booked him for the show tonight. He's headlining. It's sold a lot of tickets."

"I bet. Having Joe-Vanni Carnevale on the marquee doesn't exactly draw a crowd, I guess." I can feel her discomfort from where she stands. "What?"

"You're not on the marquee, Vanni," she says. Since she uses my real name, I gather she's serious.

"I don't understand. What was the point of this whole week if I'm not going to perform?"

"Maybe that's not how she needs you to perform," she suggests with a wry smile. "I'm sorry, Vanni. When I recommended you for this show, I really sold you to sing, I swear."

My eyes meet hers. "You recommended me for this?"

She shrugs. "I mean, it was just such a random thing. She wanted to plug some holes in the show and I said that I had seen a really great band. So of course when you showed up, I pointed you out to her. When she approached you, I thought for sure she was going to give you a chance."

I glance back up at the singer on stage, who is running the show with Arturo instead of the other way around. He wasn't being led around by his nose. That was just me. A plain, ol' regular Joe. Now I know why she thought I needed more swagger.

"Maybe she did and I just blew it."

"Vanni, don't say that. You really have something special. And if Tina can't see that, then that's her loss."

I nod. I know she means well. "Thanks for the chance anyway," I say. "Can I get a beer?" Off her look, I add, "I may not be performing but I think it's time to get this party started."

I drink at least three more before I return to the house that afternoon. Tina hasn't arrived yet, which allows me time to dress. I'm ready for the ball by the time she gets home. She hasn't changed into her gown yet, but her hair and makeup are stunning.

I meet her at the door with a glass of champagne. "For you," I say, enveloping her with my dark eyes. I finally know the rules to the game she's playing, so I feel a lot more confident than I had when she left me the night before.

She holds up the glass. "For us," she says. I offer a slight nod as I clink my glass to hers. I never take my eyes off of her as I tip the glass and slowly let the bubbly liquid slide down my throat.

She finishes her drink as well and hands me the glass. "I'll go change into my dress. I should be ready in about a half-hour or so."

I move away and gesture grandly towards the stairs with my arm. "After you."

I give her a ten-minute head start before I climb the stairs towards her personal suite on the top floor. I try the knob gently, which turns with ease. It makes me grin to myself. She didn't bother to lock it, which means she clearly expects a visitor. Maybe she's been expecting one all along. The closed door had simply been a challenge.

    I decided to play into her hands one more time.

    By no surprise, Tina's room color is a regal purple. The dark, vibrant color is broken up by ivory colored accents, with corner bookshelves, stately pillars and crown molding along the ceiling. The centerpiece of her bedroom is a large, king-sized bed that is round in shape, and covered with purple satin, and surrounded by wisps of sheer purple netting suspended like a canopy over her bed. A large crystal domed chandelier shines overhead, with a plush light mauve carpet underfoot, accented with a black filigree pattern.

    It is a room befitting a queen, and that queen sits at her vanity table overlooking a large window facing Central Park South, wearing only a pink silk dressing gown. She leans close to a mirror to apply her makeup, and that is when she spots me on the other side of the room. When our eyes meet in the reflective glass, I lock the door behind me.

    She says nothing as I walk up behind her. I don't stop until I reach her chair. I take both of her shoulders in my hands to rub them softly.

    "What are you doing, Vanni?" she asks.

    "What you pay me for, Tina," I say. I kneel down to look at her reflection in the mirror. "You know, since I'm not on the roster for tonight's show."

    "What can I say? Justin offered to play for free. And his name–"

    "Sells tickets," I finish for her. "Right. But that's not why I'm not performing tonight. I'm not stupid, Tina. I know what this week was about. You want a primped and preening poodle to walk on your leash to piss off your ex. I get that. I've got a bitch of an ex too. And that's why," I say as I lean forward, surrounding her with my arms to pull the strings on her dressing gown, "I know how this should go down."

    I'm rewarded by the hitch in her voice. "What do you mean?"

    I slip the dressing gown from her bare shoulders. She's not wearing a bra, and I inspect those firm, perfect tits in the mirror. Whether they are God-given or manmade makes no difference to me. "If you didn't hire me so that I could prove my prowess behind the mic, then that means you hired me to prove my prowess elsewhere."

"I hired you as my escort."

At least she admits it, I think to myself as I chuckle against her skin. Goose bumps spring up to my mouth as I kiss her bare shoulder. "You could have hired a professional escort if you wanted," I say. "Face it, Tina. You wanted me. And I know why."

Her face screws into a sneer. I know she's on the ropes now. "And why's that?"

I snake one hand up the back of her neck to tangle my fingers in her long hair. "Because you want your ex to know how well you're getting fucked, that's why."

I turn her face to me and deliver a scorching kiss on her partially opened lips. She wrenches back and slaps me hard across the face. It smarts, but I smile anyway. "Who do you think you are?" she demands hotly.

I lean forward, backing her against her chair. "I'm the guy you've wanted to fuck since you first laid eyes on me. You made me chase you, and I did. You made me grovel and beg, and I did. You made me jump through all your hoops. And I did. But that's not what you wanted me to do. You wanted me to take what I wanted, from that very first night. You leveraged my career for it, made me literally sing and dance for it, and even strip for it. You've done everything to piss me off and make me snap, just so I could fuck you like you've wanted to be fucked for a very long time. And now that I know that, you're about to get exactly what you want."

This time my kiss is way more demanding. I'm going to punish her for making me beg like a dog. I force her lips open with my tongue, taking full command of her mouth until she moans underneath me. She's breathless when I pull away.

"You want swagger, baby? Hang on." I wrap my arms around her and lift her up effortlessly. Her dressing gown falls away, revealing her tanned, lean body to me at last. I'm hard as a rock just thinking about the things I'm going to do to her.

I carry her easily to the king-sized, satin-covered bed, where I deposit her in a wide-eyed, panting heap. I rip away my expensive jacket and toss it to the floor as I perch myself over her on my knees. I tug my dress shirt free from my trousers before I land on top of her, pushing her down onto her back.

I don't ask for permission as I steal another kiss. I feel her bare chest pressed into mine, so I know she can feel every hard muscle. She trembles underneath me, but I know she's not scared. This is exactly what she wanted, I have no doubts.

This powerful woman wants someone else to call the shots for once.

I kiss my way down her torso to capture one of her hard nipples in my mouth. Her long, manicured fingers wind themselves into my long hair, which spills over my shoulders. I use the tip of my tongue to tease her, and I don't stop until she is gyrating underneath me. I switch to the other breast, taking my time, making her pay for this slow game of seduction she's been playing with me.

The ball's in my fucking court, goddammit. And I want to make sure it stays there.

I rub myself against her, just so she can see how hard she's made me. But I'm not going to give it to her until she makes me beg.

My mouth drifts even lower on her sweet-smelling body, across her taut tummy and down to her perfectly trimmed patch, freshly groomed. I use one large hand to impatiently part her legs before dipping my head even lower. I open her like a flower, blowing cool air on that hot little pussy. I target her clit at once, causing her to jerk against me with a suppressed cry. I grin before I latch onto it, swirling my tongue around it, lazily at first, making her groan and writhe beneath me. I gradually speed up, until she clamps both of her thighs against my head. I don't stop. Instead I take her from zero to sixty in less than two minutes, when she's coming hard and loud.

I don't stop either. As self-contained as she is, I get the sense that this woman hasn't enjoyed a proper orgasm in a while. I plan to make every sex toy she's likely to have hidden in every drawer in her bedroom obsolete. I finger her ever so gently, but just on the outside, teasing her with the idea of penetration without actually doing it.

I'm saving that particular honor for my dick.

Her hips buck against me. She wants more and she wants it bad. Her whole body is like an exposed nerve. "Now," she begs as she comes again.

"Not yet," I tell her as I keep fingering her. Her hips gyrate underneath me and her thighs shudder around me. She's coming again, even harder than before. But I don't stop. She's one exposed nerve and I'm going to keep pressing on it, swirling my fingers and tongue around it, until she's incoherent with need.

"Vanni, now!"

"No," I tell her again. "Not till I'm ready." I latch onto her and suck her clit into my mouth until she's clawing at the sheets.

She's practically in tears from the intense pleasure when I lift up only to dispense with my pants, socks and shoes. She's trembling from her last orgasm when I crawl up her body. I plant a deep kiss on her mouth. I know she can taste herself on me. She groans against me because it makes it even hotter for her, like the dirty, dirty girl she wants to be.

Her hand disappears between us to guide my cock where she wants it to go. I shake my head with a low chuckle as I raise her hand up over her head, securing it in my large palm. Her eyes widen as I do the same with her other hand, all while rubbing her clit with my dick. She shudders hard against me. I know she's aching for me to fill her. I capture her hooded gaze. "Tell me how much you want it."

She has the whole damned world at her feet, and yet she wants me. I want to hear her say it. I *need* to hear her say it.

"I want it," she ekes out. I rub a little firmer.

"Tell me like you mean it, Tina. You've wanted this cock since the first time you laid eyes on me. Admit it."

She nods her head. She can't deny it. Every cell in her body is reaching for me. "I did. I do. Fuck me, dammit." Then, in a croaked whisper, "Please."

I chuckle again as I bury my face in her neck, nibbling my way up to her ear as my free hand cups her breast. "Now tell me you want my band to perform at Sedução."

Her eyes widen as she focuses on my face. "What?"

I tease her nipple between my forefinger and my thumb. "Tit for tat, darlin'. Remember? You know I've got what it takes. You didn't just play dress up with me all week for a one-and-done dinner with your ex. You know I'm a star, and that's why you're grooming me. Admit it." I tweak her nipple again and she cries out. I capture it in my mouth, to swirl my tongue around it and lap over it until she's crazed with need.

I break away to nuzzle her ear again as my hand curls under her to cup her luscious ass. "You wanted me to take what I want? This is what I want. Tell me you'll make it happen and I'll make that big bad ache inside you go away." She groans in her throat as she stares into my eyes. I grind against her. "You want me to push this big, hard dick up inside you, pumping inside you, making you come harder than you've ever come before? You know I can do that now, don't you?" I tease her further, with kisses and touches and the promise of my rock hard cock against her. She's practically coming already. "I'll make you forget every other man who has ever fucked you before. All you gotta do is promise me one show by the end of the year. Then we both get what we want," I tell her in between slow, open-mouthed kisses.

Finally she nods her head. And I know it's not just because I'm withholding yet another orgasm for her. I know it's because that was always how this was supposed to go. I was her pet project from the moment we danced in that bar. She was turning me into the kind of man who could sweep a woman off her feet and seduce her with no regret, so that I could be a superstar that would make every little girl in the audience hungry for a piece of me.

If they were lucky, they might just get it.

"Say it," I urge as I flick the engorged head of my cock against her hard clit.

"You can play at the club," she murmurs.

"For real this time," I clarify and she nods.

"Good girl," I say before I slam myself up inside of her and make her scream. Normally I would never fuck without a condom, but there's no time, and really no need. Tina is a professional woman, whose domestic gene must have been flushed right out of her with all the champagne.

And it's so fucking nice to be inside a woman and actually *feel* her as she clamps down on me, sucking me in tighter. God, it's so amazing I can't even believe I'm doing it. I'm fucking Tina Nunes, Manhattan society's darling, and she's wrapped around me like a vice, locking me into her sweet body, begging for me to fuck her like a dirty, wanton slut.

Her eyes widen and I can't help but smile as I ride her hard and fast, driving her crazy all around my dick. I don't stop until she's coming hard around me, squeezing me so tight I can barely breathe. God, she's so fantastic, it's all I can do not to topple over the edge myself.

But my coming wasn't the objective.

We had to save some stuff for after the party.

I pull out, though I'm still rock hard. She appears puzzled so I give her a kiss. "I want you to be thinking, all night, of how hard I am and how much I want to fuck you. You can think about that as you listen to the music of whatshisname."

She can barely move as I roll away to grab my clothes, head into her private bathroom and change back into my new clothes.

It takes her a little longer to finish dressing. I know I've made a mess of her hair and her clothes, but I don't care. And I won't let her repair the damage, either. Her mouth is swollen from my forceful kisses, and her entire torso, chest, neck and face are flushed from the handful of orgasms I had given to her. Her eyes are dilated wide, pitch black like a shark. I can feel her hunger every time she looks at me. She looks just like the woman in the drawing downstairs.

There's a huskiness to her voice from the loud screams she couldn't withhold even if she had wanted to. Even her nipples are still hard as she slips into her silk slip of a dress that gathers at her neck in a jeweled collar, but is backless all the way to her tailbone.

Just knowing that I get to fuck her again at the end of the night keeps me semi-hard. I steal a kiss as we sit in the back of the hired car. "Too bad you don't fuck at your club," I murmur against her skin. "Otherwise we'd haunt that entire joint before I'm done with you."

"Let's start with the house first," is all she'll say as her head tilts back and she presses my face into her perfumed neck. Diamonds drip from her ears and her skin is silk to the touch. I've never been with a woman like this before. All I can think about is how she looked underneath me, a virtual queen thrashing against me as I took her like a dirty whore.

Even from her ivory tower, she wants to be down in the gutter with the rest of us.

And maybe this makes me the biggest manwhore in Manhattan, but I have no shame about any of it. I got what I wanted, which was to play at Sedução. That I get to have sex with one of the hottest women in New York is simply a bonus.

My hands slip between her bare legs to get her worked up all over again while we ride to the club.

I keep my arm draped around her possessively as we walk the red carpet. The smirk that I flash is the only proof that anyone needs to see exactly what I had done to her prior to our arrival. That and the bulge in my pants. It's just as prominent as her hard nipples, which lift proud and high under her slinky, sexy dress.

I lean in close for every pic snapped by the paparazzi. They don't know me from Adam, but suddenly all of them are interested.

No one is more interested than Julio Nunes, who comes to pose with his ex as a united front for their charitable organization. The girl on his arm is no slouch, either, a pretty, raven-haired former model about my age. Despite any presence or lack of a baby bump, which is hidden well under her clothing, she glances me over with interest. It only makes me pay more attention to Tina. My warm hand covers her cool bare back, and I can feel how it makes her tremble. Her body still reels from the handful of orgasms I'd already given her.

I have one job to do, and I'm going to do it well.

The headlining act tears up the stage, getting everybody on the floor to dance to his sexy pop hits. I drag Tina into the fray, holding her close as we dance. I grind against her and nuzzle her neck, making sure everyone who might be watching, including her ex, knows that she's got herself a new boy toy who knows exactly what to do with her.

Who brought sexy back?

I fucking did.

If I have any attack of conscious, it's when I face Sasha. She doesn't say anything, but with that look in her eye she doesn't have to.

I'm not going to apologize though. This is the path that presented itself to me, and I'm going to take it.

When we return to the penthouse that night, I lead Tina up to her bedroom, where I pick her up at the threshold and carry her to the bed.

Dawn the next day finds us locked in yet another passionate embrace. She's insatiable, and by this time so am I. Once I allow her to touch me and please me, she shows me exactly how sexy she can be, riding my cock like a beast as she works her own body up into a fervor with a variety of toys and accessories I've never seen before.

I barely want to take a break when Bertram brings us breakfast in bed. Tina's focus turns immediately to the society pages to see how well her event went. According to the report, it was a huge success, smashing the previous year's fundraising by at least six figures.

Of course, the picture that they showed included both Julio's new girl and me. The biggest question was not whether or not the new Mrs. Nunes was expecting. Instead, they all wanted to know who the young buck was on Tina Nunes's arm, which, of course, had been her master plan.

I can't wait to show them.

I snag a piece of toast as I turn to Tina. "So when can I tell my boys we'll be playing at the club?"

She leans back against the plush pillows and upholstered headboard. "When do you think you'll be ready?"

"We're already ready," I say but she just chuckles.

"If you were ready, baby, you'd have been headlining that show last night."

My eyes narrow as I glare at her. I was afraid of this. "Are you trying to get out of our deal?"

"No," she says. "But what I told you from the beginning still stands. Sedução is for polished professionals. And frankly, you're not there yet."

I start to climb out of bed but she holds me back by the arm. "Don't get all bent out of shape. I'm not saying this to insult you. I'm saying this to help you. I can turn you into a star, Vanni, quicker and better than anyone else in this city. But just because we're fucking doesn't mean you get to circumvent the system. I'm going to expect a lot out of you. That's just how it is." I glare at her and say nothing. Finally she softens. "I'll make you a deal. I'll put you on stage New Year's Eve. If you sell me on your band, then you'll have a regular gig here throughout the spring and into the summer. We're talking a lot of exposure and a lot of money. But you have to kill it NYE, Vanni. Otherwise the deal is off. Got it?"

I study her for a long moment, wondering if I can trust her. "Got it," I finally say.

She gives me a smile before she reaches for another kiss. This time, she's the one who journeys down my body, teasing me with her long tongue and making my senses tingle with her long nails against my skin.

This time I'm the one losing control, begging for sweet release. She straddles my hips, once again in control.

I lie back against the pillow and don't fight her one bit.

CHAPTER SEVENTEEN:

Every single member of my band looks at me like I've grown another head. Yael is the first to speak. "What do you mean you booked Sedução?"

I shrugged. "I told you I was going to do it and I did. New Year's Eve, buddy. What do you think about that?"

They all share stunned looks. "I think I may have a second-hand high from whatever Felix is smoking," Yael says at last.

I laugh. "Either way, we have to be ready to deliver a killer set by New Year's Eve. Good thing Fritz's is a week beforehand."

Yael catches the meaning behind my pointed stare. "Okay, okay. You upheld your part of the deal, so I'll uphold mine. Consider it my birthday gift to you," he adds.

"Thank you," I say, and that's that. We turn our attention to the show we have that night.

I've internalized a lot of the lessons I've learned so far from Frankie and Tina, even Sasha, so that when I perform I draw even the most stoic members of the audience to the stage, just to be a part of the experience. I become a character, it seems harmless enough. None of it is real, and that's what I'm slowly learning.

After the show is over, Bobby sidles up to me, a friendly arm around my shoulder. "I don't know what you've been smoking or drinking or taking, but keep doing whatever it is you're doing. That show was flawless. Do you know how many girls I have invited to our special party already? Just guess."

I shake my head. "Thanks, but I'm going to make an early night of it."

"Wait, what? What are you talking about? We're talking primo pieces of ass, man. Willing to do anything we want."

I just shrug. "Guess I'm not in the mood to party. It's been a pretty eventful week."

Bobby studies me for a minute before he relents. "Fine. More for me."

"Exactly," I smile.

I leave the venue early, and Tina's hired car is waiting for me the minute I walk out the front doors. Several people are standing out front of the venue, who spot the fancy car I disappear into with interest. *That'll show them who's a star,* I think to myself with a smile as I pop open a split of ever-present champagne.

I don't really make the conscious decision to move into Tina's posh mansion, it just sort of happens over the next week. When I'm not rehearsing with the band, I'm at Sedução on her arm, keeping up appearances for the equally ever-present press. By then, Julio and his young model wife have announced that they are expecting, so the paparazzi circles the club to see who the scored woman might take the news.

She's all smiles on my arm, wishing her ex and his new missus all the best for their upcoming blessed event.

"My baby has always been Sedução," she tells them.

When we're at the house, we're in her bed. And in her tub. And on her dining room table. And in front of her fireplace in the living room.

"Has Bertram ever caught you?" I ask as she straddles my lap, gyrating against me with loud moans.

"He knows better," she grins, then moans even louder for emphasis.

I capture her breast in my palm as I reach for another kiss. "Or maybe he's watching," I suggest with a lascivious grin.

We both agree that only makes it that much better.

Frankie works her magic on refining my style, with more trips to the spa and more shopping excursions to keep up with my new jet-set life as Tina's arm candy. I don't bother taking any of my old vintage clothing to Tina's. Everything I want or need, including a fully furnished home gym, is housed within that 24,000-square foot property a stone's throw from Central Park.

The car takes me to and from SoHo to rehearse with the guys, but by November, Tina suggests that we start rehearsing at Sedução itself during the daylight hours. Frankie begins to infiltrate the group one at a time to refine their style as well, which doesn't go over too well with Yael. He doesn't care about image or clothes, he just wants to play music. I practically have to beg him to get with the program. "This is our big break," I keep reminding him. "If this is what it takes to play this stage, isn't it worth it?"

He'd always relent with a beleaguered sigh. He knows I'm right, he's just not happy about it. Tina had already met with everyone and laid out her plans to give us a steady gig at the club. The money was impossible to turn down, even if it meant we were all being pulled, however unwillingly, through Frankie's wringer of trend-friendly style machine.

The only real blight on this shining new development? Sasha. She has no use for any of us outside of polite exchanges when she is needed at the bar. I sense that she's angry about my hooking up with her boss, which I find a little ironic, considering she's the one who figuratively put me on Tina's hook in the first place.

I finally corner her the week before Thanksgiving, when I have some down time. Since Tina's family is primarily in Portugal, she has no real need for a traditional holiday. She decides to take the down-time and fly overseas, and since I'm just the boy-toy de jour, it's not really expected of me to go with her.

The band still comes in every day to rehearse, since it has the sound system and lighting equipment to help us develop a legitimate show. Arturo and Yael hit it off immediately, and Yael is open to many of his suggestions as a fellow musician. They're constantly bouncing ideas off of each other to make the New Year's Eve show as epic as it can be.

This gives me even more free time, so I saunter over to the bar for a bottle of water. "Hey, Joe," she greets with that same reserved smile she's worn since the gala, when I showed up on Tina's arm.

"Hey," I say in response as I climb on one of the tall barstools. "The usual, barkeep."

She is the picture of politeness as she digs a bottle of water from the refrigerator below the bar. She opens it and hands it to me before she turns back to her tasks.

"So do I have to wave an actual white flag or will a napkin do?"

She turns back to face me. "You don't owe me anything, Vanni. I know how this stuff works. I'm a big girl."

"Then why is it every time you look at me I think I need to grab a scarlet letter for my chest? G for gigolo? M for manhore? A for asshole? Which is it?"

"You seem to have a good grasp on what you're doing. You tell me."

"How about F for friend?"

Her eyebrow lifts. "I'm surprised that's the f-word you chose."

"You seem to have a good grasp on what you want," I shoot back. "You tell me."

"We already talked about this, Vanni. And it's sure as shit gotten more complicated since we had that conversation."

"So... what? You're mad at me for hooking up with Tina?"

"I don't give a shit about what you do with Tina. I guess I just figured you had a little more integrity than this." My spine draws up tight, so she leans in. "You really have something great, Vanni. I've said that from the beginning. You didn't need to sell yourself out like this to break in."

"Says someone who hasn't ever tried to break in."

"Yeah, maybe," she concedes. "And if you can still look at yourself in the mirror every day, then more power to you. You certainly don't need my permission to live your life the way you want to. Just...," she hesitates only a second, "just be careful. That line you shouldn't cross is awfully hard to see sometimes."

"All the more reason to have a friend," I say. "Someone who can tell me where that line is."

"You're a big boy, hon. You don't need me for that. In fact, you don't need me for anything." She sighs, as if frustrated with herself. "I dunno. I guess I was kinda hoping there was a good ol Brooklyn boy in there still. But the further you get from Bensonhurst, the more Joe disappears."

"Sasha," I say as she tries to turn away. She slowly turns back. There's hope in her eyes, however small. I stick out my hand. "My name is Joe-vanni Carnevale, the incredible shrinking nice guy. Nice to meet you."

She puts her hand in mine and I close my fingers around it tight. "I appreciate the gesture. But like I said, you don't owe me anything."

I just shrug. "What can I say? The holidays are coming up and orphans like me can't really afford to throw away friends."

I can see that softens her immediately. Score one for painful honesty. "Come on now. You're part of a brotherhood."

I chuckle. "A brotherhood, right. Yael is going upstate to be with his folks, Felix is flying to California to be with his family and I'm pretty sure there's an all-you-can-eat buffet at some strip joint with Bobby's name all over it."

She echoes my laughter. "Why didn't you just go to Portugal with Tina?"

I shake my head. "It's not that kind of relationship. You know that."

"Yeah," she sighs. "I guess I do." She looks me over thoughtfully for a long moment before she finally says, "If you can stand it a hectic afternoon with screaming kids and rabid sports fans, I suppose I could scrounge up a turkey leg or something for you."

My expression brightens at once. I was thinking I'd be locked up all alone in my old Brooklyn brownstone with all the ghosts that linger there. It's my first Thanksgiving without my Aunt Susan. Let's just say I'm not looking forward to it. I had even contemplated spending some time at Fritz's, but I know if I see Pam with Doug I'd probably drown myself in the bottom of a whiskey bottle.

Even Lori has someone. Last I heard she had moved in with Tony in the city.

It makes Sasha's offer even more tempting. This is more than just some casual hookup. She is offering family. "Yeah?" I ask.

"Yeah," she decides with a nod.

The next week I head into Queens to spend the day with Sasha and her family. Since her divorce, she's been living with her folks in a cramped but homey house in a regular neighborhood where kids still played ball in the streets. I bring a bottle of wine and tiramisu from Cynzia's. Sasha's mom, Kate, greets me warmly. "So nice to meet you, Joe," she says and Sasha throws up her hands behind her in a mock apology.

I don't really mind. I don't get to be Joe much anymore, so it's a welcome change. If I'm going to be around a wholesome, all-American family, it's probably best. Giovanni was a rock star, with all the debauchery that entails.

Joe is someone who could still assimilate into polite society.

"This is my husband, Carl," she says as she introduces the big, burly guy wearing a football jersey.

"Nice to meet you," I say as I grasp his hand in a self-assured grip.

"Come on in," he says, leading me towards the crowded living room where a large TV blares one of the games being played that day. I navigate around scattered toys on the brown shag rug, to take a seat on the well-worn sofa.

A Park Avenue penthouse, it ain't. But that's why I kinda dig it, especially for Thanksgiving.

I hear the kids before I see them. "Mom, Imogen won't stop copying me!" says a boy.

"Mom, Imogen won't stop copying me," mimics a young girl who tries her very best to form every word.

"You both behave. We have company."

I turn to see Sasha corral her children into the room. Five-year-old Hugo wears a jersey similar to his granddad, and three-year-old Imogen's hair sprouts off either side of her head in adorable, lopsided pigtails.

"Guys, say hi to Joe."

They both stand in front of me, polite and well-mannered now that a stranger is present. "Hi, Joe," they say in unison.

I shake Hugo's hand, which gives him a chance to introduce himself like a proper gentleman. I then turn to Imogen, whose hand I lift up to my lips for a kiss. She giggles and runs back to her mother, peeking out at me from behind one of Sasha's pant legs. Sasha just shakes her head at me. I just smile.

While Kate and Sasha work on dinner, the kids stay with Carl and me in the living room. Imogen scoots closer and closer to me, watching me with big blue eyes. Finally she climbs up onto the sofa next to me and takes a lock of my hair in her hands. "You have long hair like a girl," she announces. I have to suppress my smile. "It's even longer than Mommy's."

"Did you ever hear of the fable of Samson, from the Bible?" I say. Her eyes widen as she nods. "He had long hair. It was the source of all of his strength."

She fingers my hair as she considers that. "And what powers does your hair have?"

I lean forward and whisper, "I sing."

Her mouth falls open. "I sing too," she says.

I narrow my eyes skeptically. "Prove it." She blushes and shakes her head. I bend closer, as if whispering a secret. "I bet if you hold on to my hair you can do it. Wanna try?"

A smile spreads across her face as she nods. I pick a song from an old animated kid's movie, which, of course, she knows. She holds onto my hair as she joins in, softly at first and then with more gusto.

By the time we're done, Carl and Hugo clap for us, as do Sasha and her mother from the doorway to the dining room.

It's enough to win over the tiny tot. Eventually she plasters herself to my side, not saying much as she plays with one of her dolls and hums the song we sang under her breath. Hugo sits with Carl, and mimics him every time he hollers at the game on TV. We only break away for dinner, which is a huge feast with ham and turkey, potatoes and stuffing, four different vegetables, three kinds of salads and two types of bread. I glance down at Sasha with a smile. "I'm going to have to run around Central Park three times to work off this meal."

"You can afford it," Kate says. "You're too skinny, Joe!"

As soon as we're seated, Kate instructs everyone to join hands and say grace. I simply bow my head. I haven't prayed since Susan died. What left was there to pray for? Who was left to pray for me?

But I can't stop thinking of my beloved *prozia*, especially as I watch the loving family around the table. Sasha fusses over her kids, making sure that they're eating properly and minding their manners. She's such a doting mother it adds another layer of depth. I soften to her immediately.

Kate and Carl are affectionate and get along well together, which is quite an accomplishment for thirty-seven years of marriage. I envy them, honestly. To have someone that you know you can count on for decades on end? I find it so hard to imagine. The closest I got was Lori, and we all know how that turned out.

I glance over at Sasha again, wondering what went wrong in her marriage.

When her ex shows up to take the kids to his parents' house, all my questions are sadly answered.

Philip is a tall man with stern features and a shock of red hair. I assume that's where Hugo gets his. But that's where the similarities end between Philip and his offspring. Instead of the wide smile and playful nature of his son, Philip is picky about the clothes she's wrestled onto her kids, clothes that instantly got dirty with some whipped cream from the pie that they ate. "I thought you would have them ready, Sasha," he says, his voice dripping with disdain. He looks me up and down. "I guess you were busy."

I hold out my hand. "Joe," I greet. "So nice to meet you. Sasha's told me all about you."

Her eyes dart to mine but I just wink at her.

"Funny," he retorts stiffly. "She hasn't told me a thing about you."

"Not much to tell," I say as I wrap an arm around her drooping shoulders. "We just met."

"Good for you," he sneers. He turns back to Sasha. "Did you pack their suitcases?"

She takes a deep breath to calm herself. "Of course. They're on the stoop."

"Oh yes. The porch. What a great place for them." We follow him and the children out to the bricked porch in front. The suitcases sit, nice and tidy, on the step, but Philip makes a face anyway. "I guess I can put them in the trunk so they won't get my car dirty." He sends Sasha a venomous stare. "Maybe next time you can think ahead."

Again I step forward. "Sorry, pal. That was my bad. Here, let me help you." I take the frilly pink suitcase and pull it by the handle right through a puddle. I then sit it in his pristine trunk with a shit-eating smile. "Happy thanksgiving," I say, daring him with the glint in my eye to make an issue of it.

He grumbles a reply before he gets the kids situated in the car, a nice car that had to cost him a good chunk of money.

Funny how everything about him seemed to cost money, from the watch on his wrist to his designer clothes. And I knew they were designer clothes because I had seen enough of them in my shopping excursions with Frankie.

He wasn't that different from all the other men who paraded in and out of the spas, primping and pampering themselves courtesy of all their excess cash. And yet here his kids live in a cramped house, taken care of by a mother who has to juggle parenthood two jobs just to get them all back on their feet.

That he had the audacity to look down on Sasha just because she struggled only pissed me off even more. I already had daddy issues. I didn't want to see some elitist asshole shit all over a struggling, blue-collar working mother her young kids just because he could.

Sasha stands in the street waving at the car until it turns out of sight. I can tell by the way her expression melts from a smile into a frown just how hard it is for her. I wrap my arm around her shoulder again and guide her back into the house.

Instead of going back in to the living room with Carl, I follow Sasha into the kitchen to help her put away the bountiful buffet. "Well, he's just prince charming, isn't he?" I quip.

"He wasn't always such a dick," she assures. "Then he got a better job, made a lot of money, found another girl, or three, or ten, and voila! Instant asshole."

"That sucks," I say, unable to think of anything deeper and more meaningful to offer.

She chuckles humorlessly. "Yeah. It kinda does."

"At least he wants to be there for his kids, I guess. Though I'm not sure what's worse... an absentee dad, or an asshole dad."

She shrugs as she starts to load the dishwasher. "The grass is always greener, or so they tell me."

Once the kitchen is spotless, I suggest that we go for a walk. She doesn't fight me on it. I can tell she's still depressed about the encounter with her ex, and the fact that her children weren't there with her on a family holiday. She's quiet as we set off down the block, and I don't say much to engage her. I figure comfortable silence is probably best.

Finally she slides me a sideways glance. "Thanks for coming today, Vanni. I appreciate it."

"Oh, I'm Vanni now?" I ask with a cheeky grin. She laughs.

"You'll always be Joe to me."

"I can live with that," I tell her. "And hey, you did me a huge favor today. If I had to spend the day in my old brownstone, I'd have been a wreck. The firsts are always the worst."

"Firsts?"

"First big milestones without a loved one. Yeah," I spare her a sardonic smirk. "I know all about the firsts. At first, it was my dad who skipped out. I was really young but some of my first memories are those big events when I couldn't figure out what had happened to him. That first birthday without him, that first Christmas." I sigh. "I was three years old when I started asking Santa to bring my father back. Funny thing is I don't think I'd have recognized the fucker if Santa had managed to do it."

"I'm sorry, Vanni," she says softly and I just shrug.

"Shit happens. You know how that is." She nods. "Losing Mama hurt a lot worse. The hole was just bigger and nothing seemed to fit. I mean, Aunt Susan tried to fit. She did whatever she could to make it easy for me, especially the holidays." My heart lurches a little when I realize that this birthday will be the first one in a long, long time without my aunt's silly surprise parties. That, and Christmas Eve... I don't know how I'm going to handle it all.

"Little did I know it would be the first Christmas without the both of them. I can't even bring myself to open the gifts she gave me yet. They're still wrapped, stacked up in the attic somewhere, waiting. You want to ask me where Joe went? I think he died that day too."

She takes my hand in hers. "Oh, I don't know about that. I think Joe is alive and well and hidden under there somewhere, beneath all the hurt, wrapped and waiting like your presents. You just have to be brave enough to open that box."

"Such wisdom," I tease.

"Call me the asshole-whisperer," she says with a broad smile that makes me laugh. I pull her under one arm and she doesn't fight it. In fact, it feels rather nice.

We walk around the neighborhood, where she shows me where she went to school, where she broke her first bone (the monkey bars at the park,) and where she had her first kiss under her parent's huge sycamore tree.

I pull her to me and kiss her upturned nose. She gives me another smile before she reaches for a spontaneous hug.

It doesn't go any further than that, but it doesn't have to. Our day was spent in comfortable companionship, and I know better than to screw with that. It's nice to have a relationship where there are no expectations.

Besides, she's got kids. Now that I met them, trying to seduce their mother is out of the question. They need her more. And I'm not going to be yet another asshole who lets her down. Who lets *them* down.

Frankly the thought of living up to their expectations is frightening as hell. I'd rather remain a nice, faint memory of that guy that showed up once for Thanksgiving.

That night I go back to the brownstone. After a month in Manhattan, it looks smaller and more run-down than it did before. I can't face the bedroom where my aunt drew her last breath. I thought I had exorcised these demons months before, but now the voices dance off of the walls like tiny echoes, and I know what they're saying. My aunt would say exactly what Sasha had said to me, that I didn't have to sell out my integrity to make my dream come true.

When I face myself in the mirror, I see the New Vanni staring back at me, more so than the Old Vanni, or even Joe, my new alter ego. The New Vanni is the one in control. He's making things happen in my world, to give me everything I always thought I wanted.

And yet... surprisingly... it's hard to be thankful. I know that no matter what this new life brings me, it can't restore to me what I've lost, and that's a painful reality to accept.

The only thing that has kept me going for all these months has been my ambition to make something of myself. Something big. Something that can't be denied, no matter how humble my beginnings.

And if I don't have that dream to chase, who the hell am I?

I sigh deeply before I turn out the light in the bathroom. I walk right past the sofa I've already prepared for bed. I grab my coat and my keys and hail a cab back to Manhattan.

CHAPTER EIGHTEEN:

The first few weeks of December fly by. There's nothing quite like the holiday season in New York, especially Manhattan. There are so many things to see and to do, and Tina's social calendar is booked solid. I'm on her arm for movie premiers and Broadway shows, though I don't get mentioned much more than "guest" these days. There are new stories for the tabloids to chase now.

I'm just the no-name escort, and they probably think I'm paid to do it. After all, I'm not famous enough to truly warrant Tina's attention. So I disappear on the sidelines while they concern themselves with what designer's dresses she happens to wear.

That's all fine with me. I have bigger things to worry about. My show at Fritz's is on December 17th, the last Saturday before my birthday, possibly the hardest birthday I'll face in my life.

I mostly hammer out the details of the gig over the phone with Cheryl, who is the only one who will return my calls.

By December 15th, I head down to Fritz's to personally oversee the details. This show means a lot to me, probably more than any other show I've done thus far. Its importance is second only to the NYE show at Sedução, since that could secure a gig for us heading all the way into summer.

Money hasn't been much of an issue since moving in with Tina. She does pay me to accompany her to different events, mostly because it takes away from the shows we could be performing otherwise.

That and it keeps our relationship strictly business, which is most comfortable with both of us. We are doing things that demand a certain level of trust, with kinky sex games and role playing that lets Tina break out of her titan persona and worship at the altar of another god for once.

We're not in love. Far from it. And one day, when she gets bored of me and wants to conquer yet another challenge, I want to have a little more to show for my time than a few more chapters to my lovemaking manual.

By the time Tina's hired car arrives at Fritz's that Thursday afternoon, my bank account is slowly creeping back towards the five figure mark again. Eventually I'll get a car so I won't have to be driven everywhere, but I figure that will come when I get the steady gig at Sedução.

When I get to Fritz's, the neighborhood bar looks much smaller. I see every imperfection I never noticed before. Every chip of paint on the walls, every scratch on the bar. None of it is shiny and new like Sedução, which has become my second home.

The stage is tiny, much tinier than I remember. I have no idea how we're going to fit everything on it.

"Hey, Vanni," Cheryl greets as she approaches. "How does it look?"

I check myself immediately. Otherwise I'll hurt her feelings. "Great," I lie. "Everything ready to go?"

"I think so," she says. "I mean obviously we can't accommodate the kind of lighting rig that you wanted to bring in. No pyrotechnics, nothing like that. Sorry."

"No worries," I tell her. "If nothing else, we can do the whole thing unplugged. As long as I celebrate my birthday here, I'm golden."

"If you're sure," she says and I nod.

I'm still working on how to accommodate my show with the venue's limitations when Pam arrives. I suck in a breath when I see her stride through the door. She doesn't see me at first. Instead she has a ready smile for Cheryl, who is preparing the bar area for the evening ahead. She shrugs out of her jacket as she heads to the bar.

I can't deny it. She looks great. She's even gained a little weight since I've seen her last. Her hips are fuller, as are her breasts. Her hourglass figure makes my arms ache to hug her and pull those soft, appealing curves closer to me.

Her skin is clearer, no doubt thanks to all the marital intercourse she must be having. I try not to snarl as I think about Doug. He gets to hold her every single night, the lucky bastard.

How can I still want this woman? I'm fucking one of the hottest ladies in New York City, and yet just seeing Pam again has me salivating like a dog.

I just can't get over the fact that she will never belong to me. That subtle promise she had made with her eyes time and time again, every time she looked up at me like I could hang the moon, has come undone.

By no surprise, *"Come Undone"* is on the set list for our intimate performance at Fritz's.

The only thing worse than not being able to have her is not being able to talk to her about it. And that's what I miss most. When I was at my lowest, she was able to pick me up and set me right again. If that's not love, then what is?

And it's that love I want. I want it more than I want to screw around with Tina. I want it more than I want to stack up lovers by the dozen after each and every show.

I just want someone to give a shit. And when no one else could manage to do that, she did.

How can I let go?

I walk over to the bar. Cheryl, who spots me coming, discretely excuses herself. When Pam turns to face me, it's like an electrical current surging throughout my entire body.

From the look in her eyes, I know she feels it too. "Hi, Pam," I say. Just saying her name feels intimate, like a verbal kiss.

"Vanni," she says with a tremor in her voice. She glances over my new clothes. I reek of money and I know it. "You look good."

"So do you," I compliment in return. "Married life really agrees with you."

She turns away. It sounds like I'm baiting her for another argument, but I'm not. At least I don't think I am.

Instead she changes the subject. "Has everything been coming together for the show?"

"I think so. I mean, you were right, the stage is a little small, but we can work with it."

She nods. "Good. Gotta say, you've practically sold out. You were right. Everyone wants to know about the hometown boy who did good."

I give her a grin. "I'm still at the starting gate. There will be more to celebrate next year." Her gaze falters. "How about you? Do you have good things to celebrate this year?"

Please don't tell me you're pregnant, please don't tell me you're pregnant...

"Of course," she answers with a sunny, albeit forced, smile. "The bar is doing really well, much better than a year ago. Dad's biopsy came back clean. Mom just lost fifteen pounds...,"

I interrupt her. "I meant with you. Are you okay? Are you happy?"

She chuckles nervously. "Of course. Why wouldn't I be?"

I swallow any retort. "How's Doug?"

"He's out of town," she answers, though I can tell she doesn't want to.

"Oh?"

"He's a pilot," she explains. "No holidays off."

"I wish I had known that," I tell her. "I would have come by to say hello on Thanksgiving."

Her eyes meet mine. "I went to see you," she admits softly.

"You did?" She nods. "Why?"

"I was worried that you'd be alone in that old house by yourself, without Lori, without your aunt. And that just seemed sad to me. I know the firsts are."

My heart aches that she knows about the firsts. And that she cared enough to want to help me through one of them. That's classic Pam at her best, and what I miss most. "I wish I'd been home," is all I can say.

"Probably for the best."

Finally I nod. "I guess so."

But I can't get her out of my mind for the rest of the day. I can't stop wondering what might have happened had I chosen to stay at the brownstone that Thanksgiving, and if she had shown up, all alone, maybe with some Chinese takeout or something, so that we could share our lonely holiday together.

Just thinking of having her alone at the brownstone is enough to make my gut twist. It's like I keep getting so close to everything I want, and it just keeps skipping on past.

I'm out of sorts that night as I return to the penthouse. I prowl around the empty space, amped up with no way to release the tension. I end up in Tina's large tub overlooking the city, soaking to my neck, my hands on my body as I daydream about Pam–the only one who got away.

I know that's why I want her. I try to remind myself that she's married. She's *married*. She's **married**.

But God, how I want her. I spend my night jacking off, indulging in naughty fantasies, thinking of how she looks, how she sounds, how she feels. I come hard thinking about her, but I'm still in a state when Tina returns that night. I pick her up at the door and carry her up to her sumptuous round bed. We topple together and I make quick work of her clothes, tossing them aside.

And though she responds to my touch, and though she knows just where to touch, suck or please me, it still leaves me frustrated. Tina doesn't miss a thing. "What's wrong, Vanni?"

"Just nervous about the shows," I dismiss.

She chuckles and reaches for some lotion next to her bed, to smooth into her delicate, perfect skin. "Nerves are for amateurs. You know what you need to do on that stage. I watch you do it every day in rehearsal. No one works harder than you, except for maybe Yael."

It's high praise, especially coming from her. I open my mouth to say that it's not about the performance at all. I need everything to go well because of how wrong it all went last December. Fate fucked me over well. I'll never approach another birthday or another Christmas without wondering which shoe is going to drop. It has to be perfect because I'm too afraid of it all going to shit... because it always seems to go to shit.

So I try to micromanage everything to make sure it goes off without a hitch. Maintaining that control is the only thing that keeps me sane, because it's the only thing that keeps me from remembering.

If I can't remember, I can't dread. I can't fear.

I can get through each painful day without ticking off in my head exactly what I was doing a year ago. Aunt Susan made her last batch of chicken cacciatore a year ago tonight. Lori was still faithful a year ago tonight. I was still in the brownstone a year ago, life made sense and I lived in blissful ignorance what kind of catastrophe waited right around the corner.

But I say nothing to Tina. It's pointless. She won't get it. "You're probably right," is all I say.

"Of course I'm right. I'm always right. Which reminds me, have you talked to the guys yet about the name?"

I sigh. For the last two weeks, Tina has been trying to get us to rename the band. *The Yael Satterlee Experiment: Featuring Giovanni Carnevale* is quite the mouthful, and even harder to fit on the marquee. So far she hasn't even put our names on any of the fliers simply because there's not enough room to fit. At the moment, we're the "And Many More" acts promised under the bigger names she's booked for the event, and I trust her with that about as far as I can throw her.

I brought it up to Yael exactly once. He had gotten up, taken his guitar and left without saying another word. None of us knew if he'd even come back the next day to practice. Fortunately he had, but none of us want to wander down that prickly path again.

"I've talked. It hasn't gone well. This is Yael's band, Tina."

Her perfectly waxed eyebrow arched. "Funny, but I remember you mentioning something about how you went in on halfsies for the band transportation."

"Which we haven't used," I point out. With all the stuff we've been doing for Sedução, there hasn't been any real time to explore venues outside of the city. "It's mostly taking up space in a garage."

She purses her lips for a moment before she finally brushes off the entire conversation. "Nothing we have to solve tonight," she says as she cuddles up to me.

As it turns out, it's a problem she wants to solve the very next day. She calls for a meeting at her penthouse, which is unusual. And the day starts like any other day, where she spends much of the morning with me trying on different clothes for my stage show, although I know that's mostly because this has become a sexy habit of ours. She sits on the bed as I pose in all the clothes she suggests. I get her all worked up by singing and posing, and then, when we can't stand it anymore, I take off everything and pin her to the bed to fuck her brains out.

Hell, I don't even know that the boys are coming until Bertram announces that they've arrived.

"Thank you, Bertram," she tells him. "Is the dining room prepared?"

Bertram nods and then leaves. I turn to her. "Prepared? Prepared for what?"

"Just a little impromptu meeting," she says as she rises from the bed. "Come on. Our guests are waiting."

We enter the sunny dining room, where Yael, Felix and Bobby now sit. There are glasses of champagne in front of them, as well as delicate, tempting finger foods.

She links her arm with mine as we approach the table. "I'm so glad you could make it," she tells them before gesturing to the goodies. "Please. Help yourself."

Yael is instantly on guard. "Fattening us up for the slaughter?"

She chuckles. "Something like that," she says as she drinks from her glass. She catches my gaze and nods to a chair. I sit on command. *Good Vanni.*

"So Vanni tells me that you all have an RV or bus or something to make shows out of town?"

Yael nods. "We just haven't really been able to book anywhere but the city."

She leans back in her chair. "That's a shame. If you want to build up a fan base, you have to be willing to expand."

"We're willing," Yael insists. "But where the flesh is willing, the wallet is weak."

She chuckles again. "Fortunately for you, I have no such limitations." She reaches for the folder sitting right in front of her. She pulls out a piece of paper and slides it over to Yael, who looks it over with a furrowed brow.

"What is this?"

"Gigs if you want them. Philadelphia. Atlantic City. Almost every major city from Boston all the way to Miami. I've got a lot of friends, Yael. If I recommend a band, they usually get booked. And, if you'll note those numbers next to the names, you'll see they're willing to pay you pretty well for it."

"That's great," he says. "What's the catch?"

She leans forward with a smile. "See, that's what I like about you, Yael. You don't mince words. I shall be equally forthcoming. The name of your band is a problem. It's too long. It won't sell. I can't put it on a marquee and make it pop."

"So?"

"So, if you want to start using that dusty ol' RV and travel the country, bringing your sound to the people, you're going to have to change it. The minute you do, I'll book at least six shows for you within the first six months of 2006."

Yael smirks. "Six shows, six months, 2006. I think that's the sign of the devil."

"I wear better shoes," she assures him. "And I'm not asking for your soul. I'm asking for one tiny change that will get you more work and more respect. When I see a band with a long name, I assume they don't know who they are. Honestly, it's one of the reasons I didn't want to book you guys. The sound is good. We can work on the stage presentation. But the name of your band is the face of your band."

"I thought that was Vanni," Bobby quips.

Her answer, however, is quite serious. "It is. You're lucky to have him as your frontman. He has a very specific image that people are going to remember. It's sexy. *The Yael Satterlee Experiment: Featuring Giovanni Carnevale* is not."

Yael glares at me. I know he thinks I've put her up to this. "So I suppose you've come up with a name."

I shake my head. "I dropped it last week, man."

He leans back in his chair, staring at the paper in front of him. That's a lot of money, with more opportunities to expose our music to a wider audience. It's everything he's always wanted. I know exactly the kind of emotional conundrum he's in, because I've been in similar ever since I met Tina. And I know she's won when he says, "So what kind of name were you thinking?"

"It's your band," she assures, but I know that's just a bone she's throwing. "But I've always found that picking a name you can easily brand is always a good start."

"How so?" Felix asks.

"If I say Guns N' Roses, you immediately see the logo. It's got an instant visual that hints to the duality of the music, the edge of hard rock with the sensitive musicians who can create such beautiful ballads. You know what you can expect right away. It needs to capture your vibe. The question you need to ask yourself is what kind of vibe that is."

"I picked the *Yael Satterlee Experiment* as homage to bands in the 1970s, where music was so experimental and they could break new ground. I wanted something retro."

"Something with instant recognition," she fills in. "Okay, so you have a 1970s retro rock sound, something experimental. Maybe something drug-influenced," she says as she refers to Felix. "Maybe go with something referring to the elements or to color, something that catches the eye immediately."

It goes on like this for what seems like forever. Now that Yael is willing to consider a name change, we all have suggestions what we could do to properly brand ourselves. We volley suggestions back and forth for about an hour until we finally circle around the idea that we're all dreamers, operating in a world beyond our own.

We decide to make a color specific to our brand, and after a minute or so we all land on and agree to the new band name: Dreaming in Blue. Tina has Frankie on the phone within minutes, to work out some ideas for logos and styling, while Bobby and Yael talk about how they can use lighting during the show, kind of like Pink Floyd, to further strengthen our brand.

As I sit there and stare out at Central Park spread out below us, all I can think about is the new name of my band, which features my favorite color.

Dreaming in Blue. I can practically see the marquee now. They are just three little words, but I know that they were about to change my world.

CHAPTER NINETEEN:

The first time that we perform as Dreaming in Blue is at Fritz's the very next day. We don't have a whole lot of time to work on a logo or merchandise, but Tina wouldn't care about any of that. She has her sights fully set on New Year's Eve.

I don't even expect to see her much throughout the weekend. When I suggest that I'll stay in Brooklyn over the weekend, as sort of a getaway before the crazy weeks leading to the holidays, she consents without a fuss.

The driver drops me off at the brownstone the morning of the 17th. I carry only the clothes I'll need for the show.

This weekend is all about the Old Vanni. I figure I have one more chance to get to see him before he's gone forever, laid to rest with everything else from my ordinary past.

We arrive at Fritz's before the bar opens, where we must finagle a performance on the fly with limited resources. We already know what music we're going to do, we just have to figure out how to scale it back from the stage and effects we normally enjoy at Sedução.

In a way, we're reconnecting as a band again too, taking it back to basics and reminding ourselves who we really are. Even though we all like the new name, it almost feels like we're trying on a new suit to see if it fits.

Fortunately the thing that brought us together–the music– unites us in this endeavor, a true brotherhood. We all have our eyes on the very same prize.

The one good thing about the limitations at Fritz's is that we can use colored lighting. It's already set up for red, blue and green spotlights, so we arrange it to where it's only blue.

The effect is strangely more intimate, especially with the music we have planned to perform. Most of them are one-word titles for some reason, like *"Creep"* and *"Closer."* I also selected *"Drive,"* by the Cars.

They're all pretty depressing for a holiday set, but there's not a lot of room to run around Fritz's stage.

We break out some original tunes, including instrumentals by the band. And, for the first time ever, we'll perform an original tune called *"Dancer Girl,"* with lyrics I wrote specifically for Pam.

She won't hear her song until we play it live, however. Instead I rehearse the other songs, keeping her in my peripheral vision to see how she reacts to my set.

It's my one and only love letter to her, my greatest unrequited love. It's all hers, all the joy and pain and the wishful thinking... all the angst.

And she's where I direct all those things as I start to sing. Since the venue is small, I can see the faces before me. Some are quite familiar, like Alicia, from Cynzia's, or some of the younger members of Susan's church. Even Chelsea makes an appearance, which surprises me, since I haven't seen her in months. But to me, there's only one person in that audience. When I launch into her song, she discretely makes an exit.

I think it's that rejection that hurts the most.

After we take our bow, the entire bar wants to buy us a drink in celebration of our performance and, of course, my birthday. Chelsea immediately finds her way to my side, and it's all I can do to politely extricate myself.

I finally get Cheryl alone. "Where's Pam?"

"Said she needed a break," Cheryl shouts over the din. "This place is a madhouse thanks to you!"

I smile with her. It has been a successful event, if a sold-out crowd of clamoring fans was what I was looking for.

Instead, I find what I'm looking for out in the parking lot, sitting alone in her car. The windows are fogged over, so all I see is her silhouette. It reminds me instantly of Lori, but unlike Lori, there's only one person in Pam's car. I tap on the window. She rolls it down, and I can hear that she's listening to the CD I gave her with me singing her song and *"Make It Happen"* after I first wrote them.

The tears in her eyes break my heart. "You okay?" I ask, even though it's a stupid question. She's not okay. I squat down to bring us face to face.

She bursts into fresh tears and then shakes her head. "I'm sorry. I know this was your special day."

"Hey, don't worry about it," I say as I take her hand in mine. Her skin is so soft... so warm. I want to take her into my arms until her last tear is shed. "What's wrong, Pam?"

She takes a deep breath. The New Vanni kind of hopes she'll tell me that Doug has run off with another woman, though I know that's a terrible thing to wish on her. It would just be so much easier if he weren't in the picture. I could climb into that car, take her into my arms, kiss her soft, pouty lips and tell her everything is going to be okay. Then we could forget about the noisy crowd in the bar and head back to my brownstone, where I'd make love to her at last.

But I can't do anything like that. I can just squat here, helplessly, waiting for her to tell me what the hell is wrong.

"It's stupid," she says.

"Try me," I say back.

A loud bang echoes through the parking lot as the steel door to the bar slams open and a group of happy drunks emerge. Without waiting for permission, I walk around to the passenger side and get inside. She rolls up the window to keep the heat in. All the lights and sounds mingle in the distance, beyond the foggy glass.

She refuses to look at me. "This is going to sound so mean and so selfish, but I guess it just kind of hit me today that you're gone."

I reach for her hand. She lets me hold it. "I'm right here. Why do you think I did this show? I never want you to forget me."

Her bloodshot, teary eyes meet mine. "I'll never forget you, Vanni. Ever."

"So what's the problem?"

"A long time ago, you asked me why I married Doug so suddenly." I nod. I remember. "The truth is...the truth is that I married him because that's the normal life I wanted, and I know you can't give it to me. I knew that the minute I went to see you perform."

My jaw falls open. "You saw me perform?"

She nods, and tells me the venue where she had seen me. It's the bar where I met Tina for the first time... and the day before she flew off to Vegas to elope.

My heart drops as the realization sinks in. She had done that *because of me.*

"I went there because I wanted to see you make your dream come true. And you were so fierce and fearless. It was like you were someone else. And then there were all these girls and they were screaming for you." She trails off and shakes her head. "Before that moment, I thought...," she trails off again, nearly bursting into fresh tears. "I guess I thought that you could still be you and I could still be me and we could see where it was all going. But I knew then that your new life didn't have room for me. I'm too... normal."

The way she says it is like an insult. I shake my head as I hold her hand. "Pam."

She doesn't let me finish. "I just wanted a steady guy, who will be solid and dependable, even if he's not the most exciting person in the world. I want to know that I can count on him. The kind of guy who knows when all the bills are due, or starts a retirement account. Doug is building a stable, dependable, reliable life, and he wanted me to be a part of it. That's what I always wanted. That's what my friends always wanted. That's what my parents always strived for. And I know it's not the most exciting life in the world, but Bruce is a good man," she insists. "My family loves him. His family loves me. Everything is perfect. And if I had met him six months before I met you, there wouldn't even be a problem."

My heart stops. What is she saying?

"It's no secret that I'm attracted to you. Who wouldn't be? You're exciting. You're sexy. You're complex. Every inch the bad boy. I knew from the first time I heard you sing that you were destined to be a star. That's why it was so exciting when you would flirt with me or sing songs to me or write songs for me," she says with another tearful wail as she refers to the song playing. "But I knew then I couldn't walk that path with you. You would never just belong to me. You'd belong to the whole world. And I don't want to compete with anyone."

"There's no competition," I tell her. "I could be anywhere in the city and I wanted to spend this time with you."

"For now," she says. "Until Tina Nunes comes calling."

I swallow hard. I didn't expect her to know about Tina. But it makes sense. Clearly I've just been in denial. "Pam," I start, but again she cuts me off.

"And it's not fair of me to expect you to do anything but run right to her. I'm not Lori," she states vehemently. "I want you to succeed. I want your dreams to come true. And I know they can. You should play at Sedução. You should play bigger venues, from New York City all the way to Los Angeles. All over the world. I want that for you. You deserve to be a huge success. You're a star, Vanni."

The way she says it rips my gut out. It sounds like such a prison sentence coming from her lips, which is essentially what she's saying. Where I'm going, she doesn't want to go. "How is that a bad thing?" I ask.

She sniffs into a wadded up tissue. "Well, that's the thing about stars. You can watch in wonder as they trek across the sky, but you can never get close to one. You can never hold one. You can never do anything but watch it until it fades away."

I open my mouth, but she's not done.

"I've never wanted anyone the way I want you, Vanni. I thought if I got married, if I threw myself into a more stable relationship, I'd forget about you. But I can't. I think about you all the time, wondering what you're doing or if you're happy. When I went to your house on Thanksgiving, I knew it was the worst thing I could do. I harbored fantasies, I'll admit it. It's not right, but it's the God's honest truth. If you weren't there, I'd be reminded, again, that you completely out of my reach. If you were there, then I'd have been tempted to stay there with you. It's not fair to Doug. It's not fair to me. And it's not fair to you. I can never be what you want me to be, Vanni. We need to stop pretending otherwise."

She pulls her hand from mine. "Pam," I start again.

"I need you to go, Vanni. I need you to go and never come back. If you care about me at all, you have to let me go. I have the life I want. I'm not emotionally equipped to sign on as a lifelong groupie, trailing you around wherever you lead. That's never what I wanted for myself."

"Then we can be friends," I offer. I'm desperate now. She's about to sever some of the last fragile strings to my old life–the old me.

She shakes her head. "No, we can't. We'll always wonder what if, and you know it."

"What if we don't have to wonder?" I say. If she came looking for me on Thanksgiving, going to my house, feeling the way she does, then wasn't that a real possibility? That we could be together at last? "If this thing is too big to fight, why don't we just give in to it?"

"Because that's not the person I want to be, Vanni. And if that's the person you want me to be, then you were never really my friend at all."

I stare at her, speechless. She's admitted that she wants me. She's admitted that she can't stay away from me. Yet she's kicking me to the curb?

"Now, if you'll please go. I have to get back inside."

"No," I say at once. "I'm not going anywhere." I lean forward, grab her face in my hand. I hold her close for a moment, memorizing every lovely detail of her face. She trembles against me. I know it's what she wants and what she fears most. I can't stop myself. My lips crash upon hers and I kiss her hard. She fights me by clenching her mouth closed, pushing at my chest with her hands. She's fighting for her integrity, but I gave mine up a long time ago. I indulge that kiss, even though it's stolen. Not just from another man... but from her.

When she finally pulls away, she slaps me hard across the face. "Get the fuck out of my car!" she screeches. "Get the fuck out of my life!"

I'm rooted to the spot as she hits me again. She bursts into more tears as she pummels my chest, calling me every name in the book.

I say nothing else as I grab her hands and hold her still. My gaze never wavers from hers. I pull her close one more time. Her eyes widen as I stare at her mouth, red and puffy from my stolen kiss. "One day you're going to change your mind."

I slam out of the car and head back into the bar for two things. I want a stiff drink, and I want to find Chelsea.

Pam is right. I am a star. And I'll be damned if I go home alone.

Pam doesn't come in right away. When she does, her eyes are puffy and her makeup is gone. Our eyes meet as I finish off the first of six shots, all bought for me by my new friends. I keep the adoring Chelsea under one arm, cuddling her close. I even kiss her where Pam can see. If she was ready to throw me to the curb, then let her take the consequences that follow.

I was ready to love her... honestly and legitimately... and she pushed me away. Once again I'm abandoned by one of the very few people left in this world to give a damn about me. Fuck her. Let her go home to her boring husband and her boring life. I'm alone but I'm not lonely. Plenty of women want to be with me, including the cute young thing at my side.

I wave to all my fans as I corral Chelsea from the club. I hold her close as we walk back to the brownstone.

I barely get us in the front door before I'm all over her. My hands roam her familiar body as I kiss her deep and long. I slam the door shut behind us, where I press her against the door. "You want me?" I ask and she nods. "Tell me."

Her voice is soft and sweet in my ear. "I want you, Vanni."

"Good," I say as I nudge her bare knees apart with mine. "Because I want you."

I reach down to release my cock from my jeans. Before I can slip a condom from my back pocket, we both hear someone clear their throat.

I spin around to find Tina sitting on my sofa. "What the fuck?!"

Tina just smiles as she stands to her feet. "Surprise."

I quickly zip up and stumble away from Chelsea, who pushes down her dress. Tina looks from one of us to the other.

"Care to introduce me to your friend?"

Though I was feeling no pain thanks to the six shots at the bar, I'm shocked into sobriety by this new development. "This is Chelsea," I stammer. "She's an old friend."

"Old?" Tina repeats as she gives Chelsea the once over. "Certainly not the word that comes to my mind."

"This is Tina," I tell Chelsea. "She's a friend."

"Oh, darling. Don't be shy," she says as she walks over to me and links her arm with mine. To Chelsea she says, "We live together."

Chelsea's eyes widen as she glances between us. I turn to Tina.

"What are you doing here?" I demand in a low voice.

"I came to hear all about the show, of course." Her cool gaze slides to Chelsea. "I'm afraid you'll have to excuse us, dear. We have important business to discuss." She pulls out her cell phone and calls for the car. "My driver will take you anywhere you want to go."

Chelsea looks up at me, as if expecting me to step in. And I probably should, but in my new sober state, I realize now that everything that I've done to further the band could crumple in a heartbeat if I piss off Tina Nunes. All my eggs are in her basket, and she could crack them all with a snap of her finger. The last thing I want to do is give her any reason to back out of her promise to let us perform on NYE. "I'll call you," I offer to Chelsea instead. I know it sounds lame, but I don't know what else to do.

She nods and then slips through the front door, humiliated and frustrated. Tina steps away from me to lock it behind her.

"What the hell was that about?"

She snickers to herself. "Oh, darling. I have so much more work to do with you. That girl? Really? She looks twelve."

"She's nineteen," I grit through clenched teeth, pissed I feel even remotely compelled to defend myself.

"Yes, well. That's still too young. The more attention you get, the more of a target you put on your back for young silly girls who want to snag themselves a rock star." She walks over to the sofa and plops down. "Now come tell me how the show went."

My jaw drops open as I stare at her. "Are you serious?"

"When I talk about business, I'm always serious. You should know that by now. Or has one night in the sticks warped your reality?"

With a sinking gut I think about Pam. "My reality has always been warped," I tell her before I stalk to the kitchen to find something, anything, to drink.

I've halfway guzzled a fifth of whiskey by the time she saunters in to find me. She pulls another bottle of vino from the shelf, before digging around in the drawers for a corkscrew. Eventually I help her find it.

"So what was all that about anyway? Are we supposed to be exclusive now?"

"Heavens no," she laughs. "You were off duty tonight," she adds with a smile. "But, if the choice of bed partner is me or some pathetic groupie, you should always pick me. Friends are hard to come by in this business. You'll do well not to burn any bridges if you can help it."

I lean against the table. "So... what? You just came here to fuck?"

She rolls one of her shoulders. "Among other things. I wasn't lying before. I really am interested in how your show went."

I chug some more whiskey. "It was a smashing success. Everyone loved us. And I hated every minute of it." I kill the bottle. She simply crosses her arms and waits. Finally, "I did it for a girl, okay?"

"Of course you did," she says as she puts her glass on the counter. "My sensitive, tender-hearted Romeo. But oh, foolish boy. Haven't you figured out love has no place in the spotlight?" She walks over to me, running her hands along my arms. "Sex, drugs and rock and roll. That's the lie you're selling. You don't want to fuck it up with the truth."

"I'm not lying to anyone," I tell her.

"Of course you are," she says. "You've never stopped. You've lied to the guys in your band. You've lied to me. Hell, you're even lying to yourself. You think there's this ordinary guy underneath it all, one who can go visit regular families in Queens on Thanksgiving, watch a little football on TV and play with a couple of kids, and that'll make it easier to stomach selling your soul for fame and glory."

I glared down my nose at her. "So you know about Sasha, too."

She leans close. "I know everything, Vanni. I told you I was going to make you a star. I've invested a lot of time, money and effort into this endeavor. And I'm not going to sit back and allow you to wreck everything I've managed to do for you. You're going to have to make up your mind what you want to do, Vanni. You can stay here in this run-down house, go back to slinging pizzas at Cynzia's. Chase after some doe-eyed groupie who will land your ass in jail if you're not careful, or wind up giving you some screaming brat you have to support. You can crawl into every whiskey bottle in Brooklyn and live out the rest of your ordinary life with nothing but your unrealized dreams to keep you company. Or," she says as she steps even closer, "You can be a good boy. You can listen to what I've trying to teach you. You can make the world stand up and take notice that you are goddamn Giovanni Carnevale and that means something whether they know it yet or not. You can stop trying to piss away everything I'm doing for you to make you a fucking legend. But you better make that choice quick and stick to it. Because if I walk away, good luck trying to find anyone who can do for you what needs to be done." Her eyes capture mine. "You just need to ask yourself one question. Who do you want to be?"

I can't decide whether I love her or hate her as I stare down into her deceptively beautiful face. I know everything she is saying is the absolute truth, and it takes someone who really gives a damn to say it so bluntly. She's invested in me, way more than anyone else had been, except for maybe my aunt. She's willing to move mountains and hand me the life I want practically on a gold platter. With her I get to attend important parties, meet influential people, and live in a fucking high-rise apartment on goddamn Park Avenue.

Fuck *yes* that's the life I want.

I grab her by the waist and pull her to my body, molding her to every sinewy line. I capture her mouth in a severe kiss, where I bite at her lips and practically choke her with my tongue. I reach around her to slam everything that is on the table right onto the floor, lying her down on her back on the old scratched table where I used to eat oatmeal and do homework.

I hike up her skirt. There's a primal growl in my throat as I discover she's not wearing any underwear. Of course she's wet for me, holding my life in the palm of her hands has always turned her on. And making her scream has always turned me on, so I unzip my pants and release my hard, pulsating cock before I climb between her spread legs and impale her with precious little preamble.

There's no lovemaking about it as I ride her hard. One hand clasps handfuls of her hair as the other squeezes her breast. I bend to take a bite out of her skin. I know how far I can go with Tina, farther than I've ever gone with anyone before.

The more aggressive I get, the wilder she gets. She's screaming for me to fuck her harder and faster. The sound bounces off the fading wallpaper. I grunt like an animal as I comply. Thanks to the liquor I've been guzzling, I can see the ghosts of my past, including Old Vanni himself, linger in the shadows of that kitchen.

Let them get an eyeful of the New Vanni in all his glory. I put all the missing pieces together with every powerful stroke, filling in the full picture of the man who will lead Dreaming in Blue right into 2006. I unload in her with a victorious yell.

The shadows scatter back to their corners. This is the only truth that matters now. This is who I am. This is who I was meant to be. And if anyone doesn't like it, they can go straight to hell.

From now on, I live for no one but me.

CHAPTER TWENTY:

The rest of 2005 is a blur. I barely notice my first Christmas without my aunt because I'm busy preparing for the NYE show.

This is not an accident.

Tina's not exactly a holiday person, so the house is never decorated, which helps. Aside from a couple of parties, we can throw all our energy into the upcoming show and not think about Christmas at all.

I don't even make it back to Bensonhurst to spend any more time at the brownstone. That's part of another life now, with painful scars that have only just begun to scab over.

Instead I rehearse the band to the point of exhaustion. Tina is very hands on with the project. She's got dozens of tips and hints to make it better.

"I want you to make an entrance," she tells me. "Let them start the intro while you're back there behind the fog machine. Then, when that spotlight hits you, you fly out of that cloud of blue smoke and attack that stage like you mean it."

I nod and we set up the intro again. Like always, she's completely right. That it makes it better.

If Sasha notices that I'm not talking much anymore, she doesn't say anything. But I can tell she's watching me. I can feel her concern.

Too little, too late. I've got shit to do, and convincing everyone that I'm okay is not high on my list of priorities.

Of course I'm okay. I'm living with a sexy, powerful woman in a luxury penthouse, I'm about to play one of the hottest venues in town on one of the biggest nights of the year. I've got the next six months set up for me, with a regular gig at Sedução and six, count 'em, six, out-of-town shows.

Finally Tina proves true to her word, which makes me even more loyal to her, even though there are already some grumblings in the band.

I want to remind them that they wouldn't have all these opportunities if it wasn't for me, but I'll hold onto that little nugget until I need it.

Instead I focus on the business, on the music, and on Tina. Even in the bedroom, she's refining this new Vanni's hard edges. Since she's older than me, she teaches me things that I never learned before. She's up for anything, no matter how raunchy. There are always new toys to try out. I thought she might shatter into a million pieces with the orgasm I gave to her after I handcuffed her.

Nothing is forbidden with her. She even suggests that we could invite other women into our bed, provided that she gets to select them. "No teenagers," she repeats again as we prowl around a swanky party full of the most beautiful, successful people in the city.

We take home a model who is so beautiful she doesn't even seem real. Watching her with Tina is all the Christmas gift I need.

By December 31st, I'm so ready to hit that stage for my Sedução debut I feel like I'm going to burn up in my own skin. And this time, unlike before, we're actually on the roster. Dreaming in Blue is scheduled to perform between two up-and-coming musical acts. The crowd in the joint is insane. They go even crazier as I jump out of that smoky mist and assault them with a sexually brazen act that has all the party girls down front ready to hop up on stage with me, which of course I allow because who *doesn't* want to dance with sexy, beautiful women?

Our set is a resounding success. By midnight, I'm on stage with my band and the rest of the talent booked that night, counting down to an amazing new year. I sweep Tina up into my arms for a deep, long kiss. I can't wait to see what happens next.

We head down to Atlantic City in January, where we're booked in one of the hottest resorts. We draw the groupies like flies, but I resist any after-parties. Tina is right. I don't need to follow my dick around anymore. "Leave them wanting more," she advised as her fingers trailed down my body. "As long as they love you more than you love them, they'll never stop coming back."

But that's not the real reason I have to abstain. I know now the one painful truth: The sweet, normal girls I always seem to favor want more than the life I can give them, especially now.

Pam is certainly proof positive of that. I wouldn't give up this life for anyone, and the girls worth having understand that. Best not to open that can of worms if at all possible.

I just save it for Tina when I get home, no matter how much Bobby pouts about it.

With me in groupie lockdown, he has lost his best wingman to seduce pretty young things by the dozen. Felix has no interest playing the field, neither does Yael. They both find Bobby's behavior sophomoric and dangerous. I finally give him the same warning Tina gave me, to be careful with girls who are so young, who might have expectations that he won't be able to meet.

He just shrugs me off and finds a couple more girls to hit on.

February we hit the road again, this time heading to Boston. I keep my nose to the grindstone, trying to figure out ways to improve our performances. I'm writing like a fiend, so generally I spend road time in the back, head in a notebook, jotting down lyrics. I usually bring Yael into the process once I get the melody down, and we end up collaborating on several songs. We've got our eye on recording a demo now, though Tina thinks it's premature.

"You need more experience," she says. "We'll talk about it after June, when things slow down."

Only things don't slow down. For Spring Break we're in Florida, where we book at least three more gigs for summer.

It's May before I make it back to Bensonhurst. I don't bother with Fritz's. There's no point. Instead, I decide to renovate the brownstone. I'm not living in it, so I can pretty much gut it and change it into something a little nicer. It's my biggest investment, after all. I want to add to its value in a way that poor Aunt Susan could never afford to do.

I'm doing well by this point, with some disposable income outside of what I want to spend on the band. I even have my very own car. Of course, it's actually Tina's. She bought a brand new sports car for me to zip around town in, so the whole city knows she's grooming a star. With the expensive clothes and the fancy car, plenty of girls try to hit on me. I just tell them to come see me at a show and I'm done with it.

I follow Tina's advice to a T.

I drive by the cemetery where Aunt Susan is buried, but I don't stop. I haven't stopped since November, before Thanksgiving. I feel like a shit about it when it crosses my mind, but surely she'd understand. Building a career takes time and energy. Some people go to college. I lug equipment across the eastern seaboard, performing for larger and larger crowds, trying to perfect our brand.

It's a breakneck pace, one that takes its toll on some of the members of the group. Yael wants to record a demo, and Bobby just wants more time to party. Only Felix and I seem to understand that we need to keep our heads down and do the job.

By July, though, I'm exhausted. Tina surprises me with a trip to Portugal. I finally get to break in my first passport. We stroll along white sand and make love in the surf of our private beach. It's perfectly blissful until I bring up recording a demo record.

"I told you, you're not ready."

I heave an exasperated sigh. "You keep saying that, but I've busted my ass for seven months straight. I don't really know how much harder I have to work to be ready."

She runs her finger down my abdomen, which now sports a natural tan. "Anyone ever tell you that your worst quality is a lack of patience?" She cuddles next to me. "We're here to relax. We can think about all of that on the plane ride home."

Only we don't talk about it. She takes some anti-anxiety pills and sleeps most of the way.

July fades into August. Our work load has lessened because we're staying primarily in New York, Connecticut, Philadelphia and New Jersey. Despite our growing success, I notice that our venues stay pretty much the same. Same crowd. Same spots on the roster. Same pay.

And I'm not the only one who notices it. All the guys are vocal about how we've stagnated. When I bring it up to Tina, she just blows it off. "You'll get there," she promises again and again.

But by September, we all notice that there's a new musical act inching its way up the leaderboard at Sedução, with a super hot Latino singing lead. The very day they get to headline, which Dreaming in Blue has never done, I break every speed limit to get back to the penthouse to confront Tina about it.

Instead I find her fucking said super hot Latino in our bed.

"Are you fucking kidding me?" I scream at her before I lunge at the young man who couldn't be more than twenty-one. He puts up a fight and we exchange blows, which bloodies both of our faces and blackens both of our eyes.

"Maybe I should just go back to my brownstone," I say. I'm going to force her to make a choice like she forced me one to make one once upon a time.

"Maybe you should," she tells me as she covers herself with an expensive silk robe. "It's becoming clearer and clearer to me that might be where you belong."

It's the only time in my life I've ever wanted to hit a woman. I spent all this time as her pampered plaything, on the line, waiting for her to fulfill her promises that she never had any intention to fulfill.

I had jumped through all her hoops and did all her bidding, but in the end I realized the ball had never left her court at all. And now she was ready to take it and go home, leaving me as high and dry as the first time I had walked into her club.

Instead I take my anger out on her perfectly regal bedroom, slamming her vanity chair into the mirror and using the broken legs to smash anything that sparkles like it's worth something.

The last time I leave her penthouse, I'm escorted out.

And that fight isn't the worst one I have that week. We may not be fuck buddies anymore, but we are in business together. When I ask her what our future is at the club, she says that there are no hard feelings. However our gigs dry up at Sedução when she wants her new Latin boy toy and his band to get top billing and I flat out refuse to play before him. "It's just business," she says over and over again, but all I can think about is how she looked on top of that motherfucker. That I'm wasted on nonstop expensive champagne doesn't help. I sign the death warrant to our best venue when I slur, "Why do the whores always like it on top?"

Because I've cost us our most lucrative venue, I end up clashing with the band over how tightly Tina held the reigns on our career. "Admit it. You were fucking whipped, dude," Bobby says.

"What the fuck do you know about it?" I yell back. "You can't get a girl to fuck you if she's old enough to know better. Fuck off."

He lunges at me, taking a swing. "You followed your dick and painted us all in a corner!"

I swing back. "At least you're not in jail!"

Felix and Yael finally break us up and separate us, but the damage is done.

Bobby Rocco officially quits Dreaming in Blue on September 28. We suspend any future shows until we find a replacement.

As it turns out, that is easier said than done. We hold auditions for two weeks solid but none of the guys feels like the right fit to me. Now that I have the band whittled down to Yael and Felix, I want someone who matches our sensibilities and has our same kind of drive. We essentially have to start over, and I want someone committed to the cause.

In mid-October, a tall, lanky guy with dark hair and a British accent arrives at the loft, with a cute blonde in tow. "The name's Iain Wallis," he says. "This is my girlfriend, Alana."

I study him thoroughly. I love his look, which will fit right in with ours. He's got long hair. He's skinny but handsome. Best of all he's not some road hound ready to blow all his cash on groupies and booze. He's older than Bobby, certainly more settled with a steady girlfriend who seems to adore him. Best of all he's been in bands before, mostly in England. When he shows us he can adapt to any style of music we play, Yael, Felix and I know we've found another musical brother.

He's an official member of the band by the beginning of November, though there's not much we can promise him at this point. We have no gigs for the foreseeable future. While we were fighting to keep our band together so we could perform, every venue we had come to rely on had dried up. They simply weren't interested. Dreaming in Blue belonged to Tina Nunes, and no one wanted to touch us with a ten-foot pole.

I suck up every last iota of pride and head back to Sedução. Maybe now that Tina can see we've replaced our weak link, she'll give us another chance. My nest egg, which I got used to spending freely during my days as a free-wheeling gigolo, is depleting by the day. I know I have to do something fast or else I'll have to put this dream to rest once and for all.

I'm intercepted by Sasha, who tells me that Tina won't see me. "You never should have called her a whore," she says.

"She never should have fucked around," I respond.

"Come on, Vanni. It's not like you both were exclusive. You weren't even in love."

I lean across the bar. "There's no room for love in rock and roll."

She sighs. "You can make it without her, that's all I'm saying."

"Really?" I challenge. "Because without her we're playing crap gigs where nobody gives a shit if we're in tune or not. She's ruined me."

"She didn't ruin you, Vanni. You ruined yourself. You believed the lie because you wanted to. She was never going to give you a headlining gig. She was using you every bit as much as you were using her. And you're smart enough that I know that you know that."

I look away. "Do you know how hard it is to find someone who will believe in you in this business? Who will stick their neck out? Who will sacrifice something of themselves to help you out?"

She laughs. "Oh, honey. You really don't think she was being altruistic, do you?" She sighs and then grabs a ledger from under the bar. She opens it to show the kind of income Sedução enjoys, just on the cover charges alone. "You ever wonder why she sent you out of town? She was farming you out to her friends and keeping you far away from the competition. She had to keep you isolated and sheltered, otherwise you'll figure out what kind of stupid game she's playing. She could have found you a studio and recorded your first demo record if she wanted. You guys had a real audience here. If she was really looking after you, if she truly believed in you, why didn't she give you a percentage of what they take in at the door like all her other mid-range acts? She offered you a flat rate, and a cheap one at that." She shakes her head as she clicks her tongue. "Everyone wants that guaranteed money, though. That might have been okay when you started, but you've never failed to pack this place in all the time you've played here. This is the kind of stuff you need to be negotiating, Vanni. Do you know how many gigs you can get if you just offer a split? And you can bring the audiences in now. All you have to do is beef up your Internet presence, so people know where you're playing when you're playing. The fans you've already made will find you. The person you need to have confidence in isn't Tina, Vanni. It's you."

I noticed she hasn't called me Joe once. Somehow it makes what she's saying more important. "So what do I do?"

She leans forward. "I'm talking to the nice guy that's still left under all this polish and sheen and bullshit. You know the one, who played with my kids and watched football with my dad, who stood up for me against my asshole ex. He's still in there and I believe in him even if you don't. If you ever want to be that guy again, you'll turn around and march out of here and never look back. There are people who will eat you alive in this business, and Tina's at the top of that list. She can't help you. She won't help you. All she'll do is turn you into a soul-sucking user like she is. You're better than that. That's why you have to go, and you totally can. In the end you call the shots for your own career and that's all."

I'm scared as shit to do exactly what she says to do. It may not have been perfect, but Sedução was a helluva lot more money and exposure than we had before, even if it did keep us chained like dogs to Tina's leash. Sure it may have been skewed to her advantage, but that's how you run business, right? You have to look out for yourself.

And that's what I do as I leave Sedução for the last time.

I don't know where I'm going from here. It's more uncertain than it's ever been. I find my way to Fritz's without even trying to.

I see her face the minute I open the door. Despite how much I tried to bury them, all the old feelings rush back. I know it's the same for her the minute our eyes meet. She's panicked to see me because she still gives a damn.

And I so need someone to just give a damn.

"We're not open yet," she says.

"I'm not a customer," I reply. "I want to book Fritz's for another performance."

She shakes her head. "I'm sorry, Vanni. I can't. You shouldn't be here."

"Why?"

"I told you why."

I slam the wood flap onto the counter as I walk behind the bar. "Yeah, I know what you told me," I say as I back her into the bar, with an arm on either side of her. "But this isn't about you and me. It's about my fucking life, Pam."

The words barely eke out of my throat. The longer I stare at her, the more emotional I get. Any fear that she might have had evaporated the second she saw the tears in my eyes. She takes me into her arms without question.

"What's wrong?" she murmurs into my ear.

I clasp her tight. So soft, so warm, surrounding me everywhere in a jasmine-scented cloud. She feels like love. "Everything," I manage.

I feel like a fool, but I know Pam doesn't judge. Of all the people in my life, Pam and Sasha don't judge.

They're also completely off limits as a married lady and a single mom. Finding anything meaningful in a personal relationship seems as impossible as breaking in.

So many missed opportunities... so many stupid mistakes. For the first time in a long time, I wonder what the hell it's all for. It was this kind of hopelessness that drove me to chase after street gangs in Philadelphia, before my Mama decided to risk it all and come to Brooklyn.

Now there's nowhere to go.

"Come on," she says as she leads me from behind the bar and towards the back, where her office is located. She shuts the door behind us and I flop down on top of her big wooden desk. "I could use a drink," I mutter, suddenly embarrassed by my emotional outburst.

"You've had enough," she tells me as she sits next to me.

"Sometimes I think there will never be enough," I confess. It's one of my dirty little secrets. Whenever things get tough, I reach for the bottle. I've been doing it since I was fifteen years old, even though I know that was what drove my dad away.

Maybe I'm destined to be just like him. Drunk and alone.

"You were right to marry whatshisname," I tell her.

"That's the booze talking. Let me get you some coffee," she offers as she steps away from the desk. I pull her back by the wrist. Our eyes meet and all those old feelings spark to life.

"I don't want coffee," I say in a soft voice.

Her breath quickens as she realizes her error. She's stuck with me, three sheets to the wind, in her locked office. There's nothing now to stop us but her willpower.

"Vanni," she murmurs, and it just sets my nerve endings on fire. I've dreamed about that sweet voice saying my name.

"I know," I say as I pull her closer. "I should go."

She gulps as her body makes contact with my massive chest. She feels small and dainty in comparison. She's so flustered she can't even speak. My hand snakes up to caress her face. "Do you know how long I've wanted to kiss you?" I ask. She shakes her head. "Since the first time I held you in my arms and felt you swoon against me. Like now," I add in a whisper.

My mouth nearly lands upon hers when she utters the only two words that can stop me. "I'm pregnant," she says softly.

I stare, unblinking, into her face for a long moment. I want to ask so many questions. When? How? *Why?*

But I already know why. She's a good girl. A sweet girl. And she needs a normal love that I know in my gut I'm not capable to provide. Doug provided that for her. A decent guy. An ordinary guy.

A guy I can never, ever be.

I hold her so long that she shudders against me. "Please," she tries again. She's holding onto her honor with a death grip. "Let me go."

I run a thumb across her bottom lip, so full and ripe and ready to be kissed. And God knows I would kiss her, had she not crushed my heart with her words. There was no way that I would ever stand between a child and its family. Ever. Even for Pam, the first woman I ever came close to loving. And she knows it too, which is why she said what she said, when she did.

There's only one thing left to do.

"Not yet," I finally say, holding on as long as I possibly can. "I'm not done telling you my story."

I can feel her tremble. I tremble in return. I know she can feel it too.

"I sang for you that day. Remember?" She gulps hard again before she nods. "I had just written my first song, and you were the only one who believed I had what it takes to make it. Do you still believe it?"

Her eyes meet mine. "Of course."

My throat aches as I say, "I'm going to miss that."

My heart thunders against my chest. I have one last song to sing. I dig back into the 1970s for a bittersweet ballad from the Manhattans, about two lovers who want one final kiss before they say goodbye. It was one of my Mama's favorite songs. I could only imagine why. Pam's eyes are locked with mine as I deliver probably the most heart-felt performance of my life. My hands slide over her body, over her shoulders and down her side, over the sweet swell of her hip. I stand, and we start to sway to the song. Her eyes flutter shut as she sways against me. Her arms slide around my waist and she lays her head on my shoulder.

When I finish the song, she lifts her head to face me. Slowly my mouth descends on hers, covering her parted lips softly. I feel her swoon against me I deepen the kiss without apology. If it's going to be our last, it's going to count.

My heart swells as she kisses me back.

One hand tangles in her hair as I clutch her tight. Her full breasts press into my chest, and it's all I can do not to cup them in my hands. My palms ache to caress them. Likewise her nails dig into my shoulders as she holds on for dear life.

When I finally drag my mouth away, we're both dazed. It would be so easy to swipe all that crap from her desk and take her right there in her office. Dear God, it's all I want to do. My holy grail... my sweet Pam. I could lift that skirt and plunge inside of her, taking what I've wanted for all these long, lonely months.

But it's not just Pam anymore. It's Pam and her baby, her nice, normal baby, one that ties her forever to a man named Doug, in a life so foreign from mine now that it's like a moon orbiting a distant planet. Her body isn't mine to take. Her love isn't mine to steal. And if I ever cared about her, even a little, I know it's best for everyone if I just let her go.

So I lift her left hand up to inspect that plain gold band that rests on her third finger. The New Vanni didn't give a shit about that ring. We were here first. We have a right to take what we want, because she wants it too. I know she does. I can feel it in her body. I could taste it in her kiss. I can see it in that cloudy look in her beautiful eyes.

I lean forward and leave a long, lingering kiss on her hand. I'm a selfish, entitled shit, but I'm not a bastard. I'm not going to hurt her and I'm not going to let her hurt herself either.

I've got to make some changes if I ever want to get control of my life back–control of *me* back.

"Goodbye," I whisper against her hand.

I finally leave my neighborhood tavern. And I know I'll never return.

CHAPTER TWENTY-ONE:

The month of November is rough for a lot of reasons. I'm drinking too much, for one. I barely leave my house for two. Using Sasha's advice, we finally book some gigs using the split, but the pay is abysmal. Fortunately, Alana has a few ideas.

She works for Schuster and Beckweth, a public relations company in the city, so she understands what kind of promotion we need. She takes over the website almost immediately, working hard to make connections and polish our social media so that we get our fledgling fanbase into the clubs.

By Thanksgiving she's already adopted all of us, and we opt for an orphan's gathering at their Chelsea apartment. Since they're both vegan, it makes it an interesting dinner indeed. Felix shares one of his magical joints with me, which means I'm eating everything that isn't tied down anyway, so it's all good. And it's so far removed from the Thanksgivings of my past it barely hurts.

December limps along much like November. Again, Alana and Iain host the holidays, which makes them a bit easier to face. Despite what Tina had said, Iain and Alana had found love in the crazy rock world, so being around them actually gave me hope that, even if I couldn't have a normal life, I could have a happy one. I start writing better songs, rather than all the bitter, angry ones I had purged after everything that had happened with Tina.

Hell, I'm even able to purge what had happened with Lori, and I know that when I pass her window-shopping on Fifth Avenue. She looks nothing like the last time we saw each other. I'm not sure which change surprises me more: the wedding rings on her finger, or the massive pregnant tummy under her maternity shirt.
Apparently there's something in the water.

I decide to wave the flag first. "I guess congratulations are in order."

"Thanks," she offers awkwardly.

"Tony's?" I ask.

She nods. "We got married last year."

"Ah," I say as I scramble for something more significant to say. She holds her belly as she looks up at me, and I wonder what we had ever shared. Had I really thought that we could ever have a future together, that we had somehow managed to find forever kind of love? Maybe I don't know what the hell love is. But apparently she does, because she was willing to gamble the rest of her life for it.

After everything I'd been through, I really don't know if I'll ever be able to do that. The odds are low I'll ever find anyone I can trust that much again. Except for Alana, every good, decent girl I'd met wanted nothing to do with the chaos that surrounded the life of a rock star.

And who could blame them?

Lori, Pam and Sasha all needed dependable good guys who could put their needs first, and I had never been capable of that with any of them. It was, and is, all about my dream.

I honestly didn't see how any woman could compete with it. Not for real. And not for long.

To her credit, Lori actually looks repentant. "Listen, Vanni. I just want to say I'm sorry for how it all went down. I was such a stupid kid back then. I should have been honest with you from the beginning."

"Ditto," I reply. I know now my biggest mistake was putting my dreams on hold and acting like that was okay, when inside it was killing me.

I'll never do that again, that's for sure.

"No hard feelings," I say, and I'm surprised to find that I actually mean it. "I wish you and Tony all the best."

She smiles. "Thanks. You too." She pauses for a beat before she asks, "Are you still performing?"

I nod but don't say anything. I figure there's no room for gory details in small talk.

"Good," she says. "You should. You're really gifted, and I'm sorry I let my fears get in the way of that."

It's the best thing she could have ever said to me. I reach for a hug. She complies. I feel her belly jump against me, which makes me laugh. How weird and wonderful and alien. "Looks like you have a football player in there."

"A ballerina," she corrects. She looks so calm and serene about it, like she's unraveled some mystery of the universe. I almost envy her.

"Congratulations again," I say before we part ways. I'm glad she's found someone to make her happy, because if that was what she needed, the wedding and the babies and stability, I know I'm not the guy for her, and never had been.

My first, and as it turns out, only, true love is music.

By the time I get home, I already feel like I've been on a spiritual journey. I look around non-decorated home and suddenly miss all the Christmas stuff my aunt would haul out every Thanksgiving so that we could enjoy them from the beginning of the season to the last.

I consider putting up my tree. I even climb up to the attic to fetch some of the decorations, just a few, just so that there's some kind of hint of merriment to liven my holiday.

I stop dead in my tracks when I run across Aunt Susan's gifts to me from 2004, still wrapped, now dusty, hidden away in a forgotten box in the attic.

I sigh as I sit cross-legged on the floor. Maybe Sasha was right. Maybe it is time to open them. The first one is a big one. It's a leather jacket, one I've always wanted. My aunt must have spent a fortune on it, and here it's been hidden in this box all this time. It still smells brand new as I take it out. I run my hands along the fabric, which feels cool and textured against my hand. A tear I don't even realize I've shed splashes on it. I brush it away.

I reach for the next one. It's a long, slender box, so I figure it's a scarf to go along with the jacket. Only this time I'm wrong. Inside the slender box is an envelope. My brow furrows as I open it and read the content silently.

THIS CERTIFICATE ENTITLES THE POSSESSER TO TWENTY HOURS OF STUDIO TIME AT BELLWETHER DIGIAL AUDIO SERVICES.

I can't believe my eyes. I have to read it at least five times to fully grasp what it means. My aunt, my beloved *prozia*, my guardian angel, paved the way for me to follow my dreams and I didn't even know it. All this time I had been chasing after shadows, when a sleeping dragon lay hidden in my attic.

I reread the certificate, and realize the studio is local, right here in Brooklyn. *My Aunt Susan always had a local connection*, I think with a smile. I can't wait to tell the guys. I know that we're ready to take this next step, and that was why it was revealed to us now instead of two years ago.

But I have one thing to do first.

I go to the cemetery and say thank you in person. I take flowers, because she deserves flowers. I spread them around on her tombstone to make it pretty, and to show the world that might pass by that a wonderful person is buried here. And I loved her. More than I've ever loved anyone.

I speak in limited Italian as I sit there on the cold ground. I say all the things I haven't been able to say, because I haven't felt worthy to say them. I thank her for the gifts. I apologize for how badly I lost my way. I apologize most of all for not coming to see her. I don't promise to be better. My aunt Susan knew better than that.

She knew me best and loved me most. What more can you ask for from anyone?

By the time I reach the festive little apartment in Chelsea, everyone has gathered for our Christmas celebration. I save my gift for last.

Thanks to my Aunt Susan, Dreaming in Blue has another chance.

This time we're not going to waste it.

CHAPTER TWENTY-TWO:

As 2006 gives way to 2007, some magical things start to happen for Dreaming in Blue. Alana books us a gig in midtown, where we have a special–and familiar–face in the crowd. I recognize her from the minute she speaks. It's the bubbly blonde from Tennessee, the one I had tried to pick up the day Tina Nunes sucked me into her web.

"Of course I remember you!" she exclaims as she embraces me without any preamble. This bubbly girl is the human equivalent of champagne. She's full of life and best of all, full of big plans. The minute she sees our band, she decides then and there she's going to represent us and take us straight to the top.

We have heard that before, of course, but she's willing to put her money where her mouth is. She waives her fee for the first month, just to prove to us what she can do. And what she can do is miraculous. She gets us booked in higher-end clubs, the ones that we never dared approach before because they were Sedução's competition. These were the places that only booked top-billing artists, and that was exactly why Iris Kimble wanted them.

Part of Iris's plan is to catch the eye, and ears, of Jasper Carrington of Carrington Entertainment, the biggest label on the east coast. She has some clients there, so she has some connections, but it's nothing major. She had been searching for the act that could really turn his head. That is her passion, taking undiscovered talent and taking it straight to the top. And she decides almost immediately that we're the band that will do it.

"Are you sure we're ready?" I ask.

"No one is ever ready," she responds. "Sometimes you just have to jump right in and go for it. You can't count on second chances in this business."

I nod. She speaks the gospel truth.

During the month of January, she books us through April, including a venue in my hometown of Philadelphia. She swears she will get Jasper to one of them, even if she has to hogtie him and drag him there herself.

Of course, it's much cuter the way she says it.

In the meantime, we spend every waking hour either rehearsing or writing. We finally get into the studio by March. Thanks to Iris, our first demo lands on Jasper's desk April 1st. When Iris calls that afternoon to let us know that Jasper will be flying down to the show in Philadelphia, we all think she's joking.

"I never kid about business," she says in that bombastic twang. "I've also asked my friend Andy to fly in, so she can interview the band and we can start circulating some press."

"She?" I ask, confused by the name, which I assumed at first was a male.

"Andy Foster," Iris says. "She's a freelance writer. Mostly travel right now, but she's really interested in breaking into entertainment. If this works out the way I think it will, it'll be a huge win for all of us."

"Just do us a favor," Felix says to me. "Don't try to get this one into bed."

Everyone laughs, especially Iris, who well remembers my hound dog ways when I tried to pick her up the night we met. "Don't worry. Andy isn't that kind of girl. She's very professional and strictly by the book. In fact, she was there that night when we first met at Sedução."

I think back, trying to remember. The picture is cloudy, but I remember that she was a curvy girl with black-rimmed glasses and funky hair. For some reason this reminds me of Pam.

"I'll be a good boy," I promise, but no one in the room believes me.

Hell, I don't even know if I believe myself. Truthfully it's been a long time since I've even thought about being with a woman. After learning about Pam's pregnancy, I simply withdrew. I am a character on a stage, and that's it.

Surprisingly, we've had more success with fans ever since we closed the revolving door. There are more fans than ever before, and they're every bit as devoted, maybe even more so.

"*As long as they love you more than you love them,*" I hear Tina's ghost echo in my ear, "*they'll never stop coming back.*"

She was a self-serving bitch, but she was right.

But I'm too busy with my career to worry about my personal life. We play every venue we can to polish our show for Jasper. We know we only get one shot to make a first impression.

By the time we pile into the RV to head down to Philadelphia, all I really want to do is sleep. I'm exhausted. But I've never felt more prepared for a gig. With Iain, we start to operate like a well-tuned machine, with a lot more diversity in our playlist, steering away from all the sex stuff to really show we can rock, too. This gives the musicians their own chance to shine. We also dig out covers that really show off my voice, and every single member of the band helps me stretch and grow beyond my comfort zone.

Iain in particular is mellow and insightful. Best of all he's a stabilizing influence on all of us. He's not the bad boy bassist or a wistful wingman. He barely even touches any kind of alcohol. He has two goals: music and Alana, and not necessarily in that order.

I'm still not sure love is compatible with my dream to be a star. I'd like to believe it is, but I've been burned more than once. I'm perfectly happy flirting with some of the groupies who visit the shows, giving them a bit of a thrill without risking my ass to do it.

Instead I focus on the last details for our show. Without a doubt, this one is going to change my life. Yeah, I've said that before, but this time I really can't see how it wouldn't. Jasper is coming to see our show based on the strength of our demo. It's either going to give me everything I want, or it's going to prove to me that the things I want aren't possible to have.

I guess no matter what happens I'm pretty sure I'm never going to have to sleep with Jasper to further my career.

I'm erring on the side of hope, so I'm pretty pumped when we hit the venue where we'll be playing. Iris and Alana whisk away to fetch Andy, the unusually named woman who will be reviewing our band for an actual nationwide publication. Though Iris has planned to bring Andy to dinner, she's there to work on her "real" job and write a review for a couple of restaurants.

It's just as well. I collapse into my bed at nine o'clock that night. I'm going to need a good night's sleep for this one.

We're one of the first to go on, so we get to set up ahead of the club opening. Time feels like it's going both in slow motion and fast forward. I'm practically jogging in place to get rid of some of my excess nervous energy.

I change into some leather pants and biker boots, but I don't bother with a shirt. Sex sells and I know it. If there's one thing I'm good at, it's the marketing of sex.

I style my hair, wild and long and wavy. My new trademark.

In fact, I use every tip that has been given to me. I use black polish on my fingers, which are adorned with rings on every finger. I rock the studded cuffs on both wrists. I shine up my chest and then fuss with my package, to give them all something to see.

By the time they hit the intro to *"Run to the Hills,"* a song that really shows off how well the band plays as a whole, I'm ready to tear the roof off of the place. I explode out of the blue mist and get a good look at my crowd for the first time. Alana and Iris are right up front, along with a full-figured beauty I assume is Andy.

It's Andy, in fact, that nearly shocks me mute as I stand there. She's wearing a low-cut top with her ample cleavage on full display. Turns out I didn't need to fondle myself into a semi. Just seeing her creamy curves is enough to shock my dick into consciousness. I can't think about it though. I've got to nail this performance. I've already started over too many times already simply because I couldn't keep the blood flow going to the right brain. I'm ready to make this dream happen or die trying. No woman is worth getting distracted with this much on the line.

I hit those impossible notes because I have no choice.

However, Andy is hard to ignore. I can see her delicious curves in my peripheral vision, which means I have to work extra hard to keep my focus. Was I really going to do this again? Self-destruct my one real shot at becoming a legitimate artist just for a piece of ass?

I try not to look at her as best as I can, but as is the norm, I sing *"Feel Like Making Love"* to every girl in the front row. I can't avoid her now, even if I want to.

And I kind of don't want to. It'd be awkward to skip this part of the performance, but Jasper would be none the wiser. Still, it'd be nice to know if I could throw her off kilter as much as she has done to me. I mean, it only seems fair.

I move along down the line, until finally I reach her. I hook a finger in the loops on my leather pants, subtly (or not so subtly) drawing her attention there. The minute our eyes meet, it's like being hit by lightning. A volt shoots right through me. She's so lovely I wish I knew how to draw just so I could immortalize her beautiful face, her haunting eyes. It's like every melody I've ever heard exploding into my brain at once in perfect, beautiful, crazy chaos.

And it may be because I've been in a sexual drought for so long, especially following such a hedonistic period, but in a flash I can see underneath me as I lose myself inside of her. It's a fantasy so strong, and so foreign, that I have to look away or else I'll forget how to breathe.

I can't help but notice that she immediately flusters as well, which doesn't help. This is my danger zone. It's not just a beautiful woman that turns my eye, otherwise I'd never get anything done.

It's finding a beautiful woman who can feel the same spark I do, something deep and forbidden, but undeniable and true. Whatever *it* is, she feels it.

I can't even look at her during *"Fat Bottomed Girls."* I can tell she has a luscious ass from where I stand over her, and if I let my thoughts linger there I'll fumble my performance like an amateur.

What's wrong with me? It's not like I can't get laid. I've made a choice to avoid these kinds of pitfalls. It's the mature, adult thing to do.

But all I want to do when I finish my set is to find that unusual girl and explore this weird, wild connection I feel. I'm drawn to her instantly and undeniably.

I'm so relieved to finish, I blow a kiss to Iris. On impulse, I wink at Andy, who instantly flushes. I feel my ego, among other things, swell.

I head backstage and I wait for what comes next, whatever that might be. I laid it all on the stage. It's up to Fate now.

Once backstage, Iris herds Andy my direction. Now that the performance is behind me, I can finally inspect this beauty a little more closely.

"This is Andy Foster," she introduces, "the writer I was telling you about."

I smile a little wider as I take her hand. "Andy, from Tennessee. It's so nice to finally meet you."

She flushes immediately. It's quite adorable. "Geez, Iris, what have you been telling these people?"

Her voice pours out of her mouth like butter, in a sexy southern lilt that immediately tantalizes. I've always been a sucker for accents. That it's coming out of this curvy beauty only makes it more irresistible.

And in fact I don't resist it. I pull her into a side hug as I answer her question. "All good but obviously not nearly enough."

God, she even feels good in the crook of my arm, like a custom fit. I have to turn to Iris or else I can't be held responsible for my actions. "You think he liked it?" I ask, referring to Jasper.

"All aces, baby," she assures me with a smile. Maybe I'm imagining things, but she quickly steals Andy back from my embrace. "Come on," she says to Andy. "Time to meet the rest of the band."

Andy looks back at me as Iris drags her towards the other members of Dreaming in Blue. I know she doesn't want to go, and I suspect that's why Iris decided to intervene. Nobody wants me to hook up with the important people who can help us in our career, and I can't say I blame them. It hasn't worked out well in our favor so far.

So I turn to a voluptuous redhead and start chatting her up instead. She's probably perfectly harmless to charm, and to seduce if I so choose. Just get the monkey off my back, so to speak. A one-night-stand in my hometown, then back to real life in New York tomorrow.

Sounds like a perfect plan.

Only I can't stop looking at Andy. There's something so familiar about her, like we have met before. Like we have known each other before. I'm not sure what it is, but it both scares me and attracts me.

Actually it scares me how much it attracts me. I haven't felt this way for a woman since Pam. If Andy is married, I might just have to kill myself.

When I see her alone at the bar, I decide to approach. Maybe if I see she's just some ordinary girl…

Alarm bells sound off in my head. Haven't I learned my lesson with ordinary girls *yet*?

Oh, who am I kidding? I want to get close to her. I want to talk to her. What's the harm, really? By tomorrow she heads back to Tennessee and I head back to New York. It's not like would complicate anything just to *talk* to her.

As she fumbles for some money from her purse to pay for her drink, I withdraw some cash from my tight pocket and toss it on the bar in front of her. "It's on me."

When she turns to face me, her eyes dart to mine. She hides behind her beer bottle. If she's doing all this to put me off, it's not working. She's adorable. Young, but not too young, probably close to mid-20s. And she's sweet. I can tell by the way the blush rises in her cheek. She's clearly not used to a guy like me, and I find that endearing after the last few years I've had.

"Thanks," she says with all the proper manners I'd expect from a girl from Tennessee.

"Thank you," I say.

She's instantly confused. "For what?"

I can't help but smirk as I lean closer to that spectacular cleavage. It's all I can do not to dive right in. "Great scenery during the show."

She blushes a deep crimson. This girl is killing me. "I didn't think you noticed," she said as she looks away.

I'm quick to assure her. "I notice everything. Especially when it's put there for me to notice."

The look in her eyes is enough to convict her. She knew what she was doing when she put on that top for the show. *Mission accomplished, baby.* "You know what they say. Play the hand you're dealt."

I have to laugh. "That wasn't a complaint. I quite enjoyed the view. I wanted to see more but it was a bit like looking into the sun during an eclipse. Be careful how you wield that weapon."

She tips her beer towards my chest. "Ditto."

Oh, so she's a smart girl, too. Even better. "I guess we're even then."

"Not really," she says.

I cock an eyebrow. "No?"

She chugs more beer before she has the guts to say, "To be even I'd have to take my shirt off."

What a naughty little thing, and I bet she doesn't even know it yet. How much fun would it be to show her? "You have a point," I say as I lean closer. I just want to touch her. I want to feel her. It's completely crazy but the New Vanni, the one who was taught to take what he wants, springs forward. I can't even stop him. "Maybe we should go somewhere and rectify this grievous injustice."

Instead she cocks her eyebrow right back at me. "Or you could just put your shirt on."

It's there and then I know I want her. She's not dropping at my feet. She's making me work for it. I like girls who make me work for it. "Well played," I salute.

She clears her throat. "Shouldn't you hang around to see what Jasper Carrington has to say?"

I fire off my sexiest smirk. "Iris tells me I should always leave them wanting more. What's more attractive than a star you can't quite catch?"

I can tell by the way her eyes darken that she gets the innuendo.

Good.

I motion to the dance floor. "Care to dance?"

"I don't really…," she starts, but I don't let her finish her sentence. It's too negative for my tastes. I grab her hand and drag her through the crowd to the middle of the crowded dance floor. Because it's so crowded, she's pressed up flush against me, with that incredible chest pressing into mine. It doesn't matter if she knows how to dance. She feels like paradise in my arms. I lock my arm around her waist and pull her closer. I know she can feel me. Her breath catches when my hands roam across her generous backside.

The song they're playing is "*Closer,*" which I've sung many times before to many women. I lean to sing directly in her ear so she can hear me. She swoons against me a little, which makes me even harder. Suddenly all I want to do is get the fuck out of here and bring that naughty little song to life.

Despite all the warnings, from Iris and everyone in the band, and every bad experience I've had the last few years, I can't seem to resist this temptress. Worse, I don't want to. I cop a feel of her ass before I plant a kiss on the tip of her upturned nose. But with a wink, I release her and disappear through the crowd before I can't pull myself away at all.

I head off to find Iris and Jasper. This is the reason I'm here, and this has to remain my focus, rather than seducing some groupie.

I'll secure the gig first, *then* I'll take Andy back to my hotel room.

I can't think of a better way to celebrate, especially when Jasper says the words I've been waiting to hear for years. "I'd love to sign you, but I need a hit song to get behind. You bring me that and I'll put you in the studio tomorrow."

Iris practically squeals where she stands. I nearly squeal myself. After all these years, after all these false starts, I finally sank the basket.

Well, in a manner of speaking, anyway. I still have to write a hit song. I glance across the room at Andy, where she sits chatting with Alana. No doubt she's warning her about me.

She totally should. Because I totally want her.

I realize in that moment I haven't felt this captivated by a woman in a long, long time–possibly ever. With Lori and Pam, even Sasha, I was trying to hold on to the guy I always was. With Tina, I was trying to wedge myself into the person I thought I wanted to be.

With Andy, it's all brand new. She's smart, she's accomplished, she's beautiful and she's funny–she's the whole package. And that appeals to a whole new Vanni. I'm kind of excited to find out who that is.

Before I can figure it out, she disappears to her hotel room. Predictably, it only makes me like her more.

I get Andy's number from Iris, to thank her for flying in for the show and helping us get some national exposure. I know when she gives it to me that she thinks I'm full of shit, and, of course, I am. Thanking her for what she was doing is merely an excuse... a reason to connect with her and talk to her.

Truth is I can't stop thinking about her. When we all leave the club at closing time, I send Miss Foster a text, inviting her to New York to see the band. *"Shirts optional. V."*

I dream about her that night, where I'm showing her my city in a hansom cab. I taste her lips in my dream, which makes it that much harder to wake up.

The next morning I find her text. *Sounds like fun. I look forward to it."*

As do I, baby. As do I.

When we head back to New York, I try to sort my fevered thoughts on paper, through lyrics, like always. It all comes back to the moment I first saw her.

The curve of her face, a wisp of her hair, I knew when I saw her standing there, I wanted her...

I'd never been hit by a thunderbolt before, but that was what Andy Foster had turned out to be.

Seeing her, wanting her, what I'd give for just one kiss...

Who knows what might have happened had Tina not intercepted me that first night so long ago? I probably would have had her then, but I knew instantly that wasn't the Vanni someone like her would have deserved. No girl did, except maybe Tina, who had assembled me like Frankenstein's monster into the rock star she wanted me to be... a rock star that wasn't going anywhere.

Does she know how I feel/ How much I want this to be real...

It got me thinking about fate, and how one moment can alter an entire course of action.

An angel from a dream I can't claim...

Fate hasn't always worked out in my favor. But what if it had decided to throw me a bone just once? What would I say to my soul mate, if I only had a split second to tell her how I feel?

Someday I'll wake from this dream and hold my angel in my arms. And she'll know all along I've wanted her.

Within a few days I have the lyrics. Within a week, we have the song. Within the four minutes it takes to listen to it, we have our first major contract with a legitimate record label.

Dreaming in Blue, and Giovanni Carnevale, had officially arrived.

Whether anyone else in the band can figure it out or not, I know that Andy is the reason why. It *was* fate that we met that night. We gravitated towards each other because we were supposed to, no matter what dire warnings the people around me might say.

It's almost like she was wrapped up in a box somewhere, a hidden present in the attic, just waiting for me to find her and set her free.

Okay, maybe I'm romanticizing, but hey. I'm Italian. I'm supposed to be a hopeless romantic. It's in my blood. And thanks to that one night in Philadelphia, so is Andy Foster.

I know what you're thinking. Here we go again, right? Me chasing my dick after some fantasy girl when I should just keep it in my pants and work hard to impress Jasper, to do anything he wants in order for Dreaming in Blue to get the shot we all deserve.

Let's face it. I'm no winner in the romance department, not by a long shot. And Andy's too good for me, I knew that the moment she told me to put on my shirt rather than fall at my feet and beg me to take her to my hotel. She's an ordinary girl, and, if the last few years have taught me anything at all, ordinary girls need more than I can ever provide. It's the price you pay for an extraordinary life, which I want more than I've ever wanted *any* woman. I couldn't give it up, not for Lori, Sasha *or* Pam. Even I can admit how much better off all those girls are without me. They want marriage and kids, and I work best with those relationships that require none of that. Deep inside I know I'm my father's son, only instead of booze, I overdose on music, attention and sex. Ordinary girls, good girls, demand that I be better than some character on a stage, and I'm not entirely sure that I'm capable of that anymore.

To be frank, the idea scares the ever loving shit out of me.

Why I want them, why I need them, why I can't stay the fuck away from them remains a mystery to me.

But Andy did stand apart from Lori, Pam or Sasha in one very important way. She had proven to be my most successful muse, connecting this enticing creature forever in my brain with my biggest break. Dreaming in Blue is about to rocket into the stratosphere, and I really don't think that would have happened without her. I honestly don't know what that means, if anything at all. I don't know where it's going or what's going to happen. All I know is every time I think about her, I smile. I feel better than I have in a long, long time.

And I truly can't wait to see her again.

ABOUT THE AUTHOR:

Ginger Voight is a screenwriter and bestselling author with more than twenty published titles in fiction and nonfiction. Her nonfiction works cover everything from travel to politics, while her works of fiction range from romance to the paranormal, as well as dark "ripped-from-the-headlines" topics, such as those featured in her book *Dirty Little Secrets*.

Ginger discovered her love for writing in the sixth grade, courtesy of a Halloween assignment. From then on, writing became a thing of solace, reflection, and security. When she found herself homeless in L.A. at the age of nineteen, she wrote her first novel in longhand on notebook paper while living out of her car.

In 1995, after she lost her nine-day-old son, she worked through her grief by writing the story that would eventually become *The Fullerton Family Saga*. In 2011, she embarked on a new journey: to publish romance novels starring heroines who look like the average American woman. These "Rubenesque romances" have developed a following thanks to her bestselling *Groupie* series. Other titles, such as the highly-rated *Fierce* series, tap into the American preoccupation with reality TV, giving her contemporary stories a current, pop-culture edge.

Ginger isn't afraid to push the envelope with characters who are perfectly imperfect. Rich or poor, sweet or selfish, gay or straight, plus-size or svelte, her characters are beautifully flawed and three-dimensional. They populate her lavish fictional landscapes and teach us more about the real world in which we live, through their interactions with each other, and often through gut-wrenching angst. Ginger's goal with every book is to give her readers a little bit more than they were expecting, with stories they'll never forget.

For more, please visit gingervoight.com. Follow Ginger on Twitter (twitter.com/gingervoight) and "like" her author page on Facebook (facebook.com/gingervoight) for all the latest news on her public appearances and new releases.

Made in the USA
Lexington, KY
03 January 2017